**Praise for Robert Jordan and The Wheel of Time®**

"His huge, ambitious Wheel of Time series helped redefine the genre."           —George R. R. Martin, internationally bestselling author of *A Game of Thrones*

"Anyone who's writing epic secondary world fantasy knows Robert Jordan isn't just a part of the landscape, he's a monolith within the landscape."           —Patrick Rothfuss, internationally bestselling author of The Kingkiller Chronicle

"*The Eye of the World* was a turning point in my life. I read, I enjoyed. (Then continued on to write my larger fantasy novels.)"           —Robin Hobb, *New York Times* bestselling author of The Farseer Trilogy

"Robert Jordan's work has been a formative influence and an inspiration for a generation of fantasy writers."           —Brent Weeks, *New York Times* bestselling author of *The Way of Shadows*

"Jordan has come to dominate the world Tolkien began to reveal."           —*The New York Times*

"One of fantasy's most acclaimed series."           —*USA Today*

"Robert Jordan was a giant of fiction whose words helped a whole generation of fantasy writers, including myself, find our true voices. I thanked him then, but I didn't thank him enough."

—Peter V. Brett, internationally bestselling author of The Demon Cycle

"[Robert Jordan's] impact on the place of fantasy in the culture is colossal. . . . He brought innumerable readers to fantasy. He became the *New York Times* Best Seller List's face of fantasy."

—Guy Gavriel Kay, internationally bestselling author of *Tigana*

"Jordan's writing is so amazing! The characterization, the attention to detail!"

—Clint McElroy, cocreator of the #1 podcast *The Adventure Zone*

"The Wheel of Time [is] rapidly becoming the definitive American fantasy saga. It is a fantasy tale seldom equaled and still less often surpassed in English."          —*Chicago Sun-Times*

"Hard to put down for even a moment. A fittingly epic conclusion to a fantasy series that many consider one of the best of all time."

—*San Francisco Book Review* on *A Memory of Light*

# BOOKS BY ROBERT JORDAN

*Warrior of the Altaii*

**THE WHEEL OF TIME®**
*New Spring: The Novel*
*The Eye of the World*
*The Great Hunt*
*The Dragon Reborn*
*The Shadow Rising*
*The Fires of Heaven*
*Lord of Chaos*
*A Crown of Swords*
*The Path of Daggers*
*Winter's Heart*
*Crossroads of Twilight*
*Knife of Dreams*

**BY ROBERT JORDAN AND BRANDON SANDERSON**
*The Gathering Storm*
*Towers of Midnight*
*A Memory of Light*

**BY ROBERT JORDAN AND TERESA PATTERSON**
*The World of Robert Jordan's The Wheel of Time*

**BY ROBERT JORDAN, HARRIET McDOUGAL,
ALAN ROMANCZUK, AND MARIA SIMONS**
*The Wheel of Time Companion*

# ROBERT JORDAN

# WARRIOR OF THE ALTAII

**TOR**®
fantasy

A TOM DOHERTY ASSOCIATES BOOK

NEW YORK

This is a work of fiction. All of the characters, organizations, and events portrayed in this novel are either products of the author's imagination or are used fictitiously.

WARRIOR OF THE ALTAII

Copyright © 2019 by Bandersnatch Group, Inc.

All rights reserved.

Maps by Ellisa Mitchell

A Tor Book
Published by Tom Doherty Associates
120 Broadway
New York, NY 10271

www.tor-forge.com

Tor® is a registered trademark of Macmillan Publishing Group, LLC.

ISBN 978-1-250-24767-4

Our books may be purchased in bulk for promotional, educational, or business use. Please contact your local bookseller or the Macmillan Corporate and Premium Sales Department at 1-800-221-7945, extension 5442, or by email at MacmillanSpecialMarkets@macmillan.com.

First Edition: October 2019
First Mass Market Edition: November 2021

Printed in the United States of America

0  9  8  7  6  5  4  3  2  1

# FOREWORD

*Warrior of the Altaii* has been sold twice, but has never been published. Until now.

How could this happen?

As Wulfgar will say, draw near and listen.

I first read the manuscript in 1978—forty years ago—just a year or so after I had relocated from New York, where I was Editorial Director of Ace Books (and Tom Doherty was Publisher), to my hometown, Charleston, South Carolina. I had a one-page contract with a guy named Richard Gallen, who played a much larger part than I knew in the founding of small publishing companies. My deal with Gallen was, I would find the writers, Gallen would invest the advance money, and we would split the profits. Profits? Hah. But that's another story.

So, where would you go to find writers? A bookstore! I went to a store owned by the local magazine wholesaler, where you could find paperback books, magazines, and newspapers from all over the place. Sure enough, the manager said there was a guy who came in for paperbacks and said he was writing something. She didn't remember his name.

I asked for an index card and a pencil, wrote my name and phone number on it, and asked her to give it to him when he next came in. She did.

He stared at it in disbelief—pencil? index card?— and was about to tear it up when she told him that I had been Editorial Director of Ace. I had told the manager I was looking for writers—actually, I wanted a new Kathleen Woodiwiss, a writer who could write bodice rippers, sexy historicals aimed at a female audience.

He called me. And made up a bodice ripper synopsis on the drive to my house. OMG, it was awful. All I remember was that the obligatory sex scene involved a duck. I thanked him and couldn't wait to close the door behind him. Turned out he had as much estrogen in him as Conan the Barbarian.

Twelve months went by. Unbeknownst to me, he had sold *Warrior of the Altaii* to DAW Books in August 1977. He had received the contract and asked for some changes in it. DAW had withdrawn their offer in September 1977. First sale, first reversion of rights.

After those eight months, I hit a slow patch and thumbed through my Rolodex looking for new prospects. I called him. He said he had written a barbarian fantasy called *Warrior of the Altaii,* and

I asked to see it. It had a beginning, a middle, and an end, and it was *good*.

Meanwhile, Tom Doherty had agreed to have Ace distribute the books of my imprint. Tom had a splendid science fiction editor, Jim Baen, and it seemed to me that this kind of book was exactly what Tom wouldn't want in *my* imprint.

I sent it to Tom, asking if he was interested in publishing it in Ace. Baen bought it in 1979. Sort of. The contract was dated April 1980. Second sale.

Meanwhile, Ace didn't stand still. It became part of "Berkley Publishing Group, Publishers of Berkley, Jove, Ace Science Fiction, Charter, Tempo and Second Chance." A myth floated around the industry that someone on the switchboard answered a call by saying "Pac-Man Books" and was out of a job by sunset.

Anyway, the editor in chief of science fiction at this unwieldy entity said she wanted some revisions. He said, just let me know what you want me to do—and then she didn't send any requests for said revisions.

He wrote to her in January 1983, "My manuscript is fast becoming a mushroom farm on a back shelf in some dark corner of your offices. In that fashion it is doing neither of us any good."

Berkley gave the rights back in June 1983. Second reversion.

Now, turn back to 1979.

Robert Jordan—then James Oliver Rigney, Jr., the name he had from birth—who was about to morph into Reagan O'Neal—told me that he had some new ideas. I made a date for a meeting. He came in and overlapped with my earlier appointment, who wanted to write a novel about Joseph of Arimathea taking the Christ child to the west of England. She was known for her historical expertise, and I had been hoping she'd want to write a historical novel set in South Carolina, but *not* in Civil War days, and said so in Rigney's presence.

So he said he was passionately interested in doing a South Carolina novel set in the American Revolution. (I am pretty sure he had no such idea when he entered the room.) He promised me an outline the next day.

He delivered an outline of a novel telling the adventures of one Michael Fallon during the Revolution. Two more Fallon books would follow, roaming through the War of 1812 to the founding of the Republic of Texas.

I gave him a contract for the first Fallon, to be written by Reagan O'Neal, on March 20, 1979.

A sale made *because* of Altaii. Most people who start a first novel never finish it, but he had done so. And he had written a good novel, head and shoulders above most first novels.

Well, he and I married on March 28, 1981.

Not so long after that, Tom Doherty got the rights from Conan Properties to do a new Conan novel, but Tom wanted to publish it in time for the first Conan movie, and Baen didn't have any writers who could do a credible Conan. So I told him

Rigney could (because of *Altaii*), and I asked Rigney to do it.

He said no.

I hoped Tom would forget about it, but that is not his way. Weeks later, he came back to me.

I went back to Rigney, pleading with him. He said, "Harriet, don't wiggle that thing" (my trembling chin) "at me. I'll do it."

So he did. Under the name Robert Jordan, his work was reviewed as "the best of the modern *Conan*s," thus establishing a name in fantasy. He liked doing it, and did six more.

And all the while he was writing them, as in the time he had been writing the Fallon books, he was thinking of the themes and shadows, the people and events of The Wheel of Time.

When I reread *Warrior of the Altaii* this winter, after this long intermission, I was amazed at the foreshadowing of The Wheel of Time. You will find many hints of what is to come. One of the most obvious is the name of the major mountain range—the Backbone of the World. In The Wheel, it is the Spine of the World. I think you'll have fun finding them as you read this brand-new Robert Jordan—a fine wine that has reached its perfect maturity.

Now go see what Wulfgar wants to tell you.

Best regards,
Harriet P. McDougal

*I am Wulfgar, Lord of Two Horsetails, warrior of the Altaii people.*

*Come near and I will tell you of Lanta, the City of Twelve Gates, the Unconquerable, the Pearl of the Plain.*

*I will tell you of the Twin Thrones of Lanta, and of the twin queens who ruled from them.*

*I will tell of the Morassa and of Brecon and Ivo, who led them to war.*

*I will tell of the Most High, and of the powers that covered the Plain in the Year of the Stone Lizard.*

*Come near and listen.*

# CONTENTS

| | Map | xviii–xix |
|---|---|---|
| I. | Sign of Morassa | 1 |
| II. | Into the Palace | 14 |
| III. | The Most High | 31 |
| IV. | A Wanderer | 37 |
| V. | A Question of Languages | 48 |
| VI. | The Price | 58 |
| VII. | A Warrior Brand | 64 |
| VIII. | The Shells | 78 |
| IX. | Out of the Trap | 93 |
| X. | Tangled Fates | 108 |
| XI. | An Honor, and a Command | 120 |
| XII. | Pride, or Honor | 129 |
| XIII. | The New Pet | 143 |

| | | |
|---|---|---|
| XIV. | Twisting Shadows | 156 |
| XV. | The Feather | 167 |
| XVI. | Kitchen Slops | 171 |
| XVII. | A Bell Note | 181 |
| XVIII. | Women's Justice | 187 |
| XIX. | A Glimmer | 209 |
| XX. | The Last Fork of the Varna | 215 |
| XXI. | To Break the Rules | 220 |
| XXII. | The Nexus | 229 |
| XXIII. | A Cloud of Dust | 237 |
| XXIV. | Blood and Steel | 244 |
| XXV. | Oaths | 258 |
| XXVI. | A Thick Tangle | 272 |
| XXVII. | A Small Spell | 286 |
| XXVIII. | A Curtain of Steel | 299 |
| XXIX. | To Come So Far | 314 |
| XXX. | Drumbeats | 322 |
| XXXI. | A Green Branch | 338 |
| XXXII. | Leash and Collar | 346 |
| XXXIII. | That Cold Wind | 355 |
| XXXIV. | And So, We Ride | 362 |

# WARRIOR
## OF THE ALTAII

SNOW COU
TALLIS
ASYAT
MIRZA
DEVIA
The PLAIN
Heights of Tybal
SIFR SENAKA THE BACKBONE of the WORLD
LANTA
River Xandra
Great Ravine
River Varna
CERDU
HYKSOS
EFHEIM
TELMARK

NTRY
NORLAND
TAFAWRI
LAND of LIAU
KNORROS
CASELLE
TYRIA
GHALT
VARANGIA

# I

## SIGN OF MORASSA

In the fifth month of the Year of the Stone Lizard, in the Kafhara Wind, I sat on my horse on a small hill not far from the great city of Lanta. They called this the Plain, the Lantans did, here where green things grew all around. Only a short ride beyond the city there were trees taller than a man on horseback. Still, to soft men of the cities perhaps it seemed like the Plain.

To the north a pack of dril circled slowly in the sky, sunlight glinting on their wing scales. Out there something was dead, or soon to be.

It was a time for it, a time for dying. Above, Loewin chased across the sky, driven there in its battle with Ban and Wilaf, with t'Fie and Mondra. It is a well-known sign of ill fortune. In addition the Kafhara Wind had come early that year. To have an early Wind and Loewin in the sky at the same time, that is an omen seldom seen, and blessings are given when it passes.

My purpose there was not to read omens, though. I adjusted my face cloth against the dust picked up by the wind, even there where green things grew, and waited for the one I knew would come. The wind lifted a screen of dust before me. When it fell, they were coming.

Twenty men rode in two columns. Their lance tips were blackened against reflecting light, and their arms were bare. They were not men to sheathe their arms in armor, or even in cloth against the wind. They had honor. It was their leader I had come to meet.

"Come," I said. My horse moved down the hill at the pressure of my knees, and twenty of my own lances followed.

The other riders halted to await us, the man I had come to meet a little in front. He was tall, taller even than I, and I am accounted tall for an Altaii.

I motioned my followers to stop and rode to meet him. He dropped his sand cloth, watching me unsmiling. After a time I held out my left hand. It is the custom of some peoples to offer the weapon hand, the right hand, to be clasped as a sign of harmlessness. This is not a custom of the Altaii. He grasped my left hand firmly in his.

"It has been a long time, Harald." I could contain my smiles no longer. "It has been a long time, and I am glad to see you again."

"It is good to see you, too, Wulfgar. There has

been a time or two this year past when I thought I would not."

Harald, son of Bohemund, who was King and Warlord of the Altaii nation, was as close to me as any man has ever been or could be. If no brother of blood remains to me, if all have fallen to steel or the Plain, this man was my brother.

When my father fell, in the great victory over the Emperor Basrath at the Heights of Tybal, it was Bohemund who took me into his household. As his son I was raised, as brother to Harald. We kept more of that closeness than most brothers of blood.

"Mayra saw that you would come this way to Lanta," I said. "Has the raiding been good?"

"No fewer than three large caravans have crossed my path in the last four tendays." He shook his head. "The caravan masters curse the fates, as usual. If they're going to cross the Plain they should learn to expect that some of them will fall to us now and again. They should look on it as a tax. And how has it been with you?"

The smile faded from my face, and I took a deep breath. "I have seen one caravan in the last six tendays, and one other in seven before that. Nine times in that space a fanghorn has raided the herds. Twice I found waterholes broken and dry, and only four days ago thirty of my lances were beset by Runners. They killed more than a hundred before they went down, as closely as we could tell, but as we found nothing but bones it was hard to be certain."

"Harsh words, Wulfgar. Hard words."

He hesitated before he spoke again, and when he spoke the laughter was gone. "The caravans were all small, and only one carried slaves. The smallest one at that. One carried cloth and pots and things made out of clay. The third carried empty casks headed back to the winery at Thisk. Such a scrawny bunch of strawmen running it I turned them loose. Had I kept them I'd never have gotten rid of them. No one in his right mind would have taken the lot as a gift."

"And the fanghorns? The Runners?"

"No Runners, and there are always fanghorns."

"More this year," I said. "There are more this year than ever before."

"All right, there are more. The Plain has never been easy. You do not live on the Plain, you make war with it."

"Don't quote sayings to me, Harald. I know you must make war on the Plain, but I never before thought it was winning."

He shifted uncomfortably. No doubt he was thinking of some other saying, one about enduring. Suddenly he frowned.

"You spoke of finding waterholes broken apart. I found three of them, myself. And at one"—he fumbled under his tunic—"in the dried mud, I found this."

It was a scarf he handed me, a small, crudely woven scarf with a simple three-cornered pattern repeated over and over again.

"Morassa," I said. "No one else would bother

with this poor a piece, so it wasn't traded. Morassa at the waterhole when it was broken?"

"Had to be. It was dried into the mud, and in that part of the Plain the mud would have dried very quickly."

"Morassa." I whispered it. They were scavengers, picking over the leavings of other men's raids. If ever they raided themselves, it was against someone they were sure was weaker. And still, even with the evidence in my hands, I found it hard to believe.

On the Plain, water is life. A waterhole is life. The absence of water is death. It is just that simple. The fact breeds respect. The man who poisoned or destroyed a waterhole would be killed immediately. If he did it to keep the water from an enemy it would make no difference. The day would surely come, would, not could, when his own people would need that water. Not even the Morassa would destroy water.

"Did you ask a Sister of Wisdom to look at the waterhole?"

He nodded. "She found nothing. There had been a spell cast over the hole for a period of time. Before, it was complete. After, it was broken. During was clouded. At the next broken waterhole I asked her to look again, and again she found the clouding."

"So someone is out to—to what? Destroy all the water on the Plain? Why?"

The wind quickened, and Harald pulled his cloak tighter around him. "I don't know, Wulfgar, and I don't intend to stay here thinking about it until I freeze."

"All right, then. To Lanta. To the Pearl of the Plain. We'll let them know we're here in peace, and maybe some of them will scrape up enough courage to come out and buy. Any goods that they might recognize in your booty? Any friends they might see on the block?"

"Has that ever stopped them before?"

"It has not. Let us ride." I spurred away, and Harald raced to catch me, our lances trailing behind.

If I made no more mention of the waterholes, they did not leave my mind. The destruction of water argued for madmen, but no madman could afford the price a Sister of Wisdom would demand for that many cloakings. Someone of wealth was destroying water, but who? And why? The questions kept ringing in my mind, but no answers came, not a glimmer of one. And then there was no more time for vague questions. We topped a rise, and Lanta was before us.

Lanta the Unconquerable, the Pearl of the Plain. Victor over Basrath they styled themselves, also, but in truth he had turned his armies away when he realized that the city would not fall to his siege. They never defeated him, or even met him in open combat. He simply grew tired of waiting with no end in sight.

At that they had reason for their pride. Only Caselle itself, among the cities I have seen, rivaled it in size. It is said that there are three or four cities as large or larger in the lands of the Liau, but I have never seen them. It is perhaps the idle talk of travelers.

The walls alone were marvels, and men who had interest in such things came great distances to see them. The Outer Wall was ten times the height of a man and had a road on top for carrying soldiers. The Inner Wall was even higher, perhaps twice as high, and it, too, had a road. The men who came to see the walls said that their construction was marvelous, that their size and length made them a wonder. The only interest they had for me was the fact that they had never been breached. Never, not even by Basrath.

We rode toward the Barbarian Gate openly, without fear of attack. It is so called, this gate, because it is the only one of the Twelve Gates that faces directly out into the Plain. Caravans leaving through it faced the worst chance of meeting with Altaii lances, or Eikonan or even Morassa. They came, though. They came because their losses to the people of the Plain were worth it if ever so often a caravan made it to the mountains to trade for gems and precious metals, for furs and perfumes and for strange things from the lands beyond the mountains. Also, a merchant often rejoiced to buy his rival's goods from us, and sometimes his rival.

At the gate an officer of the City Guard stepped out to confront us, and we slowed until he should wave us on. He did not. Nervously he looked from Harald to me and back again, tugging at his beard. As we came to a halt he drew himself up.

"Who are you? What are you doing here?"

Some of my men laughed. They thought he was making a joke or trying to build up to an insult. I thought of the Wind and Loewin running overhead and was not so certain. There had been a two-toed gromit in my tent three days past, too. Darkness was gathering, but was this just another omen or was it the place of ending?

Suddenly I realized that everyone had fallen silent, waiting for me to answer. Harald had an expectant smile on his face. I leaned down, smiling a smile that was perhaps grimmer than I intended.

"Have you no eyes to see with? Surely it is plain that I am a merchant of Devia, and these are a troupe of Cerduan dancing girls."

The lances fell to laughing and slapping their thighs. Even a few of the Lantans were hiding smiles. The officer had no smiles.

"I must know what you are doing here. You will not be allowed into the city until I do."

At last Harald realized that this was not the usual banter of the gates. "Why all this questioning?" he growled. "Are you afraid that forty Altaii lances will take your city?"

The officer swallowed hard, his face paling. Stumbling backward he raised his hand. Suddenly we faced a dozen crossbows, the bowmen spread in an arc across the gateway. There were shiftings behind me, men loosening swords in their scabbards, freeing lances.

I studied the men before me, and I knew that this had not been planned. They were uncertain and as nervous as their officer. Besides, had they meant to kill us, had they had orders to do so, there would have been more of them. Even if every crossbowman hit his mark, there would still be twice their number of lances to cut them down and ride away.

"Enough," I said. "It has been the custom of our people for centuries to come to the Twin Thrones when we passed your city, to let your people know that we come for trade, not fighting. You know that as well as I do. Now you have two choices. The first is to tell your men to fire. You will not kill all of us. Some will live to ride back to our tents with word of what happened here. Then my spirit"—I freed my lance from the stirrup socket—"and your spirit will see how many Altaii lances it takes to tear down the walls of Lanta. Otherwise, stand aside. We enter now." I kneed my horse forward.

For just an instant he hesitated. Then he broke. "Stand aside," he shouted. Seeing us bearing down on him he forgot his dignity and scrambled out of the way, falling on his face in the dirt.

The crossbowmen split, moving to the sides of the road in confusion. We moved from a walk to a trot and went through them in a cloud of dust.

Once past I raised my fist, and we slowed again

to a walk. The bowmen made no move to hinder us. They stood watching as the dust of our passage settled around them.

From the Outer Wall to the Inner Wall was a distance of perhaps two hundred and fifty paces. All of that distance between the roads was a tangle of hovels, taverns and thieves' markets called Low Town. It was always a noisy place, full of bargainers' cries and drunken gaiety, where a man could have his purse cut three times and be propositioned seven times for acts he'd never before heard of, all in a five-minute walk. Now we rode toward the inner gate through an empty, silent quarter. Obeying some instinct natural to dwellers in such places, they had sensed the trouble at the outer gate and gone to ground. When we had left they would come out again.

At the inner gate some dozens of Low Town peddlers seemed torn between obeying their impulse to run and staying to save their wares. These they had laid out for those people of the city who would come as far as the gate, but would never enter the city shanties. The guards there looked at us suspiciously as we rode through. They peered toward the outer gate, but seeing no signal or alarm they contented themselves with fingering their weapons and glowering at us as we passed.

Harald released his breath in a rush, and I realized I had been holding my own. "We are in, Wulfgar, but I'll tell you straight out that I don't like it. Not at all. I have had words with the City Guard before at the gates, angry words, curses. I've never had anything like that, though."

"We had better hope the way out is no harder than the way in."

He looked at me as if he had not thought of that possibility. "Do you think it will not be?"

"Loewin is in the sky during the daylight. The Wind is early this year. I saw a two-toed gromit in my tent three days ago."

"You're a man of good tidings today. Have you seen blood in the wine? Has a dril entered your tent?"

"I don't know," I said calmly. "I'll check when I get back."

"Well, at least you're willing to talk about getting back. I was beginning to think, with all the portents flying about, that we should just open our veins and have it over with."

"Not yet. Orne," I called, turning back to the lances. "Bartu."

The two men moved up beside me. Neither looked like an Altaii, though both had been born in the tents. Bartu was short and bowlegged, with dark eyes. Orne was even taller than Harald, and his hair was as red as a sea rover's.

"Pass the word back to the others," I said. "Be ready for trouble at any instant, trouble beyond the ordinary, but don't get into any fights unless you're attacked. Is that understood?"

"It's understood, Wulfgar," said Orne. Bartu looked disappointed.

"And stay away from the women."

Bartu made a sound of protest. It was an even gamble whether he loved women or fighting more. To be deprived of either was a hardship.

Orne nodded, and the two of them slowed to fall back into the lances.

"Do you really expect trouble here?" Harald asked.

In truth it was not the place one would usually expect to be attacked. The streets were crowded. In the market square outside the Mar'yan Arena busy merchants making deals for the shipment of thousands of gold imperials' worth of goods rubbed shoulders with beggars selling sweets for a copper.

A few, perhaps those soon to leave on caravans that would try to cross the Plain, eyed us anxiously. Most ignored us. In this city a few horsemen from the Plain could cause no stir. Such could not compare with the travelers from distant lands who thronged the streets. Indeed, fully half of those I saw seemed to be from some far place.

A dealer in gems in the purple and red of Tyria, his people trailing behind, pushed past a group of Hyksos from the south. Merchants from Tallis and Asyat argued loudly over bales of snow-crawler fur. Two sea rovers from Telmark or Varangia haggled over the price of fish. A hooded Tafawri warrior sat before a tavern sipping tea, disdainful of entering with unbelievers, oblivious of the crowd around him.

No, there was no attraction in a few men from the Plain. Or there should not be. Why then did I have this feeling that somewhere there were those who watched us, as I might watch the pieces in the Game of War?

And then we were at the huge square that was the center of the city. On that broad expanse of polished stone there were no crowds, no bargainers, no noise. There was nothing but the wide, empty square and the place we sought. The Palace of the Twin Thrones, the palace of the Queens of Lanta.

# II

## INTO THE PALACE

~

The palace gave the appearance of frivolous beauty, of crystal towers and huge expanses of wall inlaid with gems from every land known to man. It glittered in the sun, twinkling from a thousand facets, and beneath the glitter was a fortress.

The Palace Guard, the men who stood watch on the walls and gates of the palace, were also splendid to see, nearly as much so as the palace. Their armor was covered with precious metals and set with gems. Some of the officers appeared to be covered with jewels from head to foot. There were rumors that they were chosen for their looks and promoted for their vigor in the beds of the queens. Whether that was true or not, it was well to remember that they had held the Twin Thrones inviolate for over a thousand years. In that time, no one had taken the thrones by force, and those who had tried had screamed away their lives in the dungeons beneath the palace or been impaled on its walls.

We crossed the square at a gallop. The guards at the main gate of the palace shifted uncomfortably as we approached, and more than one hand went to a jeweled sword hilt. It seemed that no one in Lanta wanted to see Altaii warriors this day. That bothered me not at all. The Altaii go where they will, when they will. Indeed, it is said we are most often seen when least expected.

Harald and I reined in before the gate, and our lances broke to either side behind us. For a moment they seemed to mill around aimlessly, but when they stopped they had formed two lines, back to back, one facing the palace and one facing away. Their lines were not the straight, rigid lines of a Lantan formation, and I heard some of the Palace Guardsmen laugh. They had no service with the caravans, or they would have known that those undisciplined riders could take ten times their number of well-ordered city troops.

I dismounted and handed my lance and reins to Orne, and Harald and I approached the gates together. Almost without thinking I eased my short swords in their sheaths. There was the smell of trouble in the air, the sharp, brassy smell of blood.

"Are you certain it was a two-toed gromit?" Harald asked.

"It could have been a three-toed."

We both spat to ward off the evil of such a thing. Everyone knows the three-toed gromit is a sure and certain harbinger of death.

"You like to live dangerously, Wulfgar."

The guards before the gate drew up in a four-deep formation, spears aimed at our chests. "No one is allowed to enter."

It was impossible to tell which one of them had spoken. Leather and armor creaked as the lances shifted position. My hands went again to my sword hilts, and briefly I wondered if it had indeed been three-toed. The sands of a man's life may run out at any time. Their number is known to no one. And that smell was growing stronger.

"These—ah—people are an exception."

A short, bearded man with an oily voice stepped through a small door in the wall beside the gate. His tunic was of many colors, slashed after the fashion of Lanta so that other colors showed when he bowed to us. "You are expected, of course." His eyes darted like a bird's, and he couldn't suppress a sneer as they came to rest on our plain and dusty garb. He motioned toward the door. "If you will come in. My name is Ara. I am seneschal of the Royal Palace."

I ducked through, then stopped so suddenly that he almost trod on my heels. "You have heard of what happened at the gate." It was not a question. I was certain that he had.

"Yes." He smiled unctuously. "It was unfortunate. You may be assured that the officer in question has already been disciplined."

"That doesn't concern me," I said. "What you do to your officers is up to you. We are here to visit the rulers of your city, according to custom."

In truth I was interested, though I did not want him to know it. Whether they had actually done anything to the officer or not, they wanted me to think they had. They wanted to soothe us, and that was even more unusual than our reception at the gate. Lanta had never cared for our feelings before. I saw Harald's ears pricking and shook my head.

"If you have no interest in how the man has been disciplined, perhaps you would enjoy some wine and a chance to refresh yourselves after your ride. A girl, perhaps, fresh from the training pens of Asmara? Or two?" He smiled again.

He smiled too much for my liking, this Ara, and I was beginning to get angry about these attempts to stop us from what should have been a simple visit. Also, I was beginning to tire of waiting for the lightning. If it was going to strike, let it strike.

"Lord Harald and I came for a purpose. Enjoy the girl and the wine yourself. We will go to the great hall."

I started down the hall, and in a step Harald was with me. In two steps Ara was fluttering around us.

"You cannot! The great hall is, ah, that is, it is being used for a ceremony at present, a most sacred ceremony. You will understand, of course, that outsiders, if you will pardon me for naming you so, cannot be allowed to witness it. My lords? My lords!"

I turned to him, and he backed away hurriedly. "I have a mind to see this ceremony that is so secret. I suggest you cease hindering me before I forget your honorable position."

"It may mean your death," the seneschal warned.

"The omens say my life hangs by a thread. Perhaps I choose to cut the thread."

"But your friend—"

Harald laughed. "If an Altaii chooses to die, what can another Altaii do but kill his slayer and die beside him?"

"You are mad, both of you."

"If we are," I growled, "it is our madness, and no concern of yours. It would be a shame to get blood on that fashionable tunic." I fingered a sword hilt significantly. "The great hall?"

"You would offer violence here, in the very halls of the palace?"

"I'll not only offer it, I'll give it. And there's been enough of this delaying. Lead us, or we'll go alone, and leave you here for the guards to find."

His fingers plucked restlessly at his tunic, and he looked at us as if he had never seen the like before.

"The great hall," Harald prompted.

"If I do," he muttered, almost to himself, "both your heads and mine may decorate the palace walls by first moonrise. If I do not, you will surely—" He shook himself. "Very well, barbarians. It seems I have little choice."

"Lead, seneschal," I said.

Without another word he moved ahead of us

down the hall, as if anxious to be done with whatever might come. He did not slow until we came to great wooden doors, their surfaces covered with intricate carvings. Four guards stood stiffly before them.

"Open," he ordered.

The guards looked at one another doubtfully, and Ara made a harsh gesture. Slowly two of them moved to take handles set in the doors. Straining, they drew the doors open. From inside came music and the sounds of drunken revelry.

"A ceremony," I said sarcastically, and we followed Ara into the great hall.

The musicians faltered in their playing, then raggedly picked up the tune again. Murmuring spread through the gathered nobles as they became aware of our presence. The dancing girls did not miss a step. They would be whipped if they did not perform beautifully, or if they stopped without command, no matter the reason.

All that happened, but to me it was as if it happened somewhere else. My eyes were on the tall, carved ivory thrones at the end of the hall, or rather on the two women who sat in them. Eilinn and Elana, the Queens of Lanta.

According to their legends the city was founded by two sisters, goddesses who descended from the sky and ruled from the Twin Thrones. Each was succeeded by her eldest daughter, and that became the Lantan line of succession. Eldest daughter succeeded eldest daughter. If one queen died without an heir, then the eldest daughter of the other queen succeeded her, and the second daughter succeeded her mother. By such a thing had Eilinn and Elana reached the thrones, so that the Twin Thrones were indeed occupied by twins.

By not so much as the smallest point could they be told apart. Silver-blond hair was braided identically, piled high and set with pearls that could have been duplicates, one of the other. Four identical green eyes surveyed the hall imperiously from faces that appeared to be mirror images. And yet I knew them. I had not been this way since they took the thrones, but I knew them. And somehow, I knew also, they were tied to the omens of my fate. If the dril picked my bones, it would be because of these two women. And if they did not—If they did not—Now, there was a thought to be reckoned with.

"You may approach us, Ara," said Eilinn.

As the seneschal hurried forward to prostrate himself, the sweat of fear gleaming on his face, Harald touched my arm. "Look you what is here before us."

"Morassa," I breathed.

To the right of the dais on which the Twin Thrones stood, in a place of honor, sat three men I had never thought to see within these walls, much less seated on the right hand of the throne. Bryar sat there, the best-known war leader of the Morassa, and Daiman, who was thought to be their most successful raider, if there was such a thing among the Morassa. More importantly, Ivo sat there. Ivo, who sat on the right hand of Brecon, king of all the Morassa.

"If you would clear the cattle dung from your ears, barbarian, perhaps you could hear when you are spoken to."

Eilinn's scornful voice broke my chain of thought. The dancers had cleared the floor, the musicians were silent and everyone stared at Harald and myself.

"You are bidden to attend our audience, to present your petitions and be entertained as befits your station," she continued.

My jaw tightened at the laughter that greeted her sally. Ivo laughed so hard to hear her class us with her vassals and petitioners that the great scar across his face stood out white against the red. I forced myself to relax, forced a smile to my face.

"I am sorry, Your Highness. I was merely admiring the hangings of your great hall and wondering what we will do with them in the tents. I think that after they are cut up they will do for carpets."

There was silence in the hall. The nobles waited to see how the queens would take a barbarian who spoke of taking hangings from the walls of the very palace itself. When they smiled, Elana a bit stiffly, the rest roared with laughter. Ivo looked a bit disappointed. Perhaps he would rather have seen our blood on the floor and had it over with.

"It would be interesting to see you do this thing, barbarian," Eilinn said dryly. "When and how do you intend to steal the hangings?"

"How must remain my secret, and as to when, not yet. But I will let you and your sister know when I do. It would be rude to do otherwise."

"Of course. You would not wish to be rude." Her contempt was plain. Her sister, Elana, still watched us silently, as if we were some strange and rare animals. "You will be given places at the audience now, as I said."

Servants came to lead us to a place among the gathering, and as they did my anger rose again. Harald stiffened and would have spoken, but I gestured, and he went without the words I also wanted to say. His face, however, was as bleak as the Plain in midwinter.

We were not seated at the head of the hall, among the ranking lords, as was our due. Not only were we placed with the merchants and lesser nobles, but at the very end of the hall, where a wandering beggar who had been brought in to amuse the gathering might be seated.

Other servants came forward and, with great show, placed bowls of perfume on the floor around us, as if to shield our neighbors from the aroma of horses and leather. Platters of meat, small pieces, half burned and half raw, were offered to us, and goblets of sour-smelling wine. The girls who served us were untrained kitchen laborers dressed in greasy, ragged shifts of coarse cloth. Even the soldiers near us were being served by perfumed girls clad in sheer silks.

The men across the hall from us were grinning

openly, nudging one another and telling jokes behind their hands. Ivo did not seem to think much of it, but Bryar and Daiman laughed until they seemed ready to slide from their chairs. Bryar was spilling wine all over the floor.

Such things were not completely unheard of. Sometimes the ruler of a city would amuse themselves and their court by insulting visitors they called barbarians. What worried me now was that the insult was being offered while the Morassa sat in places of honor. And they had been willing to bribe us with sensuously trained girls, forgoing the insults and affronts, to keep us from this hall. These things worried me.

Once more Eilinn broke into my thoughts. "My sister and I wonder why you have come to our city."

An innocuous question, casually asked, and yet, like the officer at the gate, she should not have had to ask it.

"It has been our custom for centuries to stop at cities we pass to trade," I said. "Always we visit the ruler of the city to make it known that we are there for trade, not to fight. Surely it has not been that long since other Altaii have stopped here."

Eilinn brushed past my words, as I had known she would, for after all I had only told her what she already knew.

"You have no other reason for coming here at this time?"

Someone shifted in the shadows behind the thrones, but the anger was on me again, and I paid no mind. She probed at me clumsily, as if I were too stupid to realize what she did. Whether she did it because to her I was only a barbarian from the Plain or for a deeper reason, I did not care.

"In truth, there is another reason for my coming, a reason of little importance, involving nothing of note, but a reason."

Harald gave me a sidelong glance, for this was news to him. Eilinn leaned forward eagerly, and even Elana, her composure seemingly broken, listened more intently.

"And the reason is?"

"I am looking for slave girls."

"Slave girls?" she said blankly.

"Slave girls," I repeated. "Not just any girls, of course. I want a matched pair, twins in fact. Their hair should be the palest blond, and their eyes green. If they are untrained or clumsy, it does not matter. My slave mistress will no doubt train them to perfection."

Harald spoke softly from the side of his mouth. "I think it was the three-toed gromit after all."

Stunned silence filled the hall. Eilinn stared at me in shock, and Elana seemed to no longer breathe. Then the silence was ripped away by an explosion of shouts and oaths. Fists were shaken, and hands went to sword hilts.

Eilinn rose from her throne, eyes flashing. "How dare you," she hissed. "You barbarian animal! You hulking, dung-soaked—"

At the touch from her sister she stopped, though

with obvious difficulty, and the rest of the hall did the same. Elana smiled, almost warmly, and spoke for the first time.

"Perhaps, dear sister, our—ah—guests would like to see their futures. They speak so confidently of stealing hangings and"—her mouth twisted in distaste—"of other things. Let them see the truth of matters."

Instantly Eilinn's humor was restored. "Yes." She laughed. "Let them see their future. Sayene! Sayene, come out and show these men what awaits."

From the shadows behind the thrones a woman stepped out. Even without the robes she wore I would have known her by the respectful silence with which everyone but the two queens greeted her. She was a Sister of Wisdom, a seeress. Her presence firmed my resolve to consult Mayra, the Sister of Wisdom among my own tents.

Sayene bowed slightly toward the thrones, but only slightly. "I advise against this, my queens. I—"

"And I say it is to be done," Eilinn broke in.

The seeress nodded, but her mouth was tight. It was not important enough for her to oppose the queen, but it still angered her. "An acolyte will suffice for this," she said.

Another woman came forward, also in the robes of a Sister of Wisdom, but with the scarf of an acolyte, a learner, about her head. She bowed, to Sayene before the queens, then took a pouch from her belt and began. Slowly she poured a powder out, and a five-pointed star took shape on the floor.

Harald shifted, and in truth I was not comfortable myself. Magic is a thing foreign to the male, and therefore disquieting.

A second acolyte came forward with candles, and the first placed them, one at each point of the star. With an incantation and the ringing of a bell each candle was lit. The acolyte who had been chosen surveyed the pattern she had set, then smiled unpleasantly at Harald and me. The stage was laid. I could only hope the play was to our liking.

The chosen one unfastened her robes and let them fall.

All of the light in the room seemed suddenly to focus on her. It was as if her skin took on a glow.

She moved to face the topmost point of the star and raised her arms. There was silence. And then she began to chant. At first the words were understandable, but they began to change. Although her voice grew no softer the meaning of her words seemed to somehow slip away, as though they had not quite been heard. Then, slowly, a change began inside the figure on the floor.

The air within the star began to shimmer, like heat waves rising from the Plain at midday. The shimmers increased, grew stronger, began to thicken and jell. Before our eyes the empty air was filled with a dark tube, a tube that began to show images.

From indistinct shapes the images became clearer, sharper, until they were plain to all. Inside the tube knelt Harald and myself, naked, chained, cowering as though in fear. Sitting there, knowing that I did sit there and was not kneeling on the floor, still I felt a sense of drifting, of doubt as to whether I was real or the things before me were.

Harald's breath came in rasps, and his knuckles were white, but the set of his face showed rage replacing fear. The other men, Lantans and Morassa alike, took the vision with little more welcome than I. A few laughed weakly, prompted by their serving girls' giggles, but they, too, felt the alienness of it to men.

Once more the images were moving. They cringed away from something unseen. And images of Eilinn and Elana stepped out of nowhere. They were perfect images, and yet different from the real women, taller in some way, more regal, more commanding.

The fake Eilinn and Elana walked toward the fake Wulfgar and Harald. Suddenly they held whips, and began to ply them with laughter and cries of delight. The images of us also cried out, but with howls and screams and pleas for mercy, writhing and twisting on the stone floor.

With a muttered oath Harald started to rise, but I grabbed his arm and held him back.

"Let me go, Wulfgar. There are worse places to die."

"And there are better," I replied. "Keep your head, and we may yet walk out of here."

Even as I rose I did not know what I was going to do, but something guided my hand to the dagger at my belt. I realized that I was smiling. The test of the image, and maybe our way out, was right there.

Quickly, before any could move to stop me, I drew the dagger and threw it, and if I threw for the heart of the fake queen who whipped the fake Wulfgar, it is to be understood.

The men around me stared dully, wondering what I was about, but the acolyte saw, saw and screamed, a scream of fear and fury and denial. The dagger touched the image, and the light of a thousand suns blossomed in the center of the hall. Light beat at us, tearing through closed eyes and sheltering arms to burrow into the center of the brain. And the sound began. It was a sound that turned the blood to jelly, that knifed to the very marrow, a sound beside which the earlier scream of the acolyte was as the laughter of children.

The sound faded and was gone, and the light died. Spots danced before my eyes when I tried to see, but I made my way down onto the floor. The candles were melted puddles, still bubbling from the heat. The star was still there, burned into the stone of the floor. In the center of the star lay my dagger, unharmed and not even warm to the touch.

The acolyte lay halfway down the hall, lying as if thrown there by a giant hand. She seemed twisted, unnatural in some way. It was as if her body seemed to blur when the eye tried to focus on it. Sayene said something sharply, and the other acolytes rushed forward to cover the body. They also avoided looking at it, as if the sight were more than they could bear.

At Sayene's voice the silence broke. People began to speak again, to breathe and move, but none loudly. I slid the dagger back into its sheath.

"The blade has been with me since I can remember," I said. "It was given to me when I could barely grasp it. My imprint is on it as surely as if it was my own hand or my foot. Had the image been true, the power would have recoiled against me."

I did not look at the covered shape on the floor, but my message was clear to all.

Sayene wasn't interested in the truth of the image. "You risked putting cold steel into a spell-star, cold steel that carried part of your life force. Why?"

What answer I would have given I can't say, but I was spared answering by Eilinn.

"I don't care why he did it," she shrieked. "He has killed an acolyte in my service, killed her in my own palace, and in my own great hall."

"Her own lie killed her," I said. "My life was also in balance against the truth of her image."

She laughed in disbelief. "You think I'm going to let you walk out of here after this. You actually think—"

"I no longer care what you think," I interrupted. "I came here to announce our presence. Our tents lie to the west and south, an hour's ride away. If your merchants wish to trade, they are welcome."

With that I turned on my heel. Harald joined me, and we began the long walk from the hall. Eilinn shouted behind us in fury, with Elana and Sayene struggling to calm her. With every step I expected an arrow through my back, and the prickling between my shoulder blades stopped only when the doors to the great hall closed behind us.

Harald looked at me and raised an eyebrow. "Perhaps," he said, "it wasn't a three-toed gromit after all."

# III

## THE MOST HIGH

Once out of the great hall we picked up our pace from a dignified walk to a hurried trot. If Sayene and Elana won the argument we would be allowed to leave unimpeded, though why they were willing to argue for the lives of two barbarians I could not understand. On the other hand, if Eilinn prevailed, warriors would come pouring out of every opening any moment. Within paces of the door I slid to a halt. Harald nearly ran into me, then cursed as he saw why I had stopped.

From a side corridor glided three figures, man-sized, hooded and robed in shimmering bluish gray. Each carried a rod, longer than he was tall, a Staff of Power. The Most High were in the palace.

We Altaii have little to do with gods, living or otherwise, but a man must give some measure of respect to beings who have wagons that fly through the air and powers as great as, or perhaps greater than, the Sisters of Wisdom. A measure of respect I will give them, but now, on top of all that had gone before, I wished more than anything else to know why they had come.

The Most High do not visit the houses of men casually. Their appearance always foretells great events, times to shake the earth and move the sky. For them to give their favor to Lanta while the Morassa sat within the palace walls could tell of no good for the Altaii.

At the same instant that we became aware of them, they became aware of us. To my surprise they jerked away from us, as though startled or frightened. The bird-like trillings they call speech rose as if from a stirred nest of timir, and before either of us could move, one of them lifted its Staff toward us, and we could move no longer.

I struggled, but my body was turned to stone for all the control I had over it. I could not even turn my head to look at Harald, but his ragged breathing told me he was still there, as frozen as I.

The Most High seemed to ignore us. There was little enough reason for them not to, in truth. They faced each other in a circle, and though the trilling speech had died away I had the feeling that they still conversed.

Finally they stopped and turned back to us, seeming to study us for the moment. Then, paying no more attention than if we were just two more pieces of statuary, they glided smoothly past and on down the hall.

As they moved away I felt the stiffness melt from my limbs, like water running out of a jug. I took a shuddering breath, and the feel of being free to shudder was greater than I could have believed.

"What can they be doing here?" Harald asked.

"I don't know," I replied, "but I think the odds against our leaving the city alive are growing shorter."

He laughed. "Then let us not stay to take wagers."

The guards outside eyed us curiously, but they had received no orders and so let us pass. There was a stir among the lances as we approached. They, at least, seemed to sense something, to feel the danger. Swords were eased, and lances casually freed.

Orne brought my horse and leaned down to hand me the reins. "There is trouble? We fight?"

"Not now. At least, I hope not now." I swung into the saddle. "Let's ride."

We pushed harder now, moved faster than we had on the way in. Even without words the urgency had passed to the lances, and they rode with purpose. There was an air about us now such that, where men had previously paid little attention to us, and we had had to wend our way through crowded streets, now the crowds parted before us, and men eyed us warily, as if fearing sudden violence. They had no need of fear. The gates were our only goal, the gates and the Plain beyond. There would be no violence if no one tried to stop us.

My mind was not on the ride to the gate, though. I merely rode with the others. What kept running through my mind was why. There was a pattern to the events of the day, a pattern that was as important as life to us, but I could not find it.

The Morassa apparently were destroying the water, yet they lived by the waterholes no less than anyone else. They were scavengers, pickers over better men's leavings, but the queens, with all their pride and arrogance, feted them and seated them in a place of honor. Even if their presence was strange, stranger still was the attempt to hide it from us. What about their visit must be kept from the Altaii? And why did they think we had come for some hidden reason? Why did we come at this time, she had asked. At this time. What was special about this time above any other? And the Most High. The Most High, indeed.

We rode through the inner gate, and I turned to look back. The road ran straight back to the palace. Twelve roads ran from the palace like the spokes of a wheel, one to each of the Twelve Gates, unbroken except for market squares. The wall I faced, the Inner Wall, towered impregnably, topped by ballistae, onagers and catapults that had rained boulders and firepots on the few armies that had tried to besiege Lanta.

I turned my horse slowly, and some of the peddlers gathered around the inner gate made a sign to ward off evil. Harald and the lances waited outside the outer gate impatiently, but I made no haste.

The Outer Wall had been constructed by men who knew that the winds of war blow in many directions. There was no covering facing the Inner Wall. Each level was open, and an enemy who took it would find themselves open as well, open to arrows and quarrels from the Inner Wall. The men who had built it had planned well. The men who now guarded it planned less well.

Wooden walls closed off many of the open spaces, and in some areas even small huts had been built. The men on those walls no longer stood their watches in the rain and the wind, and if the original planners' design had been ruined, it did not matter. Lanta the Unconquerable would never fall, not even so much as a part of her Outer Wall.

The officer who had been at the gate was gone, and the guards, too, had been changed. Those who manned the gate now glowered at me, but did not speak, as I slowed almost to a stop to look closely at one of the famous Iron Gates. Those gates had withstood every battering ram brought against them. They looked as solid as the walls.

When finally I joined the others outside the gate Harald shook his head. "I was beginning to wonder if you were waiting for orders to be sent to stop us. Perhaps you had some wish to fight your way out."

"I was merely thinking how to make good on a boast," I said.

He had begun to follow me, but at that he stopped.

"Did the Most High addle your brains, Wulfgar? Or did Sayene cast a spell while we watched her acolyte?"

"Neither, Harald. What wits I had before I entered Lanta are still with me. The thing you do not see is that we are set on a path, now. It may not be of our choosing, and the gods alone know where it leads, but I don't think we have any choice but to follow it."

He pulled his cloak tighter around him, though the wind seemed to be slacking a little. "If we must travel this path, as you say, perhaps we can arrange a few surprises along the way for those who set us on it."

"That we will. I will consult Mayra, and you speak to Dvere. In three days we will meet again with what we can find out."

"Done," he said, and we spat to seal the bargain.

We rode then in silence, and when he moved away with his lances to the south there were no words spoken. What must be said, had been said. It was enough.

# IV

## A WANDERER

A few minutes' ride from the tents, Orne pulled up beside me and gestured off to the right. "My lord, riders."

A dozen men were coming toward us, Altaii by their garb. One rode leaning forward in his saddle as if wounded. I halted to see if they had encountered Morassa.

As they came closer I could see that two of them carried a lance between them, resting on their saddles. Tied to it, face to the ground, was a young woman. They pulled up in a swirl of dust.

"My lord," said their leader, raising his hand in salute. He was one of those who carried the lance with the captive.

"Have you seen anything of the Morassa, warrior? Tents or riders or sign?"

"No, my lord." He smiled. "Usually they do their best to avoid us."

"And where did you find this prize?" I asked.

The young woman was securely fastened to the lance at her ankles, knees, waist and shoulders. Her arms had been pulled behind her and fastened together above the haft so that her hands rested on the swells of her buttocks. She was tall, unusually so for a woman, but she did not appear dangerous enough to warrant being bound so closely. In her nakedness she could certainly conceal no weapons.

"She is a Wanderer," he said simply.

I looked at her again at that, with more interest. Wanderers are hardly a common thing. Usually they are found well away from any city or group of people. They dress strangely, speak in unknown tongues and sometimes carry odd, even miraculous weapons.

Always they are women. I have never seen or heard of a male Wanderer. Why this should be, I don't know, for they claim, when they have learned a civilized tongue, that there are indeed men in the worlds they come from.

That is perhaps the strangest thing of all about the Wanderers. They claim to come from worlds where there are wonders unheard of, and all taken as casually as a clay pot. The worlds they claim are sometimes different, sometimes the same, but even if they are found within a year of each other may insist that a hundred years or more separates their lives. And the Sisters of Wisdom say they all speak the truth.

As if she felt my scrutiny she looked up at me. She was beautiful. Her black hair was close cropped, but it seemed to suit her. To my surprise she studied me as I studied her. Her face was dusty and tired, but her blue eyes were calm and appraising. By now the usual Wanderer would have been thinking that she was going mad, but this one studied me.

"Her garments," I said.

"She wore these." He motioned, and one of the others handed me a large bundle.

The clothes made no sense, but then they were no odder than others I have seen on Wanderers. They consisted of tunic and trousers of a sleek, black cloth, suitable for a warm or mild climate, and sandals with tall thin heels, suitable for nowhere at all. There was also a fur coat, as if she intended wearing the other flimsy things in the snow. Senseless.

She caught my eye again and worked her mouth as if she wanted the leather gag removed. Her plea was directed to the wrong man, as she would soon learn. She was not my property.

"Besides the woman and her garments," the warrior said, "there is this."

I took the object he handed me carefully. Twice before had I seen such things. Once a single dose of magic had remained inside it. This one was a finely worked piece of metal, inlaid with gold scrollwork, and small enough to fit in the palm of my hand. Such things carried death as surely as sword or lance.

"That is the reason Sweyn rides as if he had coals burning on his saddle, my lord."

"How did it happen?"

"When first we spotted her, she was making hard going of it. I don't think she's used to walking on rough ground. At any rate, we rode around her in a circle, in case she was carrying such a weapon, and it's just as well we did.

"As soon as she saw us she brought out the weapon and tried to use it. We moved and dodged, and she hit no one. Finally she fell to her knees, as if she was giving up. Sweyn had seen her first, so his was the right to bind her, if he could, but at the last instant, when he was half off his horse, with one foot in the stirrup, she raised the weapon again. He managed to knee his horse, and so received this in his buttock instead of his middle."

A ripple of laughter spread at Sweyn's expense as his leader held up a small, flattened pellet of metal. How so small a thing could be thrown hard enough to strike with the force of a war shaft was a mystery not even the Sisters of Wisdom had been able to divine.

I handed the weapon back. "Do you intend to sell it?"

"That we do, Lord Wulfgar. Artifacts of the Wanderers are things for men who have money to waste. With the gold it brings in we'll buy some useful things, horses or perhaps some cattle."

"Maybe more," I said. "What is your name, warrior?"

"I am called Aelfric, my lord."

"Well, Aelfric, follow me, and we'll ride back to the tents together. And tell Sweyn to be more careful in the future. He can't hold a lance if he has to ride on his stomach."

Sweyn laughed as hard as the rest at that.

"I will tell him, my lord," Aelfric managed to get out, "but I think he's already learned that lesson."

I spurred away, and they fell in with the other men, all still laughing, but all alert. Even here, close to the tents, each man scanned the countryside as he rode, watching for possible ambush sites. I felt pride in them, the pride of warriors. With such men as these I could indeed ride to the walls of Lanta, no, to the walls of Caselle itself.

Shortly we came in sight of the tents, three clusters of three groups each around another group of three tents in the center. Between them the life of an Altaii camp went on, men gaming, boys racing horses, girls hurrying about their chores. It was a welcome sight.

In the distance were the cattle herds, source not only of food, bone and leather, but also of the joke we often tell strangers, that we are but simple herdsmen, trading in meat and hides. No one has ever believed it that I know of.

Nearer to hand were the horse herds. The guards set on them, boys who had not yet won the warrior brand, raised their lances in salute and called out greetings as we passed. Others shouted to us from the tents, and a few asked ribald questions of

Sweyn. For all the bustle of Lanta, these tents were a cheerier place.

In the center cluster of tents the other riders split away, each heading for his own tent. Only Orne remained with me. He waited until I gave my horse to Rolf, another who lacked the warrior brand, and who, according to custom, cared for my horses and armor until he should win it.

"My lord," Orne said then, "in the city, when I asked if we would fight, you said not yet. And on the way out of the city you studied the walls as if looking for a weakness to attack. Do we fight?"

"For us there is always a fight," I replied slowly. "It is only to decide when and with whom, but the fight is always there."

After a moment he nodded. "It is answer enough." He raised a hand in salute. "Until we ride, my lord."

I watched him ride away. Answer enough, he called it. It was no answer at all, not anymore. If I could find no better the omens were sure to be fulfilled, for me and perhaps for many others.

Mayra's tent was set away from the others, away from the disturbing influences of iron and of men. I shed sword belt and armor well away from it, and did not approach too near, myself. In a short time she came to me, a knot of acolytes trailing behind her with bundles. She was to me what Sayene was to the Queens of Lanta. She was a Sister of Wisdom.

"I have an answer for you," she said, "for the question about the fanghorns and the disappearing water, but it is cryptic, I'm afraid."

I waved that away. "I have another question, now. There is something which links the Morassa, Lanta and the Most High. What is it?"

She laughed, and though I knew she was old enough to be my mother's mother, when she laughed she was a girl again. "You never bring me easy questions, do you, Wulfgar? Never anything simple, like how to make the Plain bloom like a farmer's field." She shook her head. "Never mind. Tell me what you know, and I'll see what I can find out."

I told what had happened, from our arrival at the gate of Lanta to the time we left, leaving out no detail.

Mayra looked sad for a moment, then sighed. "Sayene grows wicked. She knew the vision would be false, she knew what might happen, and instead of opposing those spoiled children she serves she used a girl without much training so there would be less loss if something did go wrong. If the girl had to go sky-clad and use so much effort to produce such a small effect," she explained, "she could not have been very far along in her training, and Sayene would not have used a half-trained acolyte before the queens unless she had a good reason. Such as risking the loss of a girl in whom she had invested more time."

"Mayra, I'm not really interested in why Sayene did what she did."

"Whenever a Sister turns to evil it is a cause for sadness. But, just the same, I will see what I can do about this new question. Seat yourself over there out of the way."

I squatted on the ground where she had pointed and she began her preparations. The acolytes set up a tripod while Mayra took a silver bowl from a box. On the bottom of the bowl was the same star pattern that had been drawn on the floor of the great hall in Lanta. She placed the bowl on the tripod and, wetting a cloth with oil, wiped the surface of it.

Hands held flat on either side of the bowl, she muttered a few words. One of the acolytes held out a red bag. Mayra took a pinch of powder from it and dropped the powder into the bowl. It flared in a tongue of flame, gone almost before it formed. Another acolyte held out a small box, and Mayra dropped another portion of powder into the bowl.

This time there was only a glow, but the glow grew until a dome of light covered the bowl. Once more she put a hand on each side of the bowl and spoke an incantation. The dome of light grew brighter.

As the incantation faded, Mayra looked down into the bowl. For a long time she stood like that, staring down. Finally she motioned to me to come and look for myself.

Looking into the bowl was like looking into a window, but a window that looked down from the sky on a field. Only here and there on the field did something move. Suddenly, I realized what it was I saw. The moving things were dril, and they crawled over heaped mounds of bodies. Everywhere on the field, and the view seemed to stretch to the horizon, were heaps and mounds of dead and dying men and horses. And the men were Altaii.

I could not imagine a disaster of this size. To supply that many dead the Altaii nation would have to cease to exist. Oh, there might be a few boys too young to wield a sword, but numbers such as those would take everyone else among us without exception.

"Our future?" I said finally.

"Possibly." She took a pouch from beneath her robe, then hesitated. "The future is a fan, Wulfgar, a fan that spreads out from this moment. That scene is a possible point on that fan. A strong one, or it wouldn't have come so easily, and one tied to whatever links the Morassa, the Lantans and the Most High, but it does not have to be. Let me look a little further."

She knelt on the ground and filled her hands with rune-bones from the pouch. Three times she shook them at the sky, and three times at the ground, and then she cast them. She studied the pattern carefully, and the carvings that had landed uppermost, and I thought I saw a slight start of surprise.

"Yes," she muttered, almost to herself, "I should have expected her."

"Her?" I put in quickly, but she continued as if I hadn't spoken.

Twice more the rune-bones were shaken and cast, the last time with Mayra acting as though she knew exactly what they would say. At last she straightened.

"This is very interesting," she said. "Earlier I cast for answers to your question about the Plain seeming to get more hostile each year, and I got the same answer then that I do now."

"The same answer?"

"Yes. I told you it was cryptic, and it is. It seems that there is a girl, or young woman, who holds the key both to the struggle for the survival against the Plain and to the problem of the Lantans, the Morassa and the Most High."

"Well, who is she?" I asked. "How do I find her? And where?"

"I don't know any of those things. All I know is that she is a Wanderer, very tall, with fair skin, blue eyes and black hair cut short like a man's. What is it? You recognize the description? You've seen her?"

"She's in the camp," I laughed. "I rode in with the men who found her. She must be with Talva right now."

Mayra waved to her acolytes quickly. "Go to Talva. Tell her I want the woman I've just described, and if she makes any trouble tell her I'll give her a mad passion for old men with hunchbacks if she doesn't cooperate."

The acolytes hurried away, skirts flapping around their knees. I was wondering why she expected trouble from Talva.

"If you were a woman," she said when I asked, "you'd know. She is not satisfied with the avenues open to women. Being a Sister of Wisdom would suit her, but she has no talent for it, though it took six testings to convince her, and I'm not really sure that she is convinced. Being a scribe or a healer or a trader doesn't interest her. What she would like to do, I think, is lead warriors."

"Lead warriors?" I laughed, and then I saw she was serious. "Mayra, even if it was thinkable, she's a small woman. How would she expect to survive her first combat?"

"I don't think she intends fighting, herself. She just wants to lead. At every gathering of Free Women she harangues everyone there about how suited to command she is. Or if not that, she goes on about Caselle or Lanta or Ghalt and how women have positions of power in those cities."

"Then why doesn't she leave?"

"She doesn't leave," Mayra said as if explaining to a child. "She has a certain position here, remember, and in the cities she might not be able to duplicate it."

"Even so—"

"The girl," she said softly.

From the tents the acolytes came running, and with them was the Wanderer.

# V

# A QUESTION OF LANGUAGES

One acolyte ran on either side of the Wanderer holding a leading strap fastened to her neck. A third ran behind with a switch to make certain she didn't lag. She didn't.

Mayra studied her closely, even after they stopped and she fell to her knees breathing like a foundered horse. Slowly her breathing came under control, and she began to be aware of her surroundings. Her eye caught Mayra's, and she became very still.

Under Mayra's gaze her face grew red. She glared at me, at the acolytes. None of us moved, and she tried to force words past the gag between her teeth. Only angry burbles emerged.

"Remove the gag," Mayra said.

The Wanderer jerked at the first touch of the acolyte's fingers, then stilled as she realized what was intended. Her mouth worked to get rid of the leather taste. She used the time to study us and make a choice. She spoke to Mayra.

The words were sounds only, of no language I'd ever heard. Mayra shook her head gently. The woman understood that, at least, for she changed her speech. At any rate, the words sounded like another tongue. They were as senseless to me as the others had been.

She was quick, this woman from nowhere. Intently she leaned forward and spoke again, a few words only, in a third language, and then in a fourth. I wondered if she had been a scholar in the world she came from.

"It's no use, Mayra," I said. "She doesn't know any language we'll understand."

"I didn't expect her to, not a fresh-caught Wanderer. I had to get the rhythms and patterns of her speech before I can spell-teach her our tongue."

"I suppose I can't wait for her to learn it naturally," I said ruefully. "Very well. How much will it cost me?"

"Nothing," she replied, digging through another of the endless number of chests her acolytes seemed able to produce on command. "At least, it won't cost you any gold."

"Then what?" My voice was sharper than I had intended, and I softened it. "What will it cost?"

"A service, Wulfgar." She poured the contents of several small bottles into a bowl and began stirring them together. "You will aid me in a spell, and that will pay for this, and for the spell-sayings this morning and this evening."

I made an effort to keep my tone steady. "I know nothing about your magics and spells, Mayra. They're not meant for men, and I don't have anything to do with them."

She folded her hands in her lap and sat back. "You'll have to do with this one, or you'll wait until this Wanderer picks up enough language to tell you what you need to know."

"Mayra, you know she has answers I need. You told me so yourself. Will you wait until there's a fanghorn inside your tent?"

"I will wait as long as I need to wait." A small smile touched her lips, and I had the feeling that she was amused at the fight she knew she would win. "You won't be harmed, or not unless I am, and worse than you. You won't be changed. You'll be the same man after that you were before. I promise that. Wulfgar, this thing may not have to be done, but if it must I will have to work through and with another. And in this case, for some strange reason, I know it must be a man. I know it must be you."

I looked at the Wanderer. She knew that in some manner our conversation had concerned her, and she returned my look curiously. Finally I nodded.

"Done," I said hollowly. In truth I felt more than a little hollow at the moment. I will face what I must, if I can find it to face, but things of magic drift and change before your eyes, melting out of your hands and altering even as you seem to have them pinned down.

"I promise," Mayra said softly. There are times when she seems to know what is in your mind as quickly as you do.

"What is the service?"

"No, Wulfgar, it is best you don't know yet. It may not have to be done, and if it is not, it should be forgotten. It's easiest to forget things you never knew." She took a deep breath and picked up the bowl. "Kesho, Sh'ta, take her arms. Teva, grab her head. Luoti, put your thumbs in her jaws. And above all, make certain as much of this as possible gets into her."

The woman had no warning and no chance. The acolytes swarmed over her like kes covering a fallen animal. She had only time for one squalling cry before Mayra was scraping the foul-smelling contents of the bowl into her mouth. There were no more cries, but the gurgles and grunts that came instead made up in force what they lacked in volume. She twisted and writhed as if her bones had melted. Once she nearly lifted all of them from the ground.

Mayra backed away, and the acolytes danced off. The Wanderer swayed and fell to her hands and knees. She shuddered once, quivering over every inch, and when she looked up her eyes looked as if she had filled herself with wine instead of the noxious mess Mayra had prepared.

"She is ready," Mayra said. "Quickly now, quickly."

Hurriedly the acolytes forced the Wanderer to her feet. From somewhere they produced paints and began to trace intricate patterns on her skin.

"She is drifting." Mayra handed a strap to one of the acolytes. "Strike her, Sh'ta, and continue on a count of ten until I say otherwise. She must fight. She must struggle, or it won't work."

Sh'ta took a stance behind the strange woman, lifted her arms and brought the strap down with all her might. The Wanderer moaned and tried to pull away. They held her and continued to paint. The pattern grew, down her arms, across her breasts and belly, down her back and buttocks, down her legs. It seemed to have no end. Nor beginning either. It seemed to shift. It seemed to move, to—

I shook myself and looked away. It would have provided material for a lifetime of jokes if I had been caught in a spell not even meant for me, one for which I had paid, or would pay, at some unspecified time in the future, with some unnamed service.

They moved back from the woman again, leaving her to stand alone. At some time during the painting they had untied her arms, but she moved them as if she were not certain they were hers. She swayed, watching us blearily, and the lines on her naked body appeared to take on a life of their own.

Mayra moved forward again, lifting a bone wand to point at the woman. Loudly she recited spellwords, and with every word the Wanderer jerked as if struck.

"Gemeente! Pacavra! Oko! Ghala! Mikate!" She

took a last step and touched the wand to the woman's forehead. "Spara't'gi!"

And the woman fell backward to the ground. From head to foot she quivered, her head tossing from side to side. Her chest heaved more violently with every breath. And then the quivering was gone. Her muscles became rigid, instead, each muscle tightening, clenching, as she began to bend, to arch into a bow, until only her toes and the top of her head and her fingers touched the ground, and every muscle stood out as if carved from stone. Her throat corded, and she screamed, a scream that went on and on and on.

"Sri Ja'ti!" intoned Mayra, and the woman collapsed bonelessly to the ground.

For a time she lay there without moving. Finally she lifted her head. "What happened to me?" she asked faintly. "Must be a dream, a dream or a nightmare. Can't be real." She pushed herself up to sit on one hip. She looked at me, then at Mayra, then back to me again and shook her head. "It just can't be real."

Mayra smiled at her gently. "Are you all right, child?"

"I'm tired," the woman replied, "and I'm cold. And I—" She froze with her mouth half open. "I understood what you said," she said softly. "It was nonsense, just noise, but I understood. And I, I'm speaking the same thing. It's not—" Her mouth searched for a word that wasn't there.

Suddenly she threw her arms around herself and

shivered. "I can't think of the name of my own language." Tears bubbled on the edge of her voice. "I can't say it, I can't even think of it. I'm going crazy." Her voice rose to a peak, and the tears that had threatened now fell.

"Be easy, child." Mayra touched her on the forehead, and her tears stopped.

She looked at the older woman in wonder. The tension and fear drained out of her almost visibly. It was a fine moment, perhaps, but I had no time for fine moments.

"Mayra, let's get on with finding out how she can help me."

"Slowly, Wulfgar."

"Mayra—"

"Slowly. Slowly." She smiled at the woman, and got a faint smile in return. "What's your name, child?"

"Elspeth. There's more, but I can't seem to remember."

"That's because Elspeth is a name in our language, too. The spell I used took the words that you knew and replaced them with the same words in our speech, but words for which we have no equivalents, or words for which you had no equivalents, you don't know. The spell couldn't give you names for things you'd never seen, or replace words that just don't exist here."

"You're saying that my, my old language is gone? Forever? But why? Why would you do something like that?"

"Because you're a key," I said, "or so the rune-bones say, and I've no reason not to trust them."

"All right, Wulfgar," Mayra sighed, "ask your questions. But don't be too hard on her. It's early for her yet."

"Who is he?" Elspeth asked. "Who are you?"

"He's our leader," Mayra replied.

"Mayra," I said, "the questions? If she's the key I have to know how to use her."

"Wait a minute," Elspeth broke in. "Nobody's going to use me for anything."

Mayra raised her hands and let them fall in her lap. "You see, Wulfgar, you'll have to be patient. And you, child, ride with this as best you can. Sooner or later you must, and it would be best to make it as easy as possible."

After a moment the girl nodded, and Mayra signaled me to continue. For all her outbursts, she was self-possessed, this Wanderer. Her body formed a fluid curve, and she wore the paint from the spell with the grace of a Tufek skin dancer. The momentary eruption of fear was gone.

"Elspeth," I began slowly, "you are the key, the answer to two problems that confront us." I stopped, for in truth I wasn't certain how to discover what I needed. I wasn't even certain what it was that I needed.

"Elspeth," I began again, "what were you in your world? Were you a Sister of Wisdom?"

She shook her head. "Whatever that is, I wasn't

it. I was a student. Another year and I would've been qualified to teach history at a university."

"A scholar." I dug a heel into the ground and glared at her. "A historian. Do you know how to keep the fanghorn from raiding the herds? Does your history teach you how to find water when there is no water, but your people and your herds will die without it?"

"Gently, Wulfgar," Mayra said. "If she doesn't know the answers, perhaps those aren't the answers you need."

"Mayra, could it be that it's not something she knows? Could it be she herself that's the answer? Could she be a catalyst?"

"I've told you what I know. I might try to find out how she fits the pattern of events, but there's already a great clouding surrounding everything. Spells and counterspells and more spells. If I try to find out anything too specific the chances are I'll see nothing at all or what Sayene or the Most High want me to see. They've moved first on this. The advantage is theirs."

"All right." I got to my feet and pulled Elspeth to hers. "Let it be. Will you send a message to Moidra about this for Bohemund?"

"If you wish it. And if you're willing to have anyone who cares to listen know all about it. Message-spells aren't very private."

I hesitated. That there was trouble brewing I had to let him know. The rest I might keep to myself for a while. "Leave the Wanderer out. Just let Moidra know about what's happening in Lanta. After all, solution or not, Elspeth's of no use until I can find out how to use her."

Instead of going straight to my own tent I headed for Talva's. Elspeth seemed more interested in looking than talking. I was happy enough with her silence, for I still couldn't understand her. She did not act naturally. A woman who'd been swept away from her own world should have been hysterical. She, once her breakdown over the language was past, had taken it all much too calmly. As we walked she acted as if the tents had been laid out like a village peddler's pack for her enjoyment. It wasn't natural.

# VI

## THE PRICE

~

Talva was waiting for us. She was inside her tent, and an apprentice had to go inside for her, but it was all for show. The apprentice hadn't time for three words before Talva was out to meet me. Besides, she wore a cape of brocade and the boots with thick soles and high heels that she used in place of sandals when she wanted to appear taller. She wouldn't have worn either while lounging around her tent.

"My lord." Her bow was smooth, and it could have been used as a study on exactly how far to bow, to the last fraction, without giving offense.

"This girl, Talva. I want to buy her. How much?"

"Buy me!" Elspeth interrupted.

She cast an eye over Elspeth, ignoring the outburst, and pursed her lips. "One hundred imperials," she said finally. "Gold imperials."

"One hundred—? Does she look like a graduate of the training pens of Asmara?"

"I'm right here," said Elspeth, but we continued to negotiate over her voice.

"The price is still one hundred. If you don't want her at that, there are others who will. My lord."

The title had been an afterthought, and a surly one at that. I wondered if she was this rude to all of her customers.

"Done," I said.

"In two or three days I'll have her speaking well enough to be understood. More than that—"

"That's taken care of. Mayra spell-taught her."

Her look was more speculative this time. "So much expense, so much trouble, for a Wanderer? Why is she so important?"

"The concerns of the Sisters of Wisdom are not for you to worry about."

Talva stared at me blankly. I wasn't sure if she believed me or not, but until I could find out what was important about her myself, I wanted no rumors started, and few dared start rumors of the Sisters of Wisdom.

"What is this?" demanded Elspeth. "No one owns me."

Talva opened her mouth to speak, but I interrupted her. "I did buy you, Elspeth, but now you are free." Talva's eyes widened in shock. "You will serve me until you pay off the debt of your freedom. Talva here will train you, teach you to live among us."

Stunned, Talva came to her senses. "Every day, for several hours a day, for tendays to come, you belong to me. I will see that you are taught the things you should know. How to dance. How to sing. You must know how to read and memorize, because you'll have to recite poetry and stories, the great sagas, to your lord. You'll learn how to cook and to clean and to care for him in a thousand ways."

Her voice trailed off, and she smiled. It wasn't a pleasant smile.

"If you think—" interrupted Elspeth.

"Tomorrow," Talva continued, "you will learn respect." She rubbed her hands together eagerly. "First thing in the morning, before it's light even, we'll hang you up by your heels and beat you. You'll scream, but after a time goes by you'll realize that screaming isn't doing much good." Her satisfaction grew. "That's when you'll begin to beg. You must do it very hard and very well before you'll convince me to let you down, but you will. Once you're down I'll let you follow me around, on your hands and knees, of course, like a dog. You'll be just the right height then for me to pat you on the head if you please me. Won't you enjoy that?"

She stopped as if for an answer, but I doubt she expected one. Elspeth looked as if she was beginning to feel sick.

"Of course, little one, you won't be good for long. Sooner or later you'll try to take advantage. You'll think you're privileged just because I'm not punishing you. And then it'll be heels up in the air again and on with the whipping. And that's all we'll do, all day, but do you know, before the day is over I think you'll have learned your proper place. When can I have her, Wulfgar?" It struck her who she was speaking to, and she modified her tone. "I meant to say, my lord."

"Tomorrow will be time enough," I said. "I want her with me tonight."

"Of course, my lord." She made that fractionally correct bow again.

Elspeth appeared thoughtful on the way to my tent. Her interest in her surroundings was gone.

"If I really believed that I had to face that tomorrow, I think I'd go crazy."

I sighed heavily. I had been going to let her worry about it for the night, then stop Talva in the morning. Now I wondered if I should let it go on as planned. I needed to know why she seemed to think it was a game, that none of what Talva had said would happen. I asked her.

"Why, this is all a dream," she said. "At first I was terrified. I thought I was going mad. But now I have it all figured out. I am in a—in a—in the care of a healer, you see. I was injured by a robber."

"Just how did you puzzle all this out?"

"Well, it just has to be. I was on my way to a party. I told the man I was going with that I'd meet him there. It was a nice night, so I decided to walk through the park on the way. Somewhere along the way, though, I got off the path. The ground was very rough, and it seemed to have gotten very hot all of a sudden. I tried to find my way back to the path, but I couldn't, and then I just tried to walk out in a straight line, but that didn't work either.

"Along the way I realized that the moon was too big. Then I realized there were three *other* moons, and one of them was moving too fast, and none of them was moving in the right direction. Finally the sun came up. Instead of being in the park, I was in some kind of desert, and the sun looked wrong in some way, and there was another moon in the sky, in the daylight, and it was colored red. Whoever heard of a red moon in the daytime? It was only a little while later that those men showed up.

"There are some tough gangs who hang out near where I go to school, but they'd all run away screaming if one of those horsemen turned up. I had my—my weapon for protection when I went out after dark, and I just pulled it out and let fly." She laughed. "It didn't do much good, but I did get one where he sits." She laughed again.

"And after that there was everything that happened here. You, with your face carved out of stone, looking like some kind of war god. That witch woman. Spells and magic. That funny little woman who says she's going to beat me. It's all too wild and strange to be anything but a dream. I was hurt somehow, or maybe I drank too much and passed out, but this is a dream." The smile faded away. "It is a dream, isn't it?"

"In the morning," I said, "you'll discover how real it all is. It'll be a painful lesson, I'm afraid, but in the long run it may save your life or your sanity if you learn it now."

She seemed a little dazed as I took her arm, and we walked back to my tent.

# VII

## A WARRIOR BRAND

With darkness the Altaii retreated to their tents, except for those on guard. There was no reason for it here, far from the Plain we normally rode, but custom is a strong thing. No man who has experienced the night winds, the sudden storms and the moving walls of sand that cross the Plain at night stays out in it without reason.

In my tent the table was set with food, the wine was cold, the toklava hot, and Sara danced for me. She was tall, an olive-skinned beauty from Keev, and she saw in the tall Elspeth a rival for her place. So she danced. Not what the men of the cities call dancing, not the pale thing that their women do in taverns. The dance that Sara did spoke of life and lust and passion. More heat came from her than from the toklava.

Mirim and Elnora served the food. On this night

I had no companions to meet, but still, according to custom, they did not eat with me. They would eat when I was done. Once I met a man from a far city who said that this proved we were barbarians. If we were civilized, he said, all would eat together. I wonder what he would have said could he have been on the Plain with us when the months of Keseru are on us, when the waterholes are dry, and the rivers gone, and the cattle die by the thousands. Then food is portioned out, but the largest portions go always to the warriors, and they are first fed.

Barbarous, that man would have said, but what would he say when the fanghorn came to drink the blood of horses and cattle and of men who were too weak to escape? Would he then have called it barbarous that there were men with strength enough to fight the fanghorn and drive it away? Should everyone have eaten alike, that all might die at the beast's attack? Twice have I seen the months of Keseru, once as a man and once as a child, and neither time did any die who was not among the warriors who faced the beast.

On this night, though, there was no thought of hunger. Even the dogs would eat better than a man during Keseru. The details of all this were still not quite clear to Elspeth. She sat and watched and fumed. When first she realized that she would have to wait before eating she thought it was a joke. Now she no longer thought it funny. Perhaps she thought we intended to starve her.

The tent flap opened, and Rolf entered, sealing

the flap behind him. "My lord? I may talk with you?"

"Come in, Rolf. Of course. What is it you want to talk about? Mirim, wine for Rolf. Or would you rather have toklava?"

"Toklava. If it please you, my lord. The Wind still blows out there, and it's enough to freeze your bones."

"Then what are you doing out in it? Couldn't it wait until morning? Mirim! Where's that toklava?"

She scurried up and bent over him with the pot, fresh from the coals. Rolf's face was a study as she leaned toward him to pour. Her own face was stiff and worried. Then she caught my eye on her, and a smile returned to her lips, but not her soft brown eyes.

"You're worried, Mirim?" I asked.

Her smile broadened. "No, my lord."

She turned and moved away in a walk that was as interesting in its own way as Sara's dance. Rolf certainly seemed to think so.

"Rolf," I said, laughing, "time enough for that when you get the warrior brand. What is it you want to talk about?"

He sniffed the steam rising from the clear liquid, and drank deeply. "There are rumors in the tents, my lord. Rumors that fly as if they had wings and seem to change completely from the first teller to the third."

"You know better than to trust rumor," I chided.

"That's why I came to you. All of the rumors have

one thing in common, and if it's true, you would be the one to know, my lord."

"And that is?"

"That we ride against Lanta." He hurried on as if fearing being stopped. "If we do, can I ride with the lances? You yourself have said I'm as good with my weapons as any man half again my age. I wouldn't embarrass you, I promise."

"Rolf, I know you wouldn't embarrass me, but are you so eager for your brand that—"

Suddenly his eyes widened. "Look out, my lord." Dropping his cup he leaped forward and pushed me from my chair.

As though time had slowed I watched a crossbow bolt slice through the back of my seat and take the boy, still leaning as he had pushed me aside, in the shoulder. He fell, his hand going to the bolt, and I rolled to my feet, hand fumbling in the cushions on the floor for my sword belt.

"The back of the tent," Rolf cried. "A killer from the shadows."

The slit the killer had made to use his weapon still quivered at the back of the tent.

"A killer," I shouted. "An outsider!"

Tearing the slit open to the ground, I ducked through into the night. The cry of "killer" spread through the tents, and men on horseback began to circle with torches.

Near a tent across from me I thought I saw something move. The lights passed by, and it moved again. I also moved. In pursuit.

Almost at once the killer became aware that I followed. He redoubled his speed to get away. That alone proved that he was not of the Altaii. If one had reason to kill me, he would have stood and taken the chance. I raised the cry again.

Horsemen began to gather in behind me. Ahead, warriors with torches moved to cut his escape. He had quietly moved from shadow to shadow, working his way ever closer until he could open the slit in my tent and make his shot. Now the shadows were denied to him. Now he must run to escape. But there was no escape.

Swiftly the circle closed around him, cutting him off, closing him in. He was surrounded by men. Men with lights. Men on horseback. And me.

He turned to face me and waited calmly. From head to foot he was dressed in tight-fitting, dull black leather. It was dress designed for skulking through shadows, for killing from darkness. Over his shoulder, hanging across his back, was a long, two-handed sword. The crossbow lay at his feet.

"Do you seek me, killer from the shadows?" I called. "Do you seek Wulfgar? If so, you have found him."

He stood, making no sound, watching like a dril hovering over the dying. My blades slid smoothly from their scabbards, and the sword belt dropped to the ground.

"You've found me," I said softly. "Let's see if you can kill me."

Still he made no sound as he drew the sword over

his shoulder and attacked. It was one smooth, swift motion, the draw and charge. One moment he was standing, the next he was on me, his blade gleaming in the torchlight.

He had no chance to live and knew it was so. An assassin would not be allowed to walk away, no matter the outcome of our battle. Still, though, he might accomplish what he had come for, kill the man he sought. In that first rush he nearly did it.

Barely did I block his whirling blade with one of my short swords. The other I swung for his side, and he leaped back in midswing to avoid a backhand slash that would have removed his head.

He stood facing me, his sword held high, hilt beside his head, blade pointing at the sky. There was no sound save for the quiet rasp of our breathing, the stamping of the horses and the creak of saddle leather. I held my swords in front of my body, a little above waist high, the points raised slightly upward, aimed toward him. Slowly I circled around him, stepping carefully, placing my feet by feel on the uneven ground. I faked a thrust, and again, harder, but he made no move except to keep turning, to keep that leather-masked face toward me.

Without warning his blade flickered toward my arm. I moved to block it, and he changed direction in midswing, down and under to strike at my side. I twisted, sword swinging down to catch his, my other blade striking at his chest.

Barely did my blade catch his as it sliced into my chest. My own point cut through leather and skittered off chain mail below. Thrusting my blades up to cross above my head I just caught his downward blow. My knee rose to smash into his crotch, and I struck at his face with fisted hilt, feeling bone crunch beneath my blow. He staggered back, but recovered on the instant. And still he made no sound.

The blood seemed cold where it trickled down my side, and the hair rose on the back of my neck. In the stillness I could hear warriors mutter charms. Close was the need in me to mutter a charm myself.

What manner of man was this? It's been said that the Most High can bring men back from the dead to do their bidding. Mayra said this is foolish, at least in the way men speak of. But in some other way? She didn't speak of that. Was this such a one, this man who made no sound, showed no reaction to injury? Had they come to regret releasing me that morning? If it was so, or if it was not so, I would end it now. In one fashion or another.

I advanced on him singing my death song. My swords sang the song in the air. I advanced, caring only that it ended, and he stepped back. With that first step came a second and then a third, until he moved only backward.

Now I began to break through his guard. Knowing that the mail was there I took care that my blows struck square on, and they struck hard enough to pierce the steel net. At each blow he dodged back, so that none struck deep, but patches of blood began to soak through the slashes in his tunic. They gleamed blackly on the leather in the torchlight.

Suddenly he kicked, his boot smashing into my chest. What breath remained in me went rushing out when I struck the ground with a thud that made my bones shiver. A moan spread through the lances, and I knew they would avenge me.

Silently the assassin moved in, raising his sword for the death stroke. At the last instant, even as his blade fell, I gathered my strength one last time. One foot hooked around his ankle, the other slammed into his knee, and the crack sounded like the splintering of a tomb. He went over backward, and, teeth bared, I forced myself up to follow, diving under his descending sword. His arms struck my shoulders, and his blade fell uselessly across my back, but my steel, in the full force of my arm and weight of my body behind it, slashed through the chain mail below his ribs, sought upward for his heart, and found it.

Pulling my sword loose I got to my feet to find myself surrounded by cheering warriors. "Remove the mask," I said over the tumult. "Let me see his face."

Bartu knelt and cut away the mask. He took a fistful of hair and lifted the killer's head. He was an ordinary-looking man, except for a burn that marked his cheek. I wondered if another of his victims had fought back, and had also managed to survive.

"Has anyone here seen him before?"

I was answered with a chorus, but all the answers were the same. No one had ever seen him before.

Bartu pried open his mouth, searching for the secret of his silence.

"My lord," he said, "he has no tongue."

It was an answer that should have come to me. In some lands it is the custom to so mutilate men who kill for hire. It's not punishment. It's to keep them from being able to betray those who hire them, even under torture. At least, though, I no longer had to fear the Most High. Whatever they could do with the dead, they didn't hire assassins. It didn't take much effort, however, to think of someone who would. Two someones.

"Foul business," I said, "to cut a man so, then send him out to murder."

Bartu nodded. "It's that and more, my lord." He looked at me shrewdly. "You have an idea of who sent him?"

"I do. Just the same, take the head around the tents. See if there's anyone who's seen him before, or knows anything about him. Then send a rider to Lord Harald." I handed him one of my messenger scarves, a square of red silk with a wind serpent from the mountains to the west picked out on it in gold. The scarf would confirm the rider as coming from me. "If I'm right about the source of this vermin, then one may try for him, also. Tell the man to ride his horse into the ground, and hope that there's been no attempt made before he gets there."

"Aye, Lord Wulfgar. We can only hope." With one stroke he severed the head and stood. He nudged the body with his toe. "And what of this?"

"Throw it in the waste pits," I said.

All the way back to my tent I mulled the new card in the game. If the Most High and the Twin Thrones did indeed conspire to some end, they would have consulted on any move against me, unless the Most High made it on their own, in which case an inhuman agency would have been used, not a hired assassin. If they had consulted, the Most High would have insisted on their own agent. That left only an attack by the Twin Thrones without the knowledge of the Most High, and the Most High could deal harshly with those who altered their plans, queens or not. Unless, of course, another player had entered the game.

Inside the tent the girls were huddled against the side. Elspeth sat quietly with her head on her knees, but the others were weeping. By the table lay a figure covered by a cloak.

Dreading what I knew I must find, I lifted the edge. It was Rolf. "How? How could it happen? He was hit in the arm only, a light hit, a scratch."

Sara spoke with a quaver. "The shaft must have been poisoned, my lord. Almost as soon as you left the tent he gasped and fell to the ground. We went to him, but there wasn't even time to send for a healer. He shivered once and died."

"There wasn't any time, my lord. We tried, but it was no use," said Elnora.

"I know," I said sadly. I dropped the cloak back over him. "Go to the healers, Elnora. Tell them there will be a funeral fire in the morning."

She ran into the darkness, but I still stood there. I seemed rooted to the spot. "I chose him," I said to no one. "Five years ago, when he won the manhood brand in the first year he was eligible. He was quick, with his mind, with his weapons, quicker than any other I saw that year. And he had three kinds of courage. The kind that makes a man brave in battle. The kind that makes a man say or do the thing that must be said or done. The kind that makes a man do what other men say can't be done. That was why I chose him, as I was chosen, as Harald was chosen, as Bohemund and my father were chosen. He would have commanded warriors. He would have been a great leader."

It wasn't much as such things counted. I am not a speaker. It would serve, however, to introduce the boy to those who waited beyond.

A hand touched my arm, trembling, and drew me back to the tents from the dark place I had been. Elspeth watched me strangely, with tremors going through her body as if she stood in the wind.

"I am sorry about your friend. I know you cared for—" Her voice faded away. "This isn't a dream," she said haltingly. She choked back a sob. "It isn't."

"What was it made you decide this wasn't a dream? Rolf?"

"That, yes. That and the other. I looked outside after you ran out. I saw what happened, or some of it anyway. It wasn't clear, but I saw enough. Those men on horses, ringed around you with torches. You and that other man, fighting. And he died out there. A man died, and another one in here. That doesn't happen in dreams, or if it does, you wake up." She shivered again. "So, this must be real."

As I started to speak the healer arrived. I let him in with his apprentices, and gave them the instructions for the funeral fire in the morning. As they cared for us in life, so they cared for us in death.

"The bolt was meant for me," I told them. "Rolf pushed me aside and took it in my stead. He earned his warrior brand. I'll come in the morning to put it on his arm."

They left with their shrouded burden, and it seemed as if the future of the Altaii left with them. We'd fight. No Altaii ever surrendered to anything. Yet now it all seemed hopeless. The Plain grew harsher day by day, and even if we survived that there were still the Most High, the Lantans and the Morassa.

"Leave me," I said, and the girls scurried away. All but Elspeth. "I said to go."

"You, you spoke of a warrior brand," she said. "I saw the brands on your arms. What are they?"

I dropped to a pile of cushions while I spoke. "The Altaii way of life is hard. To live it, to survive the Plain, takes a hard man. So, from the time a boy is big enough to walk, he begins to train. He learns to fight, with nothing but his hands and feet, first, then later with sword, dagger, lance, bow, with every weapon the Altaii have ever encountered. He learns to ride, until a horse is near a part of his body, until guiding his mount is as much an instinct as breathing.

"Possibly even more important than those lessons is the lesson of survival. The Plain is harsh, and that is a mild word to describe it. This isn't the Plain here, despite what the Lantans say. This place is lush compared to the Plain. No Lantan could live a week on the Plain unprotected.

"An Altaii must be able to live there, though. It is his home. The boy learns to survive where there doesn't seem to be anything for him to survive on, to find food where there is none, to a city man's eyes, to find water where there's only sand and rock. And he has to be able to find his way, to locate waterholes without maps or guides, for a man can live anywhere, but the herds must have the waterholes.

"If he learns all of this, and survives that long, he will receive a manhood brand sometime between his twelfth and fourteenth years."

"Which is it?" she asked. "The manhood brand?"

I touched the brand on my left arm. "This one. A bull's head. The one on the right arm is the warrior brand, the head of the tussat, the great cat of the north. It fears nothing, and a single one can pull down a tusk-beast. This brand is even harder to win than the other. I spoke to a general from Caselle once. He had served the Empire through a long career, and he was proud that he'd fought in twenty battles in its service. Before an Altaii youth wins the warrior brand, he's fought a hundred battles, some as large as any that Caselle general ever saw. That's the way it's earned. Just as the other comes from proving that he's learned enough to survive, this one proves he's learned enough to be accepted by the lances."

"Do all of your boys become warriors? What about the healer?"

"Almost all. There are other paths, of course, healer, scribe, smith and the like, but most become warriors. We are a warrior people. There's no other way for us."

# VIII

## THE SHELLS

The day dawned gloomily. Clouds hung low in the sky, and there was no sunrise as such. Gradually there was a lightening of the sky, but the heavy clouds made it a morbid light. It was a fit morning for what must be done.

The healer and his apprentices had built a low mound out of the oil-rich branches of the shagara. Rolf lay on the mound. Now on his right arm was the head of the tussat.

I motioned, and the healer touched a torch to the pyre. In an instant flames leaped toward the sky, and a billow of smoke rose to the clouds. The heat was painful against my face, but I didn't move back.

Hooves came pounding from the distance. Orne, Bartu and some of the lances had come to say farewell. Back and forth they rode, making a display for Rolf's leave-taking. Orne went past standing on the back of his horse at full gallop. Bartu slipped down beside his running horse, his feet slapping the ground to throw him back up into the air and over his horse to slap at the ground again. Another slid off the back of his mount and followed it at a dead run, holding on to the tail.

I had my own leave-taking to make, the ceremonial words of long parting. "Fare you well, warrior. We will drink together in the Lands of the Dead. We will eat lamb in the Tents of Death."

I stood there until the fire burned itself out. The healer's apprentice moved to the ashes to gather what remained, a piece of bone, some ash. This would be saved until it could be scattered on the Plain. It is the beginning of the Altaii, and it receives our ending.

Orne rode to me and dismounted to walk back to the tents with me. "It's bitter, Orne, bitter as gall. He had the seeds of greatness in him. Not just the makings of a commander, but the makings of a leader, the extra something that makes men follow, not because they must, but because they want to. It's hard to find that in a man."

"I found it in you, my lord."

"If you think to cheer me with flattery," I said, "I fear it won't work this morning."

"My lord, the rider you sent to Lord Harald returned before dawn. He rode straight through to get here."

"And?"

"There was no attack on Lord Harald, nor any sign that anyone had tried to enter the tents to make one." He paused. "My lord, it doesn't make sense."

"That it doesn't, Orne. I thought it was part of whatever the Twin Thrones plot, but it looks as if someone else has entered the picture. Only, who is it? And why?"

"I couldn't say, my lord." He walked a moment before speaking again. "My lord, Mirim's run away. The horse guards heard someone trying to steal a horse early this morning. They found no one, but this was in the grass near where the sounds were heard."

It was a necklet I had bought her at the festival at Chadra. Her name was worked into it in gold wire and rubies.

"She's not been seen by anyone since your girls went to sleep last night. I can have her tracked by the dogs. The necklet's enough for them to get a scent. My lord?"

What had made her run, I wondered. Not a desire for freedom, that much was certain. A woman alone, with no family or friends or guild to protect her, would be considered fair game by any slaver who saw her. Even a man would be if he had no weapons about him. No, something else had sent her on her way.

"My lord?"

"Yes, Orne, the dogs. But see that she is not hurt."

"She'll be as unhurt as possible, Lord Wulfgar.

I promise it. There's something else about this you should know, though. This makes six girls of Talva's training who've run in the last five tendays."

I stopped and turned to face him. "You're suggesting there's something wrong with the way Talva's carrying out her duties, that that's the reason for the running?"

"I don't know," he said with a shrug. "Perhaps she's infected them with her feelings about men, my lord."

"It seems everyone knows about these feelings of hers except me."

"She takes care not to expose them except to those who can do her no harm."

We resumed our way to the tents. I was, if it's possible, grimmer than before. "Then she's dropped me to the ranks of those who can't harm her. She made no effort to hide her thoughts yesterday. Perhaps I can arrange something."

"Perhaps, my lord, but I can't see what." He seemed to want to say something further, looking at me every other step, muttering to himself.

"What is it, Orne?" I said finally. "You've thought of a way to make Talva stop ruining the slaves?"

"No, my lord. It's not that. It's—" He took a deep breath. "My lord, there's a Morassa at your tent. He says he has to see you urgently."

"You've taken to letting vermin into my tent, Orne?"

He was shocked. "I left him outside, my lord,

with a couple of lances to make certain he doesn't go where he's not wanted."

"He's not wanted here," I said. "But since he is, I'll see what he wants before I send him on his way."

We stopped by the side of my tent, and I looked around it to see my visitor. He squatted off near the entry, scratching his greasy topknot and leering at Sara and Elnora. His clothes wouldn't have made good rags for wiping down a horse, except for a lavishly brocaded vest he'd stolen somewhere and an emerald as large as his thumb hanging from his ear.

His horse stood nearby, head down, lathered sides still heaving. It had been a fine animal once. Its lines still showed. Now it was little more than food for dril.

Angrily I motioned to an unbranded boy, and he rushed for a bucket of water. Across the way a group of warriors stood casting dice. They gave more attention to my visitor, though, than to their game.

"You want something, Morassa?" I stepped out and moved to face him.

"I see you, Wulfgar," he grunted.

"If I knew you from a goat, I'd see you, too. As it is, I smell you. What do you want here?"

"You make a joke." He laughed, and rose to his feet. It was no improvement. He was just as dirty standing, and even uglier. "You Altaii make good jokes."

"When you're finished laughing at my jokes,

maybe you'll tell me why you're here," I said impatiently.

"I come from Ivo, Sword Arm of the Lord of Thunder." He sounded as if the titles were his.

"So?"

"So? So? So Ivo sends this message to you. Ivo, his own self. He will meet with you, tomorrow."

"Why would I want to meet with Ivo? I have even less to say to him than I do to you."

"Ivo is an important man," he said angrily, "a great warrior. He is—"

"Hear me, Morassa. I don't care what Ivo is. Tell me why he wants to meet me. Without bombast. Now." I put hand to sword hilt and looked at him meaningfully.

"Ah, yes." He swallowed nervously. "Now. Of course. It is those Lantan women, you see. Such fine-looking women, eh. Well, they have made a proposal to Ivo." He stopped expectantly, but I kept silent. He began to shift from foot to foot, rubbing his hands on his greasy tunic. Finally, his impatience won. "These women," he burst out, "they have proposed to Ivo that we Morassa should unite with them to destroy the Altaii. Ay? What do you think of that?"

"What do I think? I'm wondering how many times your head will bounce when it hits the ground."

His nose twitched, and he took a step back. "Your jokes become less funny, Wulfgar. I will tell you this. Why should you want to cut off my head?"

"Now it's you who make jokes, Morassa. You ride in here, tell me that your lord, this Ivo, plots with the Lantans to destroy my people, and yet you don't know why I'm going to cut off your head. You Morassa make good jokes."

Relief flooded across his face. "No, no! You misunderstand. Ivo makes no plots. Such a thing is far from his mind. He is of the Plain, as are you. Ivo wants only to talk with you, to see how this thing can be turned to the advantage for our peoples."

Hearing him link the Altaii with the dog-ridden Morassa was enough to turn my stomach, but I kept to the business at hand. "This plot that Ivo wants to turn to our advantage, what is it?"

He shrugged, confident once more. "I do not know. Ivo told me so much and no more."

"And where is this meeting to take place? Some place where a few hundred Morassa can lie in wait, I suppose?"

"Or where Altaii lances can set an ambush, eh?" His eyes glittered now that I appeared to be going along. "No, that cannot be. It must be a place where none can bring many men, or afford to let any, shall we say, 'disturbance' start." He was trying to look open and honest. He only succeeded in looking shiftier than ever.

"I assume Ivo has some place in mind," I said dryly.

"Of course. The Blue-Backed Scal, a tavern on the Street of Five Bells in the Metalworkers' Quarter of Lanta, by the Weavers' Quarter."

"Lanta!" At least he'd succeeded in surprising me.

"Of a certainty," he said, throwing his arms wide as if to show how open he was being. "Neither you nor Ivo can bring many men. The Lantans are wary of having many men of the Plain in their city at one time. For that same reason no one will start any trouble. Those City Guardsmen are very touchy about little things like brawling."

"And when is this meeting to take place? Tomorrow, you say?"

"At the third hour after noon. You will come?" He leaned forward eagerly.

"I will come," I said, and he sighed so heavily with relief that I thought he'd deflate. "Now ride back to Ivo with your message, and don't waste any more time."

Muttering, he mounted and rode away. The smell stayed behind. A handful of lances followed after to see that he went as he'd been told.

Orne walked around the corner of the tent shaking his head. "Treachery, my lord, treachery so strong I could smell it from back there."

I laughed. "That was the Morassa you smelled."

"You don't intend to trust them? You're not going? Why—"

"I gave my word, Orne. I'll go. Trusting, now, is another matter. Tell me, how many coins have you lost playing the game of the shells and the pea?"

"None, since I was a stripling," he answered, puzzled. "What has that to do with this?"

"The youth follows the shells' every move, certain

that he knows where the pea is. And all the time the pea is in the gamester's hand. We're no longer in our youth, Orne. We know where the pea is. But does Ivo?"

"My lord, I don't understand. You say you're going to the tavern, and all this talk of peas and shells. It's beyond me."

"It's a trap, beyond question, but a trap can take the trapper, too. Ivo will expect me to arrive tomorrow afternoon, with as many lances as I think I can safely bring, but he'll expect me. If they thought I was suspicious, this meeting wouldn't have even been suggested. Now, Ivo will be there."

"He will?"

"Of course. There'll be Lantans hidden behind every peddler's cart, but if Ivo's not there, someone may say he was afraid of me."

"So, he will be there, and the Lantan guards will be there. But you say we'll be there, too. I still don't understand."

"Because you're watching the shells." I laughed. "On this afternoon I'll enter the city, not tomorrow. And it will be merchants and tradesmen and farmers who enter, not Altaii lances. By tonight we'll have rooms in The Blue-Backed Scal. Tomorrow, while the soldiers wait to take us outside, Ivo will enter the tavern, to show he isn't afraid to be there to meet me. And, to his surprise, he will meet me. We'll have a little talk in private about this plot, and when he's told me everything he knows, a party of respectable Lantans will leave the inn and walk right past the soldiers."

"It's madness," he said, "and I love it."

"Then find me six or eight men who can walk a city street without looking like they'd rather be on the Plain in high summer."

"I know them already. When do we leave?"

"Not you, Orne. My height will be hard enough to keep from attracting notice. Trying to sneak you in would be like disguising a tusk-beast as a sheep."

Exasperated, he ran both hands through his hair. "I've never before regretted being a decently sized man, but now I wish I was a runt. Well, if you must have runts for this, I'll see that they're the best runts in the tents."

He strode away, muttering all the while. I'd have bet heavily that he'd show up with the others in some disguise he'd claim would get him through the gates of Lanta. It wouldn't be easy to talk him out of it.

I noticed a pointed silence from Sara and Elnora. Elnora was kneeling by the fire, preparing a stew for the noon meal. Sara was figuring the amounts spent on food and the like. Both were silent almost to the point of not breathing. For Sara especially this was unusual. When I first told her she must do the accounts, she refused. It was her place to look beautiful and please me, she said, not to play with numbers. Although she saw them as her worst chore, she usually chattered away all the while she did the accounts. Now she worked in silence. It wasn't natural.

"You disapprove," I said to the air.

"You'll be killed," said Sara, "or maybe worse."

"And we'll have to serve someone old and ugly who'll beat us," added Elnora.

"It's none of your concern," I said. They bent back to their work. "And where is Elspeth? Did she run away as well?"

They looked at each other and giggled.

"No, my lord," said Sara. "Talva came for her."

"And what happened to rouse your mirth?"

Elnora grinned by the fire. Sara laughed. "She did tell her that there was some mistake, and that if Talva would only talk to you it could all be straightened out, my lord.

"Talva had four of her apprentices, and she was in no mood for arguing. The apprentices just picked Elspeth up and carried her away, calling all the while that you'd straighten it all out."

"Sara was busy with accounts," Elnora broke in, "so I followed to see what happened. When I got to Talva's tent Elspeth was already hanging by her heels outside. I wish I knew how to curse like that. She said things about Talva's birth and the means of her conception that—"

"I'm not interested in what she said, girl. What happened?"

"Well, two of Talva's biggest apprentices beat her with paddles, like she was a carpet. She won't be able to sit down for a long time. It took her some time to get around to begging properly. All she did at first was howl and make threats. And even after Talva let her down, she started cursing again. Talva threatened to put her in with those falcons of hers."

"She didn't," I said anxiously. "Those birds sometimes attack."

"Oh, no. She just hauled Elspeth up by her heels and beat her some more."

"I'd better stop this," I muttered to myself, "before that fool girl gets herself hurt."

"Nonsense." Mayra walked up to me and frowned at me. The two girls made obeisance, sitting back on their heels, foreheads on the ground. "You'll do her worse harm than Talva ever will if you take her away now."

I didn't stop to wonder why she'd come to the tents. She rarely did. Her spells had been part of her so long that the presence of iron or steel in large amounts made her feel ill, even if no spell was being worked.

"How?" I asked. "How will it hurt her?"

"She's learning the rules of existence, Wulfgar, the rules that a child picks up as it grows. She wasn't born here, and the rules she learned aren't the rules here. I don't think she really believes that violence can touch her. She's learning the one lesson she must learn if she's to survive. She cannot live in this world using the rules of the world she's left."

"All right," I said slowly. "I'll leave her there."

"Good. Now to why I came. Could we sit out here? There's too much iron inside."

The words hadn't left her mouth before Sara and Elnora rushed to her with a chair. They had to go back for one for me. After all, I was only a man and Mayra was a Sister of Wisdom.

"Last night," she began, when we both were seated and the girls had returned to their work, "after the attempt on your life, I decided to check the effect of your death on the vision I conjured. At dawn this morning, exactly, the most propitious hour for such things, I cast another spell and tossed the rune-bones. I found out many things, bad things for a time of day so close to life."

"And what did you find? Do I die?"

"Make no jokes about this, Wulfgar. The sands of a man's life can't be counted, not by spells or by magic."

"I'm sorry, Mayra, but what did you see?"

"First this." She took a small bag from beneath her tunic and tied it around my neck. I leaned forward to help her. It felt cold against the skin. "That will protect you against the Most High."

"I need such protection?"

"You need all the protection I can give you. If I could put you back as an egg in your mother's womb, with no one to know you were there, I would. Yes, and Harald, too. I saw nothing of the manner of your death. Only this. If both you and Harald die within the year, the Lantan plot will succeed."

"Surely—"

"Surely nothing. As the Wanderer is a key, so

too are you a key, and Harald. I should have realized that something so important would come in
a sanctified number. There are three of you who
are keys. Elspeth must be utilized in some manner
that I don't yet know, and it must be done by you
or by Harald, preferably by both. If she dies, or is
taken, there's small chance that we will survive as
a people. If you and Harald die, there's no chance."

"And nothing about how to make use of her," I
sighed. "The one thing I need to know, and instead
you tell me they'd like to see me dead. That much I
know already. Maybe I can find out something useful from Ivo."

"They don't just want you dead," she said intently. "They must have you dead. You've got to
realize the importance of that difference. And why
would Ivo tell you anything?"

"I'm meeting him tomorrow in Lanta." Her face
twisted in despair, and she shook her head. I has-
tened to reassure her. "I know it's likely to be a trap,
Mayra, but I have a plan to turn the trap on him."

"After what I've told you, you can still say
that? They'll never get a better chance to put an
end to you. You'll walk up and lay your head on
the block." She took a deep breath, and I realized
she was keeping calm with an effort. If anything
did, that underscored the urgency of her words.
She wasn't one to get overwrought about trifles,
or about great matters, either. "You'll forget about
this meeting now, I assume. You'll stay here in the
tents."

"I gave my word," I said simply.

"Then you're a fool," she snapped.

"I'm a man."

"Sometimes," she said, "I think it's the same thing."

# IX

## OUT OF THE TRAP

——

The Imperial Gate of Lanta was so named because the road that passed through it led to the great city of Caselle. Once Basrath had marched along that road, with the greatest army ever seen until that day, to add Lanta to his endless string of conquests. But Basrath was dead along with most of a still-larger army at the Heights of Tybal, and Caselle was a great city of trade. The Lantans were never ones to let the past stand in the way of a profit.

The gates were wide enough for fifty men to ride through abreast, and the whole of that width was jammed. The traffic was heavy, both in and out, from single peddlers to huge caravans going to the edge of the world. No one noticed a few more travelers among so many.

On my back I carried a roll of rugs, crudely woven on a country loom. I was bent and stooped, letting the pace of the entering throng set mine as the crowd carried me along. To any who noticed, I was a sheepherder from the hills to the east of the city, come to sell a few tendays' work with the shearings.

I couldn't see any of the others, and I worried. The guards carried their spears instead of leaning on them. They were watchful. Everything felt their scrutiny. With the weight of their eyes on my back it was hard to keep the slow walk through the gate. For a moment I wondered if Mayra had been right.

Five of the six men who followed me into the city I knew well. Two of them, Karl and Hulugai, had ridden with me many times, from my first battle on. Of the sixth, a youngling named Brion, I was less sure. He'd worn the warrior brand less than a year. Such men are often wild, going out of their way to seek glory. Orne had chosen him, though, and I would trust his judgment.

At the third street beyond the outer gate, an unpaved alley in fact, I turned off the main road. It was a different world there, only a few steps from the main thoroughfare. The crowd was less exotic, but just as colorful in its rags and cast-off finery. Jugglers and puppeteers and the like were back out on the Imperial Road, where the gold was, but there were cutpurses aplenty, here, and stands at every other step hawking fruits and foods of all descriptions, to be cooked later or eaten there on the street. I kept a hand on my purse, as any shepherd would, and ignored the odors drifting from the stands.

I counted five taverns down the street, the best of them little more than an opening in the wall, and entered the fifth one. I sat at a table by myself and set the rugs on the other bench. The disguise was still needed, and had I intended to sell the rugs, I'd not have dropped them on the dirt floor.

The tavernkeeper, wiping his hands on a greasy apron, came waddling to my table.

"Kuva," I ordered, and he shuffled away.

As I waited Hulugai entered, a net bag of carved wooden boxes over his shoulder. By the time he'd found a table and given his order, Karl was there. I began to feel better.

The proprietor returned with a mug of the dark, bitter kuva of Lanta, and I tossed him a copper. Life flickered in his eyes for the time it took to stuff the coin under his apron, and then he shambled over to Karl.

I drank the kuva slowly, waiting. It wasn't hard to be slow over the drink, but to have ordered better would've attracted the wrong kind of attention, even if the tavern had it. The waiting wasn't easy. One by one the others arrived until twenty minutes had gone, and only Brion hadn't gotten there. Thirty minutes, and still he hadn't come.

The other patrons drank on, coming and going, unaware of the tension building in the cramped room. Had he been taken, the City Guard might eventually know of our purpose at The Blue-Backed Scal. Worse, if they had access to a Sister of Wisdom, a truth-spell might have them on their way to

the hovel where we waited like victims for the sac-
rifice. We waited, because there was nothing else
to do, drinking our kuva, ignoring each other, feeling the air grow heavy and thick. Each time the
door opened six pairs of eyes went to it, six hands
groped beneath tunics to touch weapons. I began
to think of a back way out. I could see the same
thought in the glances the others cast.

The door swung open to let a patron out, and
stayed open for the entrance of another. I held my
breath and slipped my hand under my tunic again.
Brion walked in as unconcerned as if he had been
strolling among the tents. The proprietor moved
forward to take his order, and a little of the tension
drained away. From the glances thrown his way,
some of it was replaced by anger.

I gave him time only for a swallow or two before
I hoisted the roll of rugs to my back and left. In
order of their coming the others followed, until we
strung out down the street, each man keeping view
of the man ahead. I searched for a type of place, not
a particular one. When I saw it, I waited until Karl
was nearly on me before I turned in to it.

It was an even smaller alley, a bent dead end that
even the people of Low Town couldn't find use for.
But it suited my purpose as if made for it. It hid us
as we tore into our burdens.

"What happened, Brion?" I cut open the roll of
rugs and took my short swords from the bundle inside.

"It was a mistake on my part to bring erris oil,

my lord," he said. "There's almost none in the city. The perfumers are going mad for the lack."

"The guards noticed?" I asked, and everyone froze.

Except for Brion, that is. He tossed the priceless flagons away casually. "At first I thought they were a pair of agents for the palace, but it turned out they were only thieves. I led them away from the meeting place, and when they finally worked up the courage to demand the oil, I cracked their heads and laid them where they won't be found."

There was quiet laughter, quickly stifled.

I stripped off the long peasant tunic and put on the knee-length garb of a merchant of slightly above middle rank. It was somewhat high for a man who was wandering in Low Town, but I would need the prestige at The Blue-Backed Scal. I buckled on my sword belt, then wiped the road dust from my legs with a rag. Topping it all with a cloak of silk-lined scarlet and a black cap, I became another of those who came to buy where poverty made their money go further, if the poor didn't steal it first.

"These thrice-accursed Lantan cloaks hamper your sword arm so, you might as well not wear a blade," Karl muttered.

"If you want to leave the swords behind," I said, "then you can leave the cloak as well."

Karl only grunted, but a few of the others laughed. They were in high spirits for men going to beard one enemy in another enemy's city.

One at a time we left the alley. If any of the Low

Towners thought it strange to see merchants of the High City coming out of an alley, they kept it to themselves. They had likely learned that the less they said of what the High City folk did, the better.

Though far yet from our goal, we were on the final leg, and we adopted the staggered spacing that let each man watch the high places above his companions, and be guarded the same in return. We walked through the gate into the High City as casually as if we made the journey every day. The guards hardly seemed to notice us among the returnees from Low Town. In moments we were past them and gone, down the street and vanished among the crowds.

As we moved deep into the Metalworkers' Quarter the crowds thinned. The Street of Silversmiths and others like it were for selling, and they were crowded. The streets deeper in were for working.

They became narrow, winding passages, with scarcely an inhabitant to be seen. Here were no displays, no shop fronts. The few taverns were small and poorly marked, the sort patronized mainly by the metalworkers themselves and those who came to buy their products.

An acrid smell drifted over the street from the vats of the dyers. The narrowness of the street seemed to shut out the sun. Then, ahead, I could see a fanciful representation of the one-horned mountain goat, the blue-backed scal.

"Nets!" came a shout from behind me.

I dove for the wall. There was a blow to my head, on my back, and I was in the doorway with my swords out. The silence was like a scream.

Angrily I ripped the cloak away. I had no more need of the expensive garment. It was less than a rag to me now.

On the street in front of me there lay a net, but a net of heavy chains. I remembered the force of its blow and was prepared for the worst when I looked carefully around the edge of my doorway. Down the narrow street there were other heavy chain nets, and some of them covered unmoving mounds.

Mayra's words came back to me, and mine to her. I hadn't listened, and my men lay in the jaws of a trap. I had made a great plan, and someone had outthought me. I would die, as I had known I would from the day the warrior brand was put on my arm, but my death would put the Altaii in jeopardy. I hoped that Mayra managed to keep Harald safe.

I took another look along the street, and the breath stuck in my throat. There were five mounds there. Only five. One other had escaped capture. They would come, those netters of men, expecting to find us unconscious and wrapped for their taking. Instead they would find two Altaii warriors with weapons in their hands. I laughed softly to myself at the joke. As deaths go, it wouldn't be a bad way to finish.

The first guards came carelessly, talking among

themselves. One exclaimed at seeing the empty net that had been meant for me, and another made a remark about those who couldn't count how many animals there were to be taken. The others laughed, and I joined silently, but at a different joke. They came on.

The first guards had passed my hiding place before one chanced to look into the dark doorway. He looked, turned away, and jerked back in disbelief. It couldn't be, but I was there. His eyes widened. His mouth opened to yell.

I made the yell for him, a wordless roar of rage. He couldn't make it himself for my steel through his throat. The other blade found lodging in a guardsman's ribs, and then the first was sending a head rolling along the stones of the street.

The narrow way was filled with screaming, panic-stricken men, with dying men. Two more fell to my blade, then another, and then they fled. Sheathing a sword, I hastily took a fallen spear and cast it with all my strength. One guard had been slow getting out of sight, and he fell, his body pierced through by the shaft.

Quickly I moved to a doorway across the passage. I had seen no heads on the rooftops. With luck the casters of nets were gone, and no one had seen me change position. If so, when they came again, we would once more dance our dance of death in the street.

My new hiding place gave me a view down to where my companion in this last fight was himself hidden. It was Brion. A trickle of blood ran down his face. He saw me, and with a smile raised one sword and kissed the blade, kissed death. I returned the salute, and the pledge. There were bodies in front of him, also. We would neither of us be easy meat. We would take a sizable honor guard with us.

Suddenly arrows began to blossom in the doorway where I had first hidden. Five. Ten. A score or more. Then there was a moment of quiet. From down the street a measured tread came.

Warily I looked toward the noise. The guards approaching came in two ranks of five, crowded together in the narrow way. Their shields overlapped, and their spears were presented. They marched in a rigid cadence to maintain the shield wall. Now they came as if to war. And so they did, if they but knew it.

With a final rush they moved forward and wheeled as one, to face an empty doorway. This time I laughed as I fell on them from behind. For some reason that seemed to unnerve them.

They were hampered by the long spears and heavy shields, suitable for infantry in the open field, but not for twisting in alleys. I was not so encumbered. My blades dodged and darted as if alive, and Lantan guards screamed and fell. Of ten, one survived to flee for his life. The others lay bloodied in the street, dead or dying.

In the shadowed doorway I waited for them to come again. This time they'd know where I was, but the choice now lay between the other side of the street, where I could be shot like an antelope, or the side I was on, where they'd at least have to come and face me.

I wished that I could die on the Plain, instead of here in the cramped and twisted streets of an enemy city, but I would make it a good death just the same, as such things are accounted. The Lantans would pay my ferryman's fee to the next world in blood. What more could a man ask? Blood and steel. There's little else for the warrior.

I could see Brion leaning against the door behind him, binding a gash in his arm. There were more shapes on the stones in front of him. They'd tried him again, also, and he'd taught them the lesson of Altaii steel. Soon they would come again. Blood and steel. I hoped that Harald was safe.

Harness and armor creaked in the street. They were preparing for the next attack. Abruptly the sounds of preparations were replaced with an uproar of confused shouting. The cries began to die down, and one commanding voice could be heard.

"Idiots! Fools! Who ordered the use of archers? I'll have his blood. No, if he's killed Wulfgar, I'll make him drink his own blood, every drop of it. He must be taken alive. It has been ordered."

There was some further muttering, but the new man with the heavy voice had established his command. No more voices were raised. I gave silent thanks to this new leader, though. Let him send his men against me with such orders. Let them come with their hands tied. I wondered, if he sent them to me piecemeal, how much of his force I could take. A hundred, perhaps? It would be a death to sing of.

From down the street came the clatter of hooves on pavement. Brion and I exchanged glances. A rider burst around the corner just beyond Brion, a Morassa. The young warrior scarcely had the time to raise his swords before the horseman's lance pinned him to the door.

The Morassa fixed his eyes on Brion and laughed. One sword dropped from a nerveless-seeming hand. Head down Brion stood and reached out as if to paw at the shaft. The rider laughed again.

Slowly Brion raised his head, and now his eyes fixed on the horseman. The Morassa's laugh died. Suddenly he must have realized Brion's intent. He tried to back away, but it was already too late.

Tightening his grip Brion jerked himself forward along the lance to thrust his sword through the rider's body. The Morassa grabbed at the blade and toppled shrieking into the street. Brion lifted his face to the sky and laughed himself, loud and long. Then he too fell.

The Morassa took some time to die, screaming all the while. There was a stir among the Lantans. No man wants to die, but all men want to face it well when it comes. Their ally hadn't, and their shame was compounded by Brion's courage.

Under my breath I spoke the words that would

never be spoken at a funeral fire. "Fare you well, warrior. We will drink together in the Land of the Dead. We will eat lamb in the Tents of Death."

That done, there was little else to do except ready myself. It wasn't a good place for dying. There was only a thin strip of sky overhead. It was like the Lantans to be as stingy with the sky as with everything else. The time came, though, as it comes to all. Brion was a man to ride the Plain with. So were they all. It was a good time to die.

"Lantan dogs," I shouted. "Sons of dogs. Why do you lie back? Why do you hide? It's a good day to die."

"Wulfgar!"

At the shout I almost rushed out at them, but then I pressed deeper into the niche. Let them come to me.

"Wulfgar, this is Ivo. Let us talk, Wulfgar."

Ivo, who'd led me there to my death, to the deaths of my companions. "Talk, if you need it, Ivo. I've nothing to say."

"It is always pleasant to live a little while longer, Wulfgar. Let us talk."

I smiled grimly. "Come ahead, Ivo. We'll talk."

He came, picking his way past the bodies. His garments looked like a whirlwind had struck a ragpicker's cart, pieces good for wiping boots mixed with rich fabrics and expensive work. The necklet he wore had a fortune in gems worked into it, and his rings would've bought a wealth of horses. He carried his helmet in his hand. The sun gleamed off the oil on his head, bald except for the topknot.

"I see you, Wulfgar." He kept close to the far side of the street, but I could smell his perfume, heavy in the still air.

I leaned casually back against the door behind me. "I'd offer wine, but for some reason I don't seem to have any to hand."

"I understand." He grinned greasily. "Perhaps another time. Or you could join me down the street at The Blue-Backed Scal."

"I think not. I find this door quite comfortable."

"Of course." He grinned again. It seemed a habit of his. "You tried to cheat, Wulfgar. You came early?"

It was my turn to grin. "And you meant to keep the meeting as planned? These nets are just here in case leopards invade the streets of Lanta, or a fanghorn."

"Not exactly," he said slyly, "but coming early as you did, you nearly ruined my plans. So many beautiful plans."

"Have you ever stopped to wonder, Ivo, why they sent you? Do they think enough Lantans have died? They sent a Morassa to kill Brion, and he died. Now they send you to me, and you can't kill me. I heard the orders, Ivo."

He tugged at a long, scraggly mustache and pursed his lips. "Others want you alive, Wulfgar. I do not. I would like to see you dead, no matter what these, these others say, but it is best not to antagonize them at present."

"And you came just to tell me that? That you'd like to see me dead? What will these others you talk about think about that?"

"They do not know, and will not. You see," he said slyly, "if you attack me, I can kill you, and no one will fault me for defending myself. There will be much fame and glory for the man who kills Wulfgar, yes?" He gestured expansively. "Or you might kill me, eh? You would like that, I think. And there is always a chance."

So someone wanted me alive, but he wanted me dead and would take the chance of fighting me to get it. The nets seemed to bear out his claims, but Morassa are noted liars, and the Lantans must know that my death was necessary to their plan. The nets must have been used so they could kill me at their leisure, because even in a hail of arrows a man may sometimes go untouched. As the baraca had protected me from the nets. No, when I stepped out to face Ivo, I'd take an arrow in the back. I had to take him with me.

"Why should I fight you, Ivo? Why should I care if a Morassa dog has a chance for glory?"

His face paled, and he jammed his helmet on. "You have little choice in the matter. You can fight me now or wait for the others to come and haul you away like a pig for the market."

He was right. There was no choice. But I needed him as angry as I could get him. I needed him closer. "I'll not haul away easily, especially by a carrion eater like you."

Howling with rage he drew his sword and pulled his buckler around from where it hung on his back. He stepped closer. Even if the archer fired the moment I stepped clear, I'd get steel between his ribs. I moved into the street, and a chain net smashed me to the ground.

# X

## TANGLED FATES

~

I lay there on the stones, clinging to the edges of consciousness. Almost immediately a rush of men swarmed over me, pulling the net away. Weakly I struggled, but they forced me back down, lashed my wrists behind me. In moments they had bound my ankles and stripped my clothes away.

"Morassa," I rasped, "your dam was a woman of the streets, and your sire a diseased goat. Crawl back to your lair and mourn for the honor you never had."

Choking out a curse, Ivo kicked me in the head, and I lost my grip on the light. When my senses returned, I was bound naked across the back of a horse. The pavement moved past beneath my head, but the effort of trying to raise it to look made me drift back toward the shadows. I was carried through the streets like a sack of meal, with no more knowledge of where I went.

The pavement changed, became smooth, polished. In the back of my head that meant something, but I couldn't pin a thought long enough to see it. A gate creaked open, and there was something else beneath the horse's hooves. Mosaics. A courtyard.

Hands pulled me from the horse and untied my ankles. The courtyard spun as I came upright, then slowed to an unsteady stop. Columns of marble surrounded us, and statues. Wall carvings. It was a palace.

And then I remembered. The polished stone pavement. The great square in the center of the city. This was the Palace of the Twin Thrones. Why had I been brought here? Why wasn't I dead?

Rough hands pushed me forward. "Move."

I stumbled forward, acting more dazed than I was. That was the voice from the Street of Five Bells, the voice that commanded that I be taken alive. I took a misstep and twisted as if falling, to see him.

He was an officer of the Palace Guard, resplendent in gold and jewels. Not the type I'd have expected to be given the dirty job of fighting barbarians in alleys. He was handsome, handsome enough to remind me of a gibe I'd heard.

"It's said," I told him with a grin, "that officers of the Palace Guard are chosen for beauty, like dancing girls, and for much the same reason."

He jerked as if I'd struck him, and restrained himself with an effort. I wondered if I'd hit close to the mark.

"If you're still alive a few months from now," he hissed, "I'll enjoy visiting you, to see what your attitude is then."

"I don't see Ivo. Isn't he here to see the end of his plan?"

"His plan? He would say something like that. We've no need for his kind here. Soon we'll have no need for any of you barbarians and—"

"You talk too much, Stefan." Another officer, older, with more gold and gems on his armor, came into the courtyard, followed by a dozen guardsmen. "This one is to be delivered at once, as ordered. He's not to be given lectures on the plans of the Twin Thrones."

"I'm sorry, Andrus. He has a way about him that gets beneath my skin."

"Control your anger," said the newcomer coolly, "and obey your orders, else you may find the torturers getting beneath your skin. With flaying knives."

Stefan blanched. He made a motion, and two of the guards grabbed my arms. I didn't resist. If they truly wanted me alive, for whatever reason, I might live long enough to escape. Besides, just because a man should meet his end well doesn't mean he has to hasten the meeting without cause. I would wait.

We went deeper into the palace, through the little-used side corridors. Not so much as a single palace servant saw our passage. The light was dim, coming as it did from only every fourth or fifth lamp. There was no need to provide light where there was no one to use it.

Passing through a narrow doorway, we stopped in bright light. My eyes were blinded after the halls, but when they began to adjust, when only scattered spots still danced in front of me, I saw the woman. She sat facing me, in a chair that was a wooden duplicate of one of the Twin Thrones. I couldn't give a name to her, but she was one of the Queens of Lanta.

"Kneel," Stefan barked.

I stood where I was. I didn't kneel to my own king, and I wouldn't kneel to this spoiled girl. As soon as they saw I wouldn't obey, the guards began to kick me, and strike with their spear butts. She watched as if it was a show put on for her as my legs were knocked out from under me, and I fell heavily to the floor.

The taste of my own blood was in my mouth. They hauled me up as far as my knees, but when I tried to rise farther they held me there. Immediately I relaxed, as if the position was of my own choosing. They'd get no satisfaction from me.

"Well, Wulfgar," said the queen, "is this how you come to steal wall hangings, or, or"—she seemed to choke on the words—"or other things?"

Getting no answer she rose and moved toward me, her concealing robes rustling softly. Her fingertips ran down the side of my face.

"Not as handsome as I could wish," she said,

almost under her breath, "but there are other things. The eyes. So fierce, so free, so untamable." She sighed heavily, and shook herself as if coming out of a trance. "I knew you were the one, Wulfgar. From the first moment I saw you, in the great hall, I knew you were the one." She backed away, eyes still fastened on mine. "Take him, Stefan, and have him prepared."

The guards pulled me up and led me away, but I scarcely noticed. I was the one, she'd said. Had she, too, felt what I had felt on seeing her and her sister, that our fates were tangled, one with the other? Was that why I was still alive? But what of her plan? Didn't she know that I had to die for it to succeed? If she didn't, but learned it, would I be killed out of hand? So many questions, and no answers that came to me. My head would have spun even if I hadn't been dizzy to start with.

From the meeting with the queen they took me to a bath, as well appointed as any in Caselle, if smaller. The tiled walls and floors showed flowers and birds, and the ceiling represented the sky, complete with clouds. The sides and bottom of the pool had plants that grow in water, and fish so real I nearly expected one to swim.

The bath girls, a dozen of them, were beautiful. They wore only armbands, and their hair was cut short to make it easy to dry. They chattered among themselves like birds on a roost. Some of their comments were as graphic as any I'd ever heard on the furs.

Why I was being given a bath I couldn't understand, but I'd take it, no matter the reason. On the
Plain water can be used for bathing only seldom,
and the tub is little bigger than needed for one
person. Usually a girl would rub me with oil and
scrape away the dust and sweat. I wouldn't pass the
chance to wallow in that much water.

"Quiet!"

The girls paid little attention to Stefan's command. He compressed his lips angrily, but said
nothing more. The girls must have served the queen
directly. They certainly showed no fear of his anger,
and he made no effort to vent it. In a moment, long
enough to show that they didn't do so from fear,
they fell silent.

"These girls," Stefan said, "will bathe you and
prepare you."

"Prepare me for what?"

He went on as if I hadn't spoken. "You'll do as
they command. They know what to do. You might
as well forget escaping from here. There's only the
one door, and crossbowmen will be waiting outside. If you come out before I return for you, they'll
shoot you. In the legs." He smiled a sneering smile.
"You won't escape that way either."

He left, and the guards followed, but a lock
clicked in the door behind them. He wasn't trusting to threats to keep me in. Well, I had no intention of leaving yet anyway.

I turned to look at the girls. They were lined
up to study me as well. They ranged from a short

brunette with mischief in her eye to a tall blonde who looked to have the ice of Norland in her veins. One of them cut my hands free with a small knife. Its blade was no bigger than my thumbnail, and it took several strokes to cut through the ropes. I hadn't really expected a usable weapon left in easy reach.

"You look very dirty and beaten about," said a long-waisted beauty with red hair. She ran a finger across my chest and examined it disdainfully. "You appear to have last lodged in a pigsty."

The others giggled and watched for my reaction. I stood quietly. Let them have their fun. If they talked enough I might learn something.

"He must have run away," said a short girl, "and now he's being cleaned up to be sold to some rich woman." They laughed uproariously at that, and she grew bolder. She leaned against my chest and looked up at my face. "Will you be a rich woman's pet?"

"I don't think he can talk," said another, trailing a hand up my thigh.

"Perhaps he's shy," suggested the tall blonde. "If so, his new mistress will break him of it soon enough, and she'll certainly have other things for him to do with his mouth besides talk."

That caused more laughter.

The brunette ran her hand along my arm. "He must be a dancer. He's not nearly pretty enough to be a dancer, but some dealers are putting these brands on and selling them as barbarians."

"I've had enough of barbarians," the tall blonde spat. "Having to serve those Morassa is like being given to animals."

"Be easy, Maleri," the brunette answered. "Soon there'll be no more barbarians of any kind. Besides, this one's brands look wrong to be a barbarian. I've seen the ones they put on the dancers, and they're not the same."

"Not wrong, Tnay," whispered the red-haired girl. "They're right."

"What are you talking about, Lura?"

"The brands aren't wrong," she said forcefully. "The man who first put chains on me wore brands like these. Do you think I'd forget them?" She stared at me, blue eyes seeming to fill her face. "He's an Altaii. A Plain barbarian."

They all froze where they stood. The girl leaning against my chest trembled and looked as if she was going to cry.

Well, I hadn't expected to learn much. I straightened the short girl and walked into the pool. "You're supposed to bathe me," I said. "Do it."

They came slowly, timidly. All of their brash words were gone, blown away by Lura's simple statement. They brought sponges and perfumed soaps, and scrubbed as if they were scrubbing a fanghorn. Perhaps, to them, there wasn't much difference.

Sluicing away the soap I hoisted myself from the pool. Tnay ran to get toweling. She and Maleri dried me, and all the while they shivered. I wondered what stories they'd been told. Did they think an Altaii warrior ate people?

Without speaking they stretched me out on a table and began to massage me with oils. They were trained well. Their fingers felt out every ache, every tightness, and rubbed it away. It was easy to let my mind drift.

We have no need of his kind, Stefan had said. Soon we'll have no need for any of you barbarians. And Tnay had said that soon there'd be no barbarians of any kind. Andrus had threatened Stefan with torture when he spoke of it. That seemed to indicate that there really was a double plot, a plot to use the Morassa to destroy the Altaii, and then, in turn, in some way destroy the Morassa.

Of course, that might be the reason I'd been allowed to hear of this end to all the barbarians from two different sources, so that I'd believe and act in some way the Lantans wanted. Either way it was typical of the Lantans. Leave a clear-seeming path, but with a trap obvious to all but the most unobserving. Leave a second path, somewhat hidden, with a trap that only one who looked closely could find. And for those very observant ones who found the second trap, leave a third way with a trap that couldn't be found unless you knew it was there. The only thing to do was find a fourth way, and hope there was no trap there. I'd have to take the problem to Mayra when I escaped. If I escaped.

"M-master," said Lura. "The hair on your chest. We must remove it. It's not of the fashion."

I stretched lazily. "No."

"But, master—"

"No. I care nothing for your fashions." I rose as Maleri approached with a glass flagon. "What is that?"

"It's perfume, master. The finest scent from Yagri."

"I don't wear perfume."

"Master, we were ordered to perfume you. The hair on your chest wasn't mentioned. For that we may escape punishment, but the perfume was ordered."

"No."

"M-master, we m-must," Maleri stuttered. Her knuckles were white on the flagon, and all of her icy calm was gone.

"Master," Lura cried, "if you don't wear the scent, we'll be blamed. We'll all be whipped."

"Then suffer your stripes." I snatched the perfume and threw it into the pool.

"No! I don't want to be whipped!" Wailing, Lura grabbed another flask and rushed at me, at the same time trying to unstopper it and fling the contents on me.

I wrested the perfume from her and sent it to join the other. She gave another scream when I picked her up and tossed her in to join the perfume. For a moment she floundered as if she'd never seen water

before, then, coughing and crying, pulled herself out
and lay beside the pool. The others huddled around
her, comforting her and watching me warily, waiting for the beast to strike again. A fine thing for a
warrior. Reduced to frightening bath girls.

"Are there any clothes here?" I asked gently. "A
tunic, or anything I can put on."

"No, master," Maleri said, "there's nothing."

"What about wine? Surely there's some wine?"
They went silent as if at a command and stared at
me. Even Lura ceased her sobbing. "Don't worry. I
won't get angry if you don't have it."

"We have wine, master." Tnay rushed to fetch it.
Her hand shook when she poured.

She seemed eager for one so afraid. They were
all eager. Was it drugged, this wine, or poisoned?
The last was unlikely. They'd not go to all the trouble of bringing me here only to poison me in the
baths of the palace. Drugs were another matter. But
what kind? Mayra could make potions to do ten
thousand things, many of them unpleasant beyond
belief. But much the same logic followed as with
poison. Would I have been brought here merely for
that?

Well, I'd never find out by looking. Tilting the cup
up I drained it and tossed it aside. I felt like laughing. The bath girls heaved a sigh of relief when I'd
drunk. Now they held their breaths to see what
would happen.

A heaviness crept into my limbs. From somewhere came a desire to sleep. I wanted to laugh

again, but it became a yawn. So simple. They wanted me to sleep.

In some fashion the men outside must have known when I asked for the wine, for I heard the locks in the door even as I started to slide to the floor. It was Stefan, with his guards. They pulled me upright before I could finish falling and pushed me out of the room and down the hall, hurrying.

I tried to speak. The energy to form words, to think of what to say, was gone. My head was made of iron, and my arms and legs of lead.

A door opened ahead of us, and we entered apartments, large and richly furnished. There was something about some of the furnishings, something strange, but I couldn't seem to make my mind focus on what it was. They were only interested in one furnishing, anyway. A bench.

They laid me on it on my back, for in truth by that time they carried me like a bundle. Straps went around me, enough to have held me rigid if I could've moved. Roughly they forced a gag between my teeth, to stop the words I couldn't say. And then, still saying nothing, they left. In the silence and dim light I drifted into unconsciousness.

# XI

## AN HONOR, AND A COMMAND

~

I awakened slowly, with fog swirling in my head. I was still bound to the bench. I tensed in every muscle, strained against the straps, and moved not in the slightest.

Slowly I realized that I wasn't alone. The woman who had greeted me below sat beside the bench, watching with eyes like green fire.

"You're back," she said. Her fingers trailed across my chest, pointed nails scratching slightly. "I'm glad the bath girls didn't shave this hair. It's almost a shame to have them punished for it. Don't look surprised, my barbarian. It's the way Sayene taught me when I was a child. Punish hard when your orders are disobeyed, even in the slightest detail. In that way you ensure that your orders will always be obeyed to the letter. Punish twice as hard when the wishes you haven't expressed aren't carried out.

In that way everyone will constantly search for ways to please you." She sighed. "They were told to prepare you in the current fashion, but here you are, chest unshaved, no perfume. It doesn't matter that I like it. It's not the way they were told, so they'll be punished."

I didn't struggle or try to avoid her hands. It would have been useless, bound as I was. She touched me as if I was something new and exotic, something she had to feel.

"You're not very pretty, are you, my barbarian? You're barely even handsome. So why am I drawn to you in particular? Could it be your eyes? Have I told you how they fascinate me? So compelling." One finger traced its way around my eye as she spoke. "I don't think I've ever seen eyes so blue before. Like ice from a glacier, but with a fire burning inside."

She stood and moved back. "You can't know how exciting it is to have a wild male here, after so many tame ones. It'll be a shame to tame you, my sweet," she sighed, "but you're too dangerous to be left wild. Now, however, there are other matters to be taken care of. You're to be an instrument of punishment."

She walked to the wall and pulled a tasseled cord, and I watched, puzzled. For the first time I saw those furnishings that had seemed strange to me. They were things more appropriate to a slave trainer's pens than a palace.

The doors opened slowly. Through them came

two men, the biggest men I'd ever seen. They were at least a head taller than Orne, and bulkier. Between them they led a woman, each holding one of her arms in a hand that appeared able to wrap twice around it. She was blindfolded with a slave hood, but she wore the long flowing dress of a Lantan noble, with rubies at her neck and wrists. She threw her dark hair back over her shoulder and listened, seeking. She was calm.

"Well, Leah, are you more, shall we say, agreeable than before?"

At the first word the woman stiffened. "Agreeable, Elana? Agreeable? I've been kidnapped from the very courtyard of my home, hooded like a slave and brought here to I know not what. And you expect me to be agreeable?"

"When I command, girl, you're always expected to be agreeable. And in your case, penitent. Oh," she said as the woman tried to interrupt, "not for what you just said, though your words were rude for one speaking to her queen. Rather, I speak of earlier, of a few days ago." She smiled evilly. "When I invite you to my bed you're to consider it an honor, and a command. You're to come running, eager to please your queen. You do not send a message declining the invitation."

"My queen doubtless knows that I'm to be married?"

"It makes no difference. Sometimes I send a message to husband or to wife, telling them to send their spouse to me. None refuses. And you won't either.

If I send for you in your bridal bed, you'll come to me."

"Toran will hear of this," Leah said angrily. "He's a man of power, my queen, and you cannot dare to anger him too far. He has the ear of the Council of Nobles, and of the generals. He—"

"He's out of the city," Elana said sweetly. "I sent him on an embassy to Caselle. A long one."

Leah seemed to shrink. "He's gone," she said hollowly.

"Strip her," Elana commanded.

"No!" the noblewoman screamed, but the huge men paid no heed.

They tore her garments away as if her struggles weren't happening. They bound her arms behind her. While she writhed and sobbed they held her for the queen.

Elana stirred the contents of a small pot with a feather. Still using the feather she spread it over Leah's breasts, not in any pattern, but just as a coating. The woman seemed to realize what it was. She began to scream louder. The queen nodded, and the men turned the woman upside down, holding her suspended from her ankles while Elana finished her painting.

At last she stepped back. The men set Leah on her feet, and she sank to her knees, sobbing.

"You know what it is, don't you?" Elana asked casually. The huddled woman only sobbed louder, but the queen nodded. "Yes, you know. The passions grow. Fires heat the blood. And until those passions are slaked, they grow. And the longer they grow, the more it takes to slake them. By tomorrow, you'll do anything. By the next day—"

"Please," Leah moaned. "Please."

"You don't want to wait?" Elana asked as if surprised. "Well, there is a way. If you're sure you don't want to wait until tomorrow."

"Anything," Leah said. "Anything."

"If you don't want to come to my bed, perhaps you'd rather lie in the arms of a man. There's one here for you." The evil smile returned. "A slave."

"A, a slave?" Leah said thickly. "No. No, not a slave."

"Perhaps tomorrow—"

"You win." The young noblewoman sounded beaten, lifeless. "I'll do what you want."

Swiftly the two men dragged her to where I lay. Her flesh shrank from contact with mine, but the potion's effect was taking hold. Her will no longer held sway over her body. When it was over, she lay on my chest, and her sweat mingled with mine.

"Very good, Leah," Elana said softly.

Leah started to rise, but the men took her again, holding her head down as before. She swung between them, dwarfed, and moaned, but whether from pain or fright I couldn't say.

"Take her," said the queen. "Put her in the special dungeon."

Heedless of her cries the two men carried their writhing burden away.

Her screams faded with distance, but they never

seemed to decrease in intensity, as if she found new energy in the vain hope that her pleas would be answered. At last they were gone, but still they seemed to linger in the air. Elana felt it, too. She hugged herself and rubbed at her arms as if cold.

"Do you think me cruel? You're right. Your new mistress is a hard woman with those she rules, and cruel, too, when she needs to be. But she can be kind. Sometimes. For those who earn it." She looked down at me, studying. "I'll remove the gag. If you become abusive I'll have it replaced, and I'll have you beaten."

She unfastened the strap and took it away. I worked my mouth to get enough moisture to speak. It had gone dry from biting leather.

"Is this why I've been taken captive?" I asked finally. "To make love to the women of Lanta?"

She chuckled deep in her throat. "No, not all the women, my barbarian. You see, my wild one, you're going to be my slave, my personal slave." She frowned. "The others say—Well, never mind what the others say. You're going to be my slave for a long, long time."

So there were others who didn't go along with her plan for keeping me alive as a slave. Her sister? The Most High? I was glad to know that there was disunity in the enemy camp, however slight, and glad, too, that she intended keeping me alive, for a long time.

"When I was a child, before I took the throne, I saw an Altaii warrior, riding through the streets. I'd never seen anything like him. A leopard in human form. A human eagle. I wanted him. I demanded he be given to me. And I was told that gold might buy an Altaii sword, but never an Altaii. There was no such thing as an Altaii slave. They escaped, or they died, but they never remained slaves. I vowed to have one, then, and I remembered that vow, as I remembered him. Then I saw you." She drew a breath. "As soon as I saw you I knew that you were the one. In some fashion your destiny and mine were linked so strongly that I could feel it, with no help from a Sister of Wisdom. That could mean only one thing. You're the one. You were born to be the Altaii slave I've dreamed of."

"Then why try to kill me? The tongueless assassin wasn't there to capture me."

"It wasn't I who sent him," she said. "He was Eilinn's idea. You made her very angry, you know, with your talk of making her a slave." She laughed again, a throaty laugh. "She worked herself into a frenzy over the way Altaii slave girls are supposed to be treated. It made her furious. She's never had a love, man or woman, and for you to speak of her so, in public especially—" She paused and looked at me pointedly. "For some reason you make me talk. It won't matter, though. Slaves always keep secrets, at least, if they're given no chance to tell them, and you won't be."

"How do you intend to keep me alive, when your sister wants me dead? Someone will tell her I'm in the palace, surely."

"My sister doesn't know everything that happens in the palace, nor do, ah, certain others. There are enough people who owe their loyalty to me personally to keep your presence a secret. By the time she learns you're a captive, you'll be properly tamed. That will satisfy her. That should satisfy everyone."

She was growing pensive again, thinking, I was sure, about the need for me to die. If she thought about it long enough, she might change her mind, decide the others were right after all.

"Elana, why do you want to destroy us? We pose no threat to you. The caravans we take in our best years aren't a pinprick on Lanta's trade."

"Slaves aren't supposed to call their mistresses by name. Perhaps in private, though. So many questions. You Altaii stand in the way of empire. There, does that answer your question?"

"And the Morassa?"

"We need horsemen in numbers to counter your horsemen," she answered indifferently.

"I mean after," I said, and could've bitten my tongue.

Her indolence fell away. She looked at me, really looked at me, and drew a wondering breath. "You know," she said softly. "You know. But how much? And how? Almost you frighten me, my barbarian. It will not do for you to frighten me. I might begin to wonder if the others are right about you."

I kept a steady face and cursed my own stupidity. If she did change her mind, there was absolutely nothing I could do about it. Her face was as serious as my own.

"It's time, I think," she said.

I tensed for the knife, but instead she unfastened the heavy brocade robes and let them fall. Beneath them she was naked. Her breasts were firm, upstanding globes. Below them a waist my hands could nearly span swelled into beautifully rounded hips. It was the body of the goddess her people believed her to be.

"You find me beautiful," she said. "That's good. Now, my wild one."

And she descended on me.

# XII

## PRIDE, OR HONOR

I've not seen many dungeons, but the one I sat in was better than most I had. The stone walls were no softer, the iron on my ankle was no more comfortable, and the ropes that bound my wrists were no looser, but it was warm and dry, and the straw on the floor was reasonably clean. There was even a pot for slops, which made it a palace among dungeons.

There was a companion of sorts in the cell with me. He appeared to be a Lantan nobleman, or at least the rags he wore had once been a nobleman's garments, and he had the manners of one. He answered all of my questions with mutters about barbarian dogs and the indignity of being forced to share his cell with animals. He didn't speak of the indignity of being chained and having his hands tied behind him.

From his appearance I wondered if we'd be fed. His arms were no more than sticks, and I could count his ribs easily through the holes in his tunic. I had no reason to believe I'd be starved, but then I had no real reason to believe I wouldn't. I didn't know what to expect.

I'd been dragged from the bench straight to the cell, and I'd fallen asleep almost immediately. My fellow prisoner had no conversation to keep me awake. He was the only human I'd seen since entering the cell, and I'd heard no sound save his mutters. No sooner did the thought enter my head than I heard footsteps. Approaching footsteps.

The bolts on the door were drawn back. It swung open. "Well, barbarian, how do you like it here in my dungeon? This is the section reserved for those who anger Elana. Queen Elana, that is, but you'll never tell. You should be honored. Many high nobles have been where you are now. Like this one." He kicked, and the ragged nobleman doubled over, gagging.

He was heavyset, this jailer, and his clothes were a mass of filth and grease. With his many chins and his constant laughter, he seemed a jolly sort. Until, that is, you saw his eyes. Red-rimmed, they were, and vicious, like those of a wild pig in a corner. He was a man who liked his work.

On the floor in front of each of us he set a plate. I looked at him in astonishment. The food was of the best. Barro's tongue. Small roasted birds in a rich sauce. Whole osere, and I'll wager the man who dug them never got more than a smell.

Beside the plates he put large cups of wine. It was no fare for prisoners, certainly not what they'd been feeding my ragged cell-mate on. He rolled over to face the wall. His chins quivering, the jailer stood and watched. And I understood.

The food was there, rich food, food to tempt anyone, there for us to eat as we would. But our hands would remain tied behind our backs.

"Eat," I told the other prisoner. He didn't move. I dropped to my knees, put my face to the plate and ate.

The imprisoned nobleman glared at me in disgust. The jailer laughed aloud. When he left, carefully locking the door behind him, he was still laughing. Let him laugh. Let the noble fool glare. I continued to eat. When my chance to escape came, I'd not be too weak from hunger to take it.

He who lay, huddled and starving, across from me confused honor with pride. Pride said, Don't eat like this. Don't let them make you get down on your knees and eat like an animal. Don't give in so much as the width of the narrowest thread in your cloak. Honor said, Eat. Survive. Maintain your strength. Escape. And flavor every bite you take with the thought of the revenge you'll take. I ate.

The days passed, but how many I couldn't tell. The light was always the same, dim and unceasing. Food came, but the time that passed between its comings was never the same. Sometimes I ate twice in the space of what I thought was a day. Once not at all for two days. Or so I thought. It was meant to soften the will, to sow doubt. But I survived. The other kept his face turned to the wall.

One day the jailer set the plates on the floor, and getting no response to his gibes he kicked the other man hard enough to lift him off the floor. Still he got no response. With a curse, he rolled him over and stared him in the face. Then he dragged him away, sweating all the while, though not from exertion, I think.

After that I passed my days alone, except for the visits of the jailer. I wondered briefly if the other prisoner had died, but he had made his choice. I had made mine.

I tried to tell the passage of time by the growth of my beard. It was all I had that wasn't controlled by the jailer. My beard was full when the door finally opened to admit someone other than the jailer. I could understand how some men could have felt a kind of joy at seeing a different face. To me it meant only that one part was over, and new means of breaking me were about to be tried.

The guards who entered, with the jailer hovering in the background, removed my leg iron and led me away, still bound. I didn't speak, and this seemed to puzzle them. Doubtless they had taken many others from those cells, and doubtless all of them had been eager to speak, to hear a human voice. I didn't care to speak. I wanted only to reach our destination, to discover if it offered possibilities for escape.

They took me to a garden. I hadn't thought the dungeon had affected me, but going from the hard, gray drabness to bright flowers and fountains was like a blow.

A number of women in plain white robes sat on the benches among the flowers. Among them, the center of them, was Elana. Her robes were white, also, but richly embroidered, far from plain. The women gathered around me, laughing gaily, chattering like songbirds. Despite their beauty my eyes were drawn to the walls. Guards, in groups of four, three groups to each wall except for the innermost one, and it stretched into the sky like a mountain. There was no escape from there.

"Are you softened properly, my barbarian?" Elana asked. The women all laughed as if at something witty. "At any rate, you're scruffy enough. I might allow you to keep that beard, trimmed a little, of course. It's quite handsome." There was a coy tone to her voice, and the women laughed again.

"I hear that you ate well from the very first. Such submissiveness surprises me, barbarian. Some of the finest nobles of Lanta have held out to the point of death in those cells. Or beyond. I was certain you'd fight. Still, we must see if you have softened enough."

The guards hustled me to a pair of stone pillars facing a fountain. Cutting the ropes that bound my hands, they jerked my wrists up and fastened them to the posts. After being tied so long my arms became bars of fire and pain at the movement. I could no more control them than if they were sticks of wood.

The straps on my wrists were tight, but they didn't

hold me rigid. I could move my body or bend an arm. My feet weren't bound at all. Obviously it was desired that I move. Beneath the lash, it was expected, I'd forget who I was and act as a slave. Around me Elana and her women found seats to watch.

The heavyset jailer came into my sight, wearing a clean tunic and carrying a red bag under his arm. He dropped to his knees to make obeisance to the queen, behind me, but she must have dismissed him immediately, for he rose as soon as his knees touched the stones. As he opened the bag and removed its contents the disappointment at her brusque treatment disappeared behind a smile of porcine satisfaction. In his hands he held a whip. It was an instrument to break the will of a man, two paces and more in length, tightly braided black leather. It was a weapon.

He came to me, looping the whip around my neck. "I could break you easily, below, with the rack and the pincers and the hot irons, but they want it done the hard way. Now, I'm told to use this"—he shifted the whip slightly—"and even then I'm told to remove the metal barbs. You're not supposed to be damaged badly." He sneered. "But I'll break you, just the same."

I looked at him no more, but he shifted uncomfortably, then jerked back as though I had snarled at him. He scowled as he remembered that I was bound, and he was the man with the whip.

"I'll have no need of metal tips," he spat. "I'll take the flesh from your bones."

"Get on with it, Nesir," called the queen. "You'll not frighten him into submission with your whispers."

Nesir smiled his vicious smile and prepared for work. I'd seen his eyes. There'd been no smile there. There'd been shame at his fear of a bound man, and anger at the laughter of the women, and desire for revenge. We would see which of us wanted his revenge the more.

No sooner were my feet set than the first lash fell, a searing streak of fire across my shoulders. The breath caught in my throat, but no sound passed my lips, and I didn't move. The second blow fell, and I concentrated on remaining absolutely still, absolutely silent. My hands weren't clenched into fists. They hung loose in their bonds. As each blow struck I stood steady, hands open, feet unmoving. My breath was regular and controlled, and I looked straight ahead. My body was mine to command. It would not react if I willed it not to. I made no sound. I moved no muscle.

Then the whip stopped. The fires making burning lines across my back were undiminished. I could feel blood dripping down to fall and spot the stones.

Elana came to stand in front of me. "You're a very dangerous man, barbarian," she said softly. "A man who can stand like that under the whip, who doesn't cry out, such a man must be dangerous." She ran a hand over my chest and shoulders. "It seems I've made an error. While I thought I was softening you, all I was doing was keeping you well fed.

Have I made another error? Should I be keeping you alive when they tell me you must—"

She broke off, searching in my eyes for answers. I could only wait. She bit at the corner of her lips, then slowly wet them with the tip of her tongue. "Nesir!"

"Yes, my queen?" he answered fawningly.

"Remain here for instructions on how he's to be handled from here on." She smiled and patted me on the cheek. "Guards, take him to the old cell."

They freed my hands only to bind them behind my back again, and pulled me from the garden. The cell to which they took me could have been the one I'd been in before. Except, Elana had called it the old cell. What was different? The stone walls gave no clue.

They chained me to the wall by one ankle, as before, but this time they unbound my wrists. Extinguishing the light, they left, the door grating shut behind them with a sound of finality.

On my hands and knees, in the dark, I set out to explore what I could of my prison. I couldn't reach the door, or the walls at the ends of the cell. In the straw on the floor I could reach I found nothing. No scraps of bones from a previous prisoner's meal. No bits of rag. Nothing. It was as if the cell had been cleaned out after the previous occupant. The straw wasn't only clean. It smelled new. It seemed the cell had been readied only recently.

The chain I followed back to its beginning at the wall. The end seemed to grow out of a metal cap in some manner I couldn't make out in the dark. Even if I'd had the bone I'd searched for there was no way to scrape at the mortar to free that.

After a time I lay down to sleep. There was nothing else to do, except sit and stare at the darkness, and I'd already done that. So I went to sleep.

It was the motion that woke me, the feeling that the floor was sliding underneath me. I woke to find it was sliding underneath me, with a grating sound, as of rocks being ground. Across the center of the room a bar seemed darker than the rest of the darkness, and the bar was growing wider. Abruptly I realized what was happening. I leaped for the wall and caught hold with fingertips and toenails in the cracks as the floor disappeared from beneath me.

The grating noise went, but in its place, from the deep darkness below, came hissings and slitherings and sounds of slimy motion. I clung to the wall and wondered how deep the darkness was. How high could whatever made those noises leap? I thought of how far my chain would be hanging down and crept higher on the wall, carefully, finger by finger, toe by toe. And all the while those sounds continued.

When my fingers seemed frozen into hooks and my toes felt at the edge of tearing from my feet, I heard the grating again, the noise of the floor sliding back into place. Slowly I moved back down the wall, crack by crack, as carefully as I'd climbed. How far had I climbed to escape what crawled below? How far back down had I come?

Suddenly I felt a difference in the stones. They

were damp, slimy with a growth that crushed beneath my hands and feet and gave a sickly smell. I was below the level of the floor. Desperately I climbed, but in my desperation, quietly still. For the things were still beneath me. I climbed, and as I felt the cap that marked the end of my chain, the floor slid out in truth. It caught me in the ribs, knocking me free from the wall. My fingers scrabbled at the stone, bare now, as I hung over the pit. With what seemed the last of my strength I managed to throw one leg over the edge of the floor and heave myself up as the two halves slid shut at my fingertips.

I lay awake for a long time, wondering if the floor would split again, wondering what lay beneath it, but at last, against my will, sleep came. This time it was the grating that woke me. I made the leap to the wall without a thought.

After a few minutes something strange struck me. There was no widening darker space in the center of the room. I moved back down, slowly. The floor wasn't moving. Only the sound of its moving was there.

That sound went on, and so long as it continued I had to remain awake. If I slept the moving floor might not be enough to wake me. I sat and watched the darkness and listened to the grinding sound of stone sliding over stone.

When it stopped it left an emptiness behind, as if it had become as much a part of the cell as the stone and the dark. I lay down to sleep, but lightly, warily, as an animal sleeps. Like an animal I didn't dare be surprised in my sleep.

Four times more the sound of grating rock came without the floor moving. Three times it came and the floor opened. On the last of these times I nearly died.

The constant alarms, the vital clinging to the wall were taking their toll. Each time I slept, I slept deeper. At last the grating noise failed to wake me. The sliding of the floor failed to wake me.

The floor disappeared from beneath me, and only the fall woke me. In desperation I grabbed for the chain. The links slid through my hands, ripping and tearing at the flesh of my palms, but I slowed, and I stopped, and immediately I began to climb again, back up the chain that was wet with my blood.

The sounds from the pit below were still there, louder now, closer. My exertions opened the wounds on my back, and the blood dropped into the darkness. The hissings grew more agitated, the slitherings more rapid. Something jerked at the chain that hung in a loop below me, brushing against my leg.

I kicked, and my foot connected with something that mashed under my bare toes, something that gave a hissing scream, released a smell like the sour smell of the slime that grew on the stones beneath the floor. It fell away without me seeing it, and I was glad. I would face anything that runs or flies, on the Plain or in the far mountains, but that which was below made me feel unclean merely by being close.

How long I clung to the chain at the cap on the wall I could not say. It seemed like days. I couldn't go higher because I couldn't trust my bloody fingers to hold in the chinks between the stones. I had to remain on the chain. Again and again something reached from the pit to tug and pull at that chain, to try and pull me down. I swung violently to snatch the chain away. I shouted at the things below, screamed defiance. And I hung there, through endless time, endless darkness, while drops of my blood fell to whet the tastes of the beasts in the pit.

When the floor at last returned I swung onto it weakly, and lay exhausted, covered with a cold sweat. If they'd come for me then, I'd have forgotten about survival. I'd have fought, naked and chained as I was. Better to die a clean death on a blade than to fall to whatever lay in the pit.

In those first days in the cell I quickly got used to the fact that I wouldn't be fed. Elana's gibes about keeping me well fed had been warning enough on that. In truth, I could survive for some time without it. Food's often scarce enough when the lances campaign. Water, however, was a different matter.

As the days passed my lips cracked. My tongue swelled, and if Ivo had come in I couldn't have managed enough wetness to spit on him. Then my sweat no longer tasted salty, and I knew I would soon begin to die.

I was lying against the wall when I heard steps outside. Lying took less energy even than sitting, and I'd none to spare.

I watched the door swing open with as much interest as I could muster. It was Nesir. The dim light through the door behind him hurt my eyes, but I could see that much. And I could see the large clay pot in his hands. He set the pot on the floor, tossed a small packet down beside it and left. He didn't say a word.

Hastily I opened the packet. It was salt, and the pot held water, pure and sweet. The water was enough for several days, and the salt would help keep me alive to drink it. And then it came to me. I hadn't heard the bolts on the door. He hadn't fastened the door to the cell.

I didn't rush, but neither did I move slowly. I ate some of the salt and drank some water. More salt and more water. I drank until I was ready to burst, then I poured some of it over me, to wash away sweat and grime, to lessen sweating and the body's loss of moisture. And I drank more of it. When I set the pot down it couldn't have held more than a few mouthfuls.

Nesir had been waiting for the clink of the clay pot on the stones. Immediately he swung the door open and ran in. On the run he kicked the pot against the wall, dodging back out of my reach. I couldn't see his face, but he made his first sound when the lack of a splash told him the water was already gone, a snarl of disappointment. He jerked out of the cell, slamming the door behind him. This time the bolts rammed shut loudly. I lay in the darkness and laughed until tears ran down my face.

After that visit the game with the floor began again. Only, this time, something new was added. Sometimes the floor would move, but it wouldn't open. And always when this happened there was the thought in the back of my head that it really was opening, that this time I just couldn't see the gap widening in the center of the room. Added to the rest it made an interesting test of the will. How long could I let the floor move before I went to the wall, opening or no?

On the next visit with the water, the salt was in the water. I didn't discover it until I'd taken a huge swallow, and the time until the third visit was an agony of burning thirst. The water was good again at the third visit, but after that the floor began to split without warning. There was no grating sound, no grind of stone against stone. Merely a silent slide into emptiness. After that I seldom slept.

The days continued. The darkness continued. The pit below continued. I couldn't tell time by changing light, or by meals. I told it by the visits with water. Twenty-three visits with water. I kept the numbers in my head, even when I slept. Twenty-three visits with water, and all the while the pit below clamored for me.

At the twenty-fourth visit they took me from the cell.

# XIII

## THE NEW PET

The guards who pulled me out of the cell stopped in astonishment when they got into the light enough to see me. No doubt I looked like an escapee from the Lands of the Dead. I felt like one about to enter them.

"We can't take him like this," one of them protested.

"It's orders," said Nesir.

The guards were doubtful, but they wouldn't disobey orders. They half carried me to the garden I'd left so long ago.

Once again the women waited in their white dresses, sitting around a fountain. Once again Elana was the center of them all. This time, though, the laughter and talk faded as I was pushed, stumbling, into their midst and fell heavily to the tiles. There was total silence until Elana spoke.

"I didn't expect—I didn't believe—" She grabbed my matted beard and twisted my head up. "Has what I want been crushed out of you, barbarian? Has it?" She peered at me intently, then released me and held out her hands. Instantly a cloth was there to wipe them where they'd touched me. "No," she said, "it's not gone, is it, barbarian? You should be beaten, groveling, but the defiance is still alive. The fire still burns in your eyes."

"As you said, Elana," I croaked, "Altaii don't make slaves."

"You misunderstand, barbarian." She laughed. "You're doing well. I don't want to break your spirit, I just want to know you'll obey me. And you will."

"Never," I managed.

She laughed again. "Of course you will. Here." She held out a piece of meat in her fingers. "You'll eat to survive. You've proven that. And you need food. You're starving. But the only food you'll get is what you take nicely from my hand, or the hand of one of my ladies, as a pet should." She waggled the meat and smiled. "Take it, my wild one."

She was right. I would survive, and even like this the meat would taste sweet with the spice of future revenge. I took the meat from her fingers.

She laughed, and the others laughed with her, at that. Then all of the rest of them wanted to feed the new pet too. I played the part, crawling to each in turn for a piece of meat or a double handful of water or wine. I kept my head down, though. If they'd seen my eyes while I fed like that they'd have known I was nowhere near tamed.

"Might I feed your new pet also, sister?"

The women around Elana all gasped at the newcomer, and even she seemed uncomfortable at first. It didn't last very long, though. "Certainly, sister. He isn't trained, yet, but I have taught him this one trick."

Eilinn left her entourage to walk to the fountain. She was dressed as Elana was, but in blue, and her women wore every color in the garden. She held out a hand without looking, and one of Elana's women put a piece of meat on it.

"Come, barbarian pet, get the meat. Do your trick for me."

Rage seemed to bubble up in me, like the bubbles in a pool of boiling mud. I could keep it down with Elana. I could control it with her women. Why should it burn so with her sister? I gripped the tiles of the courtyard until my knuckles were white. And somehow, by the thickness of a fingernail, I managed to crawl to Eilinn and take the meat.

"He seems tame enough," she said coolly, "but it's not enough, you know, sister. He has to die. They've all said it. The Most High. Sayene. Ya'shen. Betine. They all say he has to die."

"And I say this is enough. Look at him, sister. Does he look like he can stand in the way of anything?"

"Perhaps not, but—"

"I mean to have him, Eilinn. I want him, and I mean to have him. I say enslaving him is sufficient."

"As you wish, sister." Eilinn's voice was as frosty as her sister's was hot. "If there is any failure, though, it rests on your head."

"Don't threaten me, sister," Elana spat. "I know the real reason you want him dead. He spoke of putting chains on you. That's the reason, isn't it?"

"I didn't come here for this," Eilinn said coldly, "and I won't stay for it. Just remember what I said. Failure is on your head."

Elana's face twisted with anger as her sister walked away. Her ladies sat very still, fearful of attracting the fury she meant for Eilinn. It took her a long time to calm, a time I spent still kneeling on the tiles, and when she did a sourness was left behind.

"There's no fun here anymore," she complained. "He's too dirty, and his beard looks like a rat's nest. Take him away and have him bathed. I've got to—"

Whatever it was she had to do, she hurried off without finishing the sentence. I was left with the guards.

It was still necessary for them to half carry me. One small meal hadn't done a great deal in restoring my strength. They didn't appear to relish the task. Elana had been right about the dirt.

The bath they took me to was a different one from the first I'd seen in the palace. Where the other had been supposed to be a pond in a garden, this was a river. Two of the walls showed rushes on the banks, and the other two pictured the view up and down the river.

The girls were different, too. They were not nearly as pretty, plain, in fact, for bath girls, a trade where beauty is common. They were also silent, almost cheerless. There was no banter here, not even a smile.

In my filth they wouldn't let me into the pool until I'd been cleaned off. They scrubbed me down three times from head to toe before they were satisfied, and they had all the animation they'd have had if they were scrubbing a horse.

The baths are usually a cheerful place, but these girls remained drab and lifeless. Even in the pool, where more games than a few are played, they had no spirit. I suffered them to wash me and cut my hair and beard, and it was a suffering in truth. I began to feel worse than when I came in. Even a massage didn't help.

The guards waited, then led me away, not to a cell, but to an alcove off a corridor in what seemed to be a main part of the palace. There was a sleeping pad there, but there were still no clothes of any kind. As they chained my ankle my curiosity won out.

"Those girls—" I began.

They laughed as if it was a great joke. Finally one of them spoke. "The queen has decided you'll see no woman who's not plain, except for her. You won't even be allowed to talk to a woman, except for the queen. Soon you won't even be able to think of another woman."

"And it won't matter that you told me about it?"

They froze, doubled over the way they were, but they weren't laughing anymore. "We'll have to kill him," one said.

"And how will you explain it?" I asked calmly, but I kept a wary eye on his hand, creeping toward his sword. "They'll never believe I attacked you. I can hardly stand. Kill me, and you'll die screaming in the dungeons."

"And we'll die anyway if she finds out we've ruined her plans," he said, but his hand stopped moving toward his sword.

"I certainly won't tell. She might change to another plan, one I don't know about, one that might work." They began to relax. "That is, I won't tell if you answer a few questions."

They went taut again. Then the one who'd spoken before shifted. "What kind of questions?"

"Not much. For instance, where am I, exactly, and what am I doing here?"

He began slowly, but warmed to the task as he went on. "You're not far from the queen's chambers. Elana's chambers, that is. The first turn to the right ahead leads straight to her door."

"And why I'm here?"

"Isn't it plain enough? Once you put a little meat back on your frame, you'll be spending a lot of time in those chambers, entertaining the queen." He snickered nervously.

"You don't sound very respectful," I said. "I thought she was supposed to be a goddess."

"To the rabble in the streets she's a goddess. They give their coins to buy prayers to her, and to the other one. Me, I live here in the palace, same as the rest of the Palace Guard. She's human enough to us. She's no goddess, except maybe to the officers." He snickered again.

"Have you gone mad?" the other guard hissed. "You could get the both of us impaled on the walls for saying that."

The second guard's nervousness infected the first. They looked around as if expecting to see someone standing there to accuse them. In a moment they were going to run.

"One more question," I said. "How do I get to the palace wall from here?"

"Palace wall? You're talking about escape? You're mad. If it's discovered that I've been talking to you like this—"

"It won't be, as long as I get an answer. The outer wall of the palace."

His companion was already half a dozen steps down the hall. He licked his lips and took a step. "Two crossings after the one that leads to the queen's chambers. Go to the left. At the first stairs you come to, go down three flights, then keep on the way you were headed. You'll reach a door to the outside. It leads to a walk on the palace wall. You'll never make it, you know. The guards at the queen's door will see you when you try to cross the hall. And between here and the wall there are other guards, and servants and slaves who'll raise an alarm as soon as they see you."

"Do you really care about my making it, or even trying? And Lantan, if anything makes me think you've talked about my plan, the way you did about Elana's—" I smiled at him, unpleasantly.

He took a step down the hall, and then another. "I won't talk," he said, "but you'll still never escape." And he turned and ran after the other guard.

The pad was more comfortable than anything I'd lain on since I came to the palace, and once the guards were gone I slept, a sleep untroubled by moving floors or hissing from below. I slept, and when I woke I was being watched.

The girl was pretty, but her garb and the black iron bracelets on her wrists proclaimed her a laborer. Her hair was cropped raggedly close, for cleanliness at her labors, and her nails were broken off short. But there was spirit in her brown eyes yet, and intelligence. She hadn't broken.

"What are you looking at, girl?" I growled.

"You, of course," she said calmly.

I suppressed a smile. "And why am I worth looking at?"

"Because you're the queen's new barbarian slave. She's supposed to be much taken with you." She frowned. "I don't see why."

"You have a mouth on you, girl."

"Even a kitchen girl must have a mouth." With a swing of her tunic and a laugh she disappeared down the hall, in the direction away from the queen's chamber. I wondered what had brought her. It seemed a long time before the guards returned. From where I was chained I could see the walls of my alcove, the far wall of the hall, part of a pillar and half of a plant. In the dungeon I'd had to fight for my life every second. Here the boredom was likely to kill me.

When they did come they were the first to pass since the kitchen girl. They were a different pair than the ones who'd brought me there. They didn't speak at all. They led me straight down to the garden, where Elana was waiting with her women.

Once again, I fed from their fingers, crawling on hands and knees. Once again I drank from their cupped hands. Because I was clean they patted me the way they would a dog, and they were freer with their laughter and their comments. Some were as ribald as those of Lura and Tnay and the other bath girls.

When my brief time in the garden court was done I was returned to the alcove. There I sat in utter solitude until it was time to be fed by Elana in the garden again. From the garden I went to the bath, where the same dull bath girls bathed me. So passed the day. Unrelieved drabness around two bits of color, both centered on Elana. Could her scheme work even when I knew what she tried?

The guard had given me directions for my escape. It would take more than a few days to regain my strength on the tidbits they fed me in the garden, but when I did, I had to be free of the chain to make use of the directions. It wasn't like the chain in the cell. It had no cap, merely a bolt set in the wall. I knew it wouldn't move, but I braced my feet on either side of it, took up the slack in the chain and pulled with all my strength.

"You won't get free like that."

I twisted around to find the kitchen girl regarding me studiously. "You again," I said. "Why?"

"I heard something about you. I thought I'd seen healed whip marks on your back, but I couldn't be sure until now. They say in the slave quarters that you took a hundred lashes without making a sound, or even flinching. They say that Nesir was so frightened of you that he wouldn't free you himself after."

"They seem to say a lot of things," I said dryly, "and only a little of it true."

"But how could you do it? I cry when Cook hits me with her spoon." She rubbed at her hip reflectively.

"Perhaps you don't have enough reason not to cry, or maybe you know Cook has good cause to hit you."

"Not always." She looked down the hall and frowned. "Could I sit in there with you? You wouldn't hurt me, or—I mean—"

"I won't hurt you, girl," I said, and she scurried into the alcove, a bag I hadn't noticed clutched to her breast. "I never see anyone here except for you.

And the guards, of course. I didn't think any pretty women were to be allowed near me."

She froze half seated. "You won't tell? Please?"

"If I was a slave, I'd tell."

She puzzled over that for a minute, then smiled and settled to the floor. "But you're not really a slave, so you won't carry tales like one. And thank you."

"For what? I won't tell because I don't want to."

"No," she said shyly. "For saying I'm pretty. Cook sometimes says I think I am, but then she always takes a strap to me. And she always gives me work where I'm so dirty I couldn't tell if I was or not."

"You've never seen a mirror?"

"There are no mirrors in the kitchens." She set the bag on the floor. "I brought this, because of what you did." From the bag she took a piece of meat, bread, cheese and fruit. "I tried to get wine, but I couldn't."

"Why, child?"

"Because." It was as if she thought I should know the answer. "I have to go now." She gathered up her bag and peered around the corner into the hall.

"Girl." She stopped at the word. "You've not told me your name."

"Nilla," she said. "I'm called Nilla." Like a wraith she disappeared.

Elana began to remark on my trips to the garden that the food was agreeing with me, that I was regaining lost flesh. It wasn't her food that did it, but the food that Nilla brought every night, food stolen at great risk to herself, I had no doubt, from the kitchens.

At first I asked her every time why she did it. Being caught would've meant the displeasure of Elana, and for a kitchen girl that could be worse than death. She never gave an answer, or gave the same one as the first time I asked, because. She'd try to change the subject, talk of other things, and I didn't try and force her. I've never professed to know much of the minds of women, but she began to convince me I knew nothing.

We talked at each visit until she had to leave. Sometimes she'd share the food with me, but usually she said she was fed better than I was. She did talk with intelligence, though, and one night I learned how she came to be a kitchen girl.

"I'm the daughter of a farmer near Knorros," she said. "My parents allowed me to spend my days reading and dreaming, instead of making me work on the land, but I came to realize that I was bound to be a burden to them. I looked as if I was made of sticks, and my father couldn't provide a very large dowry, so I knew I'd never be able to get a husband to help work my father's lands or grandchildren to provide for him when he was old."

"You should have waited," I said. "They'd not want a dowry if they saw you now."

"But I didn't wait. I set out for Knorros. I thought I'd find work and save enough money in a few years to hire a laborer who'd take care of the farm when they were old. I suppose I was innocent, even for a country girl. I didn't even get to Knorros before a slaver found me. When he saw what he'd gotten he said it wasn't worth stopping to take me, but since he'd already stopped, he'd carry me along. I've seen coffles of slavers since then, and all their women were beautiful, but this one was third-rate, dealing in laborers, and I was pretty enough for him. He sold me here three years ago to work in the palace kitchens."

With her talk to heal my mind and her food to heal my body I regained most of the weight I'd lost by the third tenday in the alcove. The strength, however, would take longer, I knew. I didn't get it.

On my thirtieth day there, while I waited for the afternoon journey to the garden, guards came. Not the pair who'd always come before, but a full twenty. A new page was turning in the book, and I didn't think I'd like what was written on the other side.

# XIV

## TWISTING SHADOWS

Twenty men can't be called a guard for one man. They have to be considered an escort. So they escorted me to a part of the palace I'd not seen before, a large, open room that must have been the top of a tower for all its size, for it had huge arched windows on all sides leading out onto a balcony. The ceiling was a dome that stretched out of sight, covered with strange symbols. Some of them I thought I'd seen Mayra use.

They pushed me to the center of the room and bound my hands and feet to a ring set in the floor, so I had no choice but to kneel there. When I saw what I was kneeling on, I wished I'd fought them.

I was in the middle of a large five-pointed star, worked into the stone. Inside the star was a goat's head, his ears in two points of the star, his horns in two, and his beard in the fifth. Even the pit, I thought, might be preferable.

From somewhere behind me five women entered the room. Eilinn and Elana were coldly formal toward each other. Of the others I recognized only Sayene, but something in the dress of the others made me remember names half heard in the garden, Ya'shen and Betine. Three Sisters of Wisdom, a sacred number magnifying their powers, and I knelt on a symbol of power, a focus of darkness.

"I still don't think this is necessary," Elana said angrily.

"Once again, my queen," said Sayene, "let me explain." Her voice sounded as if she'd held on to the proper tone with difficulty. "You don't want to kill him. That means he must be neutralized. If that can be done perhaps the other matter can be disposed of, and all will still be as it must be. If not—"

"I don't like this hiding of things," said a beautiful woman. "This one. The other one. These are times of power, and happenings of power. There is no time for childish hiding games."

"You forget who you're speaking to, Ya'shen," Elana snapped. "I am the power here. I am the Queen of Lanta, and I don't like you poking into what I do with your spells and magic."

"You're not the only power in Lanta," Eilinn broke in, "or the only queen."

"If you please," said the third Sister of Wisdom, the one who must be Betine, "this is not the time for squabbling. Let us do what we came here to do. Then we can all get on with more important matters."

They all fell silent, though Eilinn and Elana still eyed one another with looks that could wound flesh. The three Sisters of Wisdom ranged themselves around the star. Betine and Ya'shen each stood before a horn. Sayene stood at the beard and faced me where I knelt between the eyes. They let their robes fall to the stone.

Sayene lit a candle and stepped into the star. I heard the pad of feet behind me and knew that the others had done the same. Sayene knelt and put the candle before her. I tugged at the ropes, but there was no give in them. They cut into me from the effort.

"Maji Kwa," intoned Sayene.

"Maji Kwa," the others repeated.

"Imholith."

"Imholith."

"Catal Kendora Amarane."

"Catal Kendora Amarane."

The daylight from outside seemed cut off. The air thickened around me, caught in my throat like jelly. Their voices quickened, the responses falling hard on the heels of Sayene's lead.

"Mahera Tras!"

"Mahera Tras!"

"Rajinga!"

"Rajinga!"

"Lac Dakoro!"

"Lac Dakoro!"

Dizziness tugged at me, and only a single tube of vision remained, down which I stared at Sayene's face, wet with effort as she fought to steal my being. I wanted to shout, but I couldn't open my mouth, couldn't make a sound. And yet, yet, I felt strength seeping into me. From somewhere I felt power return to my arms and legs. I tugged at the ropes, and they creaked. I was certain if I pulled harder they'd snap like twine.

The voices rose to a crescendo, all coming at the same time.

"Dargahn! Nehmeni! Ourachi!"

"Dargahn! Nehmeni! Ourachi!"

"Dargahn! Nehmeni! Ourachi!"

Silence returned. For a moment there was no movement, but then Elana rushed forward.

"Is it done? Is it finished?"

"He's protected," Sayene said flatly. Sweat ran down her face.

"Of course he's protected," Elana said. "Every pastry seller in the streets has some protection, and a man like him would have the most of all. That's why there are three of you here. That's why you went through all of this, to break his protection."

"I don't mean simple wards, Elana," Sayene said wearily. "Somewhere there's a Sister of Wisdom who's actively protecting him. At this very moment she has her hands on his forehead. They won't stop steel, though. Kill him."

"She's a woman of unusual power, Sayene," Ya'shen mused. "I wonder who—"

"No," said Elana quietly. "He won't be killed."

"Sister," Eilinn said, "you did agree—"

"No! I want him, and I'll have him. Alive. You three are supposed to be the most powerful Sisters of Wisdom on this side of the mountains. Break that protection. Find a way."

"If you'd brought him to us when he was first taken—" said Sayene. "Now, it can be dangerous to try further."

"If," suggested Betine, "I brought my two best acolytes, Sisters, really, in all but name, and you brought yours—"

"Could you do it if there were nine of you?" demanded Elana. "Would a simple barbarian beat you then?"

"With nine in the circle," said Sayene grimly, "we could break any power that exists."

Sayene's words kept ringing in my head as the guards took me back to the alcove. *With nine in the circle, we could break any power that exists.* And the power they wanted to break was the only thing that was keeping me from being broken myself. Thinking of that protection made me think of Mayra. That it was she who had her hands on my forehead I had no doubt. And along with her hands she'd managed somehow to tamper with their spell. As they tried to strip me of will and strength she had managed to reverse their attempt so they actually forced strength on me. It was the only explanation for the way I felt. I was in the first flush of my youth again. Now, if only I could find an opening.

The lamps in the side corridors had been extinguished for the night when two guards came for me. In the darkness of my alcove I smiled.

One of them nudged me with his toe. "On your feet, slave."

"The queen wants her play pretty," the other said.

I rose slowly and waited quietly while they unfastened my leg iron. I recognized them now. The same two who'd brought me to the alcove for the first time. It was fitting.

"Come on, slave. Elana won't wait all night for you. If you make her wait at all she'll have your hide."

His eyes found mine in the darkness; remembrance of the questions I'd asked that first day, especially the question about escape, flashed across them. His hand streaked for his sword, and my left hand crushed his throat. The right pulled his sword from its scabbard as he fell. It made a shining fan in the darkness as it rushed toward the other. The second guard's fingers dropped his sword, and it and his head struck the floor at the same time.

There hadn't been much noise, but I waited for the guards at the queen's chamber to come running. Nothing happened.

Quickly I rolled the bodies into the alcove. Neither guard was as tall as I was, but I forced my way into one's tunic just the same. There might be notice taken of a naked slave running through the halls, but who would pay attention to a guard, even if his tunic was small? Luckily the Lantans wore sandals instead of boots, so the poor fit was still passable, and the helmet was actually too big. As they'd told me the way to escape, they'd also given me the means.

There was little life in the palace at that hour, save for servants and slaves hurrying on assigned chores, preparing for tomorrow. They had no time nor any desire to question anyone, certainly not a guard. They lowered their heads when they saw me and scurried by, eyes on the floor.

The few other guards, free assistants to Ara and the like, gave more problems. They appeared suddenly from side corridors as I passed, or opened doors behind me. It was as much as I could do at those times to keep walking calmly as if I had a right to be there and a right to go where I was headed. The borrowed tunic began to sweat through.

The second corridor that crossed the one of my alcove after the one that leads to the queen's chambers, the guard had said. Then go to the left. At the first stairs go down three flights.

Those first stairs were wide, sweeping things of polished white stone. They looked more like a main passageway than an escape route. Had the guard thought to give me a false route?

I'd not time to ponder it, and I couldn't afford to take the guard's route as false until I was certain. At the bottom of the third flight I turned in the direction I'd been heading above. Was it false? The door at the end was the same massive door that could be found on any of a thousand palace chambers. Was it the outer wall on the other side, or a guardroom? I drew the guard's sword, kissed the blade, and threw open the door.

Moonlight streamed through, and I could see the parapet around the palace. I dashed through and pulled the door shut behind me. Not until then did I permit myself the sigh of relief I needed.

Loewin, Mondra and Wilaf were in the sky. Together they gave light to see clearly, but their pattern on that night cast strange triple shadows that shifted and moved. It was a good night for sneaking from shadow to shadow, but in the open space of the square those shadows twisting around me would only draw the attention of the guards. I needed another way to leave.

I took advantage of those shadows on the wall, though. If there was a way out other than dropping over the side to the square below, it would be somewhere on that outer wall.

I had covered nearly a quarter of the wall, careful as a poacher to avoid guards, when I moved out of the darkness and from the corner of my eye saw a man-shape. I froze, and then realized the other hadn't moved. And he seemed to be straddling a strong cylinder as if it was a horse.

The moons continued their courses, and the clouds shifted, and as the patterns of light on the walltop changed, I saw that he was naked, and his hands were bound behind him. He sat there, head on his chest, unmoving, and as the light played across him, I recognized him.

"Hulugai," I murmured, and rushed to him. "Hulugai, I thought you all were dead. Where are the others?"

He raised his head, and I skidded to a halt. His face was beaten and bruised, his eyes near swollen shut, and a rope of blood hung from the corner of his mouth. Now that I was close I could see other marks on his body, too, whip marks, slashes and gashes as if he'd been savaged by some beast.

"The rest are dead," he said faintly, "and better I was, too."

"Nonsense," I said. "I'll get you free, and then we'll both—"

I had him half lifted off, and he muted a shriek that even so chilled the bones in me. I gave a moan of my own when I saw the spiked iron bar below him. He'd been impaled.

"S-set me down, my lord."

Gently as I was able I lowered him, and tried to close my ears to the cries he couldn't stifle. "I'm sorry, Hulugai. I've much to answer for, bringing you to this."

"Nothing to answer for, my lord," he breathed. "My right to ride with you. My right to die for you. I'm not a fat merchant, to die in bed."

"Who ordered this? Who ordered it, Hulugai?"

"Sayene, the Sister of Wisdom. For a long time they kept us locked away, hidden, I think. When Sayene found us, a tenday ago, she was furious about us being there." He tried to laugh and choked instead. "She was so mad I thought she'd have a seizure. She questioned each of us. Used a truth-spell. She didn't find what she wanted, my lord. Whatever it was, she didn't find it."

"I know, Hulugai, I know. Rest now."

He didn't seem to hear me. "That made her madder than before. The guards asked if they should kill us, but she said let the torturers use us for practice. They took us one by one, to let the rest watch, but no one gave them satisfaction. With all their whips and racks and knouts and hot irons, all they got was curses, my lord, curses and taunts at their cowardice."

"I know, Hulugai. You gave them nothing."

Sayene. She'd done this, and done it for no reason, not even to further her schemes against my people. Because she couldn't find the answers she wanted, she had my men tortured, and killed by as foul a means as existed. There was much to be answered for, and Sayene must do the answering.

"My lord," he whispered, "give me grace."

"Hulugai, I'll avenge you, you and the others. I swear it by the ashes of my father, and my father's father, and his father."

He smiled. "They don't know what they've brought on themselves. Grace, my lord."

I took his head gently in my hands. "Until the grasses grow on the Plain again, until the dry rivers flow again, until the trees turned to stone bear fruit again"—my hands twisted, and he died silently—"I give you grace. Fare you well, warrior. We will drink together in the Land of the Dead. We will eat lamb in the Tents of Death."

It must be granted, a request for grace, when the wounds are too bad and death comes slowly. Some say it's proof we're barbarians, but those same people force their dying to cling to life, or scream their way to meet the dark ones. Who is the barbarian?

I was halfway back to the door that led into the palace before I realized where I was going, and why. Sayene. I couldn't reach that Sister of Wisdom. I didn't even know where she was. But I knew where another was, another who gave commands, who plotted and schemed the death of my people. I knew where Elana was.

# XV

## THE FEATHER

—

I retraced my steps back into the palace, back near where I'd started, then down and out into the court-yard, not much different from the garden where Elana had played her games. There were some differences. There were no low walls with guards, only towering, carved walls. There were no laughing women, but there was a woman four floors above, and all I had to do was climb those four floors up the wall in the dark to get to her. It could have been a set of stairs.

I swarmed up the wall. The carvings made easier finger- and toeholds than the chinks between the stones in my cell had. I went over gods and god-desses, animals ordinary and fanciful, past huge flowers and strange designs. The wind tugged at me, and I smiled. The garden below was no pit. A fall into it held few fears.

And then I stood on a balcony, and inside, through the curtains, I saw Elana. She lounged on a couch, in a filmy robe open down the front. She watched the door, and from time to time she'd throw a cushion at the big bed against the wall. She was impatient with the delay in my coming. I'd keep her no longer.

She didn't hear me enter, and my sandals made no sound on the thick carpets. Her first warning was when my hand at her throat snatched her off the couch.

Her hands clawed for my face, but I caught them easily. A gamut of emotions ran across her face when she realized who I was. Surprise, indignation, consternation, and then amusement. When my hands began to tighten on her throat she knew her mistake. Her legs kicked wildly, beating at my sides. Her eyes began to bulge, and a rattling choked in her throat. And my hand loosened.

I couldn't do it. I couldn't kill her. It wasn't because she was a woman. She'd forfeited all the protection that gave. And I certainly wanted her death as a partial payment for Hulugai and the others. But I couldn't. I'd felt it first in the great hall that first day in Lanta. My fate was bound in some fashion to these sisters. I did not dare kill one of them, not until I knew what that binding was.

She was beginning to breathe again, her small tongue licking at her lips. She had her wits, though. But then, I had mine. When her throat expanded for the scream I tightened my grip again.

Swiftly I carried her to the huge bed. A pile of scarves lay on a table beside it. A handful did to wad up and stuff in her mouth, with another to tie them there. She watched me furiously as I tied her arms and legs to the posts of the bed, tightly. She was stretched in a taut, living cross.

Her expression had changed while I bound her. She thought desire for her had overcome the rage. I put my hands back at her throat, but her eyes were amused, contemptuous. She was sure I wouldn't hurt her. She was sure the barbarian would let lust overcome his senses.

I couldn't leave her with that thought. I had to do something to wipe the amusement off of her face. But what? Something by the couch where she'd been waiting caught my eye, a jar with a thin paste inside and a feather. Where—? Then it came. The first night that I was in the palace. Leah, the young noblewoman.

Elana watched me warily as I brought the jar and the feather to the bed. I stirred the thin paste and smiled at her.

"This was for me, wasn't it?" I said softly. "I suppose it works as well on a man as it did on Leah."

Her eyes showed I'd struck home, her eyes and the way she tugged at her bonds. The scarves didn't move, though. Nothing could move except her head.

"It's fitting, isn't it, Elana?"

The feather held a goodly enough amount of the paste to cover one of her breasts. She watched wide-eyed until the rounded mound was covered.

When the paste faded away, disappearing into the skin, she moaned deep in her throat.

"You said that it fires the blood, didn't you? That it makes the passions grow?"

She watched the second breast receive its coating with the same intensity, but when I drew a streak down her belly, she closed her eyes.

"How long before you're discovered, Elana? How long will your passions grow? I can't kill you, perhaps, but in this case I'll stoop to torture. And I think this qualifies as torture." She still glared at me, but some of the arrogance was gone. Her nostrils flared with every breath. "No one will dare disturb you tonight, and if a queen wishes to sleep late, who will dare to wake her? They won't come until you call, will they? It'd be worth their lives to disturb you before time. How long then, before someone finally decides that it's been too long, that maybe something's wrong, that they have to take the chance? Tomorrow morning sometime? Tomorrow afternoon? Tomorrow night?"

I don't think she heard me. Already she was breathing in shuddering gulps, her head tossing wildly. Every muscle in her body was flexing and twisting. She was lost in another world. It wasn't enough, I knew, but I was sure that Hulugai would've understood why I had to let her live. It wasn't a part of the payment she was owed, but maybe it was a single coin in promise of future payment.

I'd wasted all the time I could afford. Now I had to go, if I was going to leave at all.

# XVI

## KITCHEN SLOPS

~

There was a slight lessening of darkness, but not yet a glimmer of light when I climbed over the balcony rail and began to work my way across the face of the wall. I had no time to make the slow downward climb in the dark and then try and find my way back to the wall from the courtyard. I had to start in the corridors I had some knowledge of.

The moons gave light, more light than I wished at that particular time. Darkness would have done me more good if someone chanced to look out of a window and see me ghosting across the wall. When I crawled into a darkened room I was as relieved as if my escape was complete.

Once in the halls, once past the point where the guards at Elana's door might hear me, I ran. Servants who saw me stared slack-jawed before they dropped their gaze. They'd say nothing. Those in cities quickly learned that the fastest way to trouble is to become involved in anything that isn't ordered or doesn't concern them directly.

I knew I risked much in my haste, but I had to be on the wall and gone before light came, before it could be seen that there was a guard on the walls who didn't belong there. I wasn't worried about the bodies in the alcove. Only Nilla ever went there, except for the guards sent by Elana, and if Nilla found them she was levelheaded enough to leave and say nothing.

It was still dark on the walls, but barely. Loewin was gone, but a rim of light was showing at the horizon. I couldn't afford to retrace ground I'd already covered, so I turned away from Hulugai and the stone cylinder. I walked more boldly now, although I still avoided guards. There was no time for creeping in shadows.

And then I came on a small courtyard. Its gate was narrow, with only a single guard. Light spilling out of a door showed a large, two-wheeled cart with one horse. While I watched, a scrawny old man came out with a large tub and dumped its contents into the cart.

The smell told me what it was, kitchen slops. Soon the high-wheeled cart would make its way outside the walls to the dumping ground, for Lanta had no sewers as Caselle does.

When the old man went back into the kitchens, I climbed down into the courtyard, ran to the cart and clambered in. I burrowed down into scraps of spoiled meat, fruit peels, rinds and half-rotted vegetables. The stench was enough to choke a jackal, but I'd be invisible to anyone who wasn't looking for me.

Three more times waste tubs were emptied on top of me. Then, finally, the cart creaked forward, and someone woke the guard at the gate with curses.

The guard muttered about having duty where there was no one to talk to, and where he had to help the slop man get in and out. The slop man said something about if he didn't quit sleeping when he was supposed to be guarding, he'd end up being carried out with the slops himself. The guard answered with curses, but the slop man just climbed up on the seat at the front of the cart and flapped the reins. The horse moved forward, and, pursued by the guard's curses, we left the Palace of the Twin Thrones.

I shifted a melon rind from in front of my face and watched the rooflines go by in the lightening sky. Of the driver, the slop man, I could make out only a skinny back hunched in a tunic, colorless except for its stains, and a fringe of white hair. The horse moved at a trot through streets that were largely silent at that hour. Soon the Inner Wall passed, and the guards at the Outer Wall sent the cart on with only a word. Obviously, they knew it.

On the road from the city it seemed that the driver knew every rut and bump and was determined to visit all of them. I was about to make a move when the cart stopped, and the driver hopped down. From the front of the cart came sounds of activity;

then suddenly the shafts shot into the air, and the cart spilled backward, dumping the garbage, and me, onto the ground.

The driver came around the cart, a shovel in his hand, and stopped in surprise. "What are you doing there? Get out of that!" A look of puzzlement came onto his face. "How did you get in there?"

"Old man," I said, "I've always wanted to ride in a slop cart, ever since I was a boy. Today I did it."

"Are you mad?" he quavered. "I didn't stop, from the palace to here. Who are you?"

He poked the shovel out like a spear. It wasn't much, but from the rear it'd be a formidable weapon, so I took it and broke it over my knee.

"I can't stop to answer your questions, old man. You start walking back to Lanta, and I'll take your horse and be on my way. I'd leave it to you, but I have a long way to go, and you'll be home in under an hour."

"Take the horse? You've already broken my shovel. If you take the horse I'll be beaten for sure."

"It'll probably hurt the whip more than you, scrawny as you are. Look, you're not that old. Don't go back to the palace. Say you're a free man and find work. You'll not be beaten then."

"You mean run away?" He sounded shocked. "But what if I couldn't find work? How would I eat? Where would I sleep?"

I reached out and tapped the man on the eye. He staggered back two steps and sat down in the road.

He looked surprised as he sat there with one hand over the eye.

"That'll swell, soon," I said. "Tell them you were attacked. You fought, but they were too many for you. Show them your eye, and maybe they won't beat you."

A grin blossomed on his face. "Thank you, master. Thank you." He scrambled up and hurried down the road, looking over his shoulder at every other step, no doubt to see if I'd changed my mind.

Once I got a better look at his beast, I was tempted to call him back and make him take it. How he thought anyone would punish him for losing such a spavined creature was beyond my comprehension. I thought they might reward him for getting rid of it.

All the same, I scrambled up on it, and kicked it into motion. It had no gait at all, I found. It merely ambled along. But it seemed sound enough, for all its looks.

I'd head for the place where the tents had been, I decided, to pick up the trail of the lances and follow. There'd likely be a celebration when they found me returned from the Land of the Dead. I was nearing the place where we'd camped when a horseman burst from a ravine and put a lance to my chest.

"Ho, townsman," he said, "what are you doing here, riding on a goat and smelling like one, too?"

"Bartu," I said, "if you don't remove that lance from my face, I'll take it and pry out all of your teeth."

"M-my lord?" The lance point dropped, and he came closer, still not believing. "Lord Wulfgar?"

"It's me, Bartu, alive, if somewhat the worse for wear and in need of a bath."

There was moisture in his eyes, and in mine also, but then there was a lot of dust in the air.

"Mayra said you lived, my lord, but after Lord Harald disappeared also—"

"Harald gone?" I kicked the nag into a trot, or as close to one as it could manage. "We ride to the tents at once. You tell me everything that's happened, from the beginning."

"I'll try, Lord Wulfgar," he said. "When you'd been gone three days, we became worried. Orne and I went to Mayra. She chased us away. Said we were fools. Said your life was hanging by a thread and we were getting in her way while she tried to keep the thread from breaking. Said all men were fools and worse, and women were idiots for putting up with them. My lord, she ought to ride with the lances, Sister of Wisdom or no. She wouldn't need a lance, just her tongue."

"Get on with it."

"Yes, my lord. With Mayra keeping to her tent we did what we could ourselves. We sent a messenger to Lord Harald. Before he could have gotten there, a messenger from Lord Harald's tents arrived, wanting to know if we had word of him. He went to Lanta, to meet Daiman, on the same day you went to meet Ivo."

"Then he's either a captive, or, more likely, he's

dead." I said it as flatly as I could. I'd mourn later, if mourning there must be.

"Dvere says she thinks he's still alive, but she can't be sure. She didn't have the warning that Mayra had."

"If he's alive, then we can free him. If not, we'll avenge him. What else happened, Bartu?"

"Tension, my lord, tension and strife. The lances wanted to fight, to a man, but no one knew who to fight, the Morassa or the Lantans. Orne insisted you were in the Palace of the Twin Thrones, though he couldn't say why, and he wanted to raid in force, to cut our way through to the palace, free you and Lord Harald, then cut our way out again. It was only because we didn't know if you were really there that I wouldn't agree to it."

"You and Orne are good men," I said, "and fine warriors, but you'll neither of you command a thousand if you have ideas like that. You'd all have died, and for no purpose, as the men who went with me to Lanta did."

"Any man born of the Plain knows death waits with the next hour."

We rode in silence for a time, with only the wind and the creak of saddle leather to break it. Death might wait with the next hour, but there had been too much of it lately, and all of it of the dark and furtive sort.

"The merchants," Bartu went on finally, "have stopped coming to the tents. For a time some came, slinking as if they were sneaking into some slimy dive in Low Town, but now no one comes. The Council of Nobles sent a message to us, sent it by slave because they were afraid we'd kill the messenger. They said the gates of the city were closed to us, that the guards would fire if we came too close. We dressed the slave like a High Toman, gave him a string of horses, and paraded him outside the gates. You should've heard the guards howl when he went riding off toward Manhaut."

"And matters rest there?"

"Not at all. We sent a rider to Bohemund, to tell him what had happened. He sent a delegation to the Lantans, with Lord Dunstan and Lord Otogai to lead it. They weren't allowed inside the gates either. Some of the Council of Nobles came out with the commander of the City Guard. They swore oaths on the bones of their fathers, and on the doornails of their temples, that neither you nor Lord Harald was in the city. They swore they knew nothing of your whereabouts, and pledged their daughters to their word." He grimaced as if he'd bitten a rotten cos-fruit. "They have no honor at all."

"They're city men, Bartu."

He grunted as if that was explanation enough. "With oaths like those, the delegation had to accept their words, but I thought Lord Dunstan and Lord Otogai both were surprised they'd offer them before they were asked."

"The Lantans offered the oaths? Perhaps one of the Sisters of Wisdom did something to absolve them. It doesn't matter. I don't absolve them."

"No, my lord. They had an iron sky-stone, those nobles did, with the Terg carved in it by a Sister of Wisdom. Blessed by three times three Sisters of Wisdom, they said it was, and they demanded we say our words with a sword hand on it. Of course, no man would lie under those circumstances. We had to admit that a Morassa had brought the message to you, and another to Lord Harald, that he'd gone to meet Daiman and you to meet Ivo. They said that made it plain we had no call to claim they had any part in it. Whatever was done, was done by the Morassa."

"And the Lantans," I said, "did they touch the sky-stone when they spoke?"

"After the oaths they swore, who would ask them to?"

"Then they lied, and knew they lied. The oaths they never meant to keep were only meant to keep them from having to touch the sky-stone and have their hands burned off by their lies. It could be no other way."

"My lord, what happened there in the city? How could they take you?"

"They were waiting for us on the rooftops over the Street of Five Bells, with chain nets. Even though we went early, they knew we were coming." That struck me all of a sudden and I repeated it. "Even though we went early, they knew we were coming. Yes. It was so. They took us like fish from a stream. Only Brion gained glory from it. They paid a ferryman's fee for him fit for a king. They imprisoned us, but I didn't know what happened to the others until I'd escaped. They tortured them, Bartu. Not for a reason, but for the sport of it. Then they impaled them."

"Once, my lord, you spoke of finding out how many lances it would take to tear down the walls of Lanta. Do you know the number, yet?"

"I know, Bartu. I know."

# XVII

## A BELL NOTE

—

At the tents many called laughingly to Bartu to ask if he was capturing beggars these days. No one knew me, and the comments grew louder the deeper into the tents we rode. Even unbranded youths snickered behind their hands. I saw some thoughtful stares, though. Soon someone would realize who I was, and the laugh would be on the laughers.

Elspeth, Sara and Elnora were working in front of my tent when I swung down. They eyed me with distaste.

"Why are you bringing him here, Bartu?" Sara asked.

"Bring me the tub," I said, "and water. I want a bath before I get used to this smell."

They stared at me with their mouths open. Suddenly it struck them that it was indeed I who masqueraded in a beard and the smells of slop tubs. While they were laboring with the tub, Orne walked in.

"Lord Wulfgar." He started to throw his arms around me, and stopped with them spread wide. His nose twitched.

"I'm taking a bath," I said. "They're getting the tub, now."

"I'll help them, my lord."

With his help the girls wrestled the tub into the tent. Then they ran for water, and he sat to talk. I dropped the guard tunic on the ground.

"That's to be burned."

"And that so-called horse, my lord?"

"Turn it loose with the herds."

"My lord," he protested.

"It's a gelding, Orne, so there's no worry for the bloodlines. And it carried me away from Lanta. It also has more brains than its former driver. He walked back to Lanta and his chains." They had finished filling the tub, and I settled myself into it, slowly. "Orne, tell Mayra I'll be to her as soon as I'm clean. She'd not have thanked me for coming as I was."

"Yes, Lord Wulfgar."

He went on his way, and I relaxed as Elnora and Sara scrubbed away the stink. They wore the kisu, long panels of clinging, opaque silk that hung below the knees in front and back and were fastened at the waist with a belt. Elspeth stood to the side not looking at me as I bathed.

"How is your training going, Elspeth?" I asked.

"It's going fine," she said through pursed lips.

I smiled. Her spirit wasn't broken in my absence. "You're playing a game, Elspeth. Games can be dangerous."

"No games, then. It's not fair. That's how my training is. Not fair. I have to read, not only your language, but others I've never heard of, not because I might want to, but so I can read to you, or recite poems to you. And for some reason I have to learn to cook dishes in twenty different styles, and dance dances from a dozen countries, and sing. Talva beats me because I don't have a good voice. I can't make myself have a good voice. Why does she have to beat me for something I can't change?" Her eyes closed and her head fell forward. "And that's the way it's changing me. I complain because she beats me for something I can't change. Not about being beaten, but because it's for something I can't change. It's not fair, not fair."

"Your world is always fair." I didn't make it a question, and she just straightened and looked at me without speaking. I don't think she would have or could have answered it anyway. "There's no fairness to worlds. Fairness is a thing created by men. It doesn't exist. It isn't the same in different cities, or among different people. How can fairness be the same thing in two different worlds? In your world you were a scholar, in this one you're nothing. In this world I'm a warrior, but if I went to yours, I might be a beggar."

It didn't make a mark on her attitude. I could see that from the stubborn cast to her jaw. So I tried another way. "Where you were found when you first came to this world, you could have expected to live to sunset at best. With no water, no food, no knowledge of the land, and above all with no way to protect yourself from anything from a fanghorn to a kes hive, you were dead."

I was reaching for the toweling Sara held when Elspeth said, "I have an answer to your problem."

She said it so softly that it didn't register on my mind at first. When it did I whirled around with the toweling forgotten around my shoulders.

"The problem? You've—" I jerked my head toward the tent flaps. "Sara, Elnora, wait outside." When they'd gone I turned my attention back to Elspeth. She was still kneeling by the tub, frowning at the floor, a slight pout on her lips. "The problem," I said.

"It wasn't until I learned exactly what your people's problem was that I saw the solution. The weather on the Plain gets worse every year, now, and has for some years past. There's less water every year, and less forage for your herds. It's hotter in the summers, and the winters are colder. And that makes the fanghorns multiply. They breed in the summers, and give birth during the winters in hibernation. The colder winters mean they hibernate longer, and the young have gotten larger by the time they come out in the spring, so more and more of them are able to survive."

"So far," I said dryly, "you've told me a great deal that I already know."

She took a deep breath and went on. "There are many peoples who've faced the same problem, or the same sort of problem, and those who solved it did it in the same basic way. I've studied it time and time again."

"You mean you knew this all the time? You knew the answer the first day I found you?"

"That's right," she said angrily, "I knew it. But you never told me what the problem was. I never knew I had your answers. You just kept on bullying and browbeating me like I was—"

"The answers." I forced myself to back away, to stop hovering over her. "You've gone a long way with this. Now, how did those people you studied solve their problem?"

"You won't like it," she said. I just waited. "These people, when the land changed so their old lifestyle wouldn't work anymore, they changed it. The ones like you settled down, planted crops, built villages, dug wells for irrigation. They stopped being nomadic herders and became farmers."

"Farmers." I put as much venom into the word as I could muster. "You suggest the Altaii become farmers? We're not grubbers in the dirt. We live by our herds, and by our swords. By our swords most of all. If we have to die, we'll die as what we are, not like those northern dirtmen, selling their roots and pulling their forelocks to everyone who frowns at them."

"But you have to change, or that's exactly what

will happen. You'll all die. But if you do change, it doesn't have to be that bad. Your villages could become cities, in time. One day they might be as big as Lanta."

The name hung there in the air like a bell note.

"Lanta," I breathed, and it was as if the bell had been brushed again.

"M-my lord, I don't understand," she said, but she could feel it in the air too.

"If we take Lanta, we won't have to wait for our villages to grow. Lanta could serve as a center for the entire Altaii nation."

"No. Wulfgar."

"There are lands to the east of Lanta that could support our herds, all of them, for countless years to come. I said we might have to take Lanta, but now we have a hundredfold reason to do it."

"I didn't tell you this to start you off on some war of conquest."

"Elspeth, if you'll feel better about it, the Lantans moved against us first. At this moment they're plotting with the Morassa to destroy us. If we don't destroy them first, the Plain won't have a chance to kill us. We will be dead already."

"Violence doesn't excuse violence, Wulfgar. Conquering lands and keeping them is wrong."

"Conquering lands and not keeping them is stupid," I said. Hurriedly I got into tunic, trousers and boots. "Hand me my sword belt and come with me. We're going to see Mayra. She can tell me if taking Lanta is what I must do or not do."

# XVIII

## WOMEN'S JUSTICE

~

Mayra was waiting for me, impatiently, which wasn't usual for her. She barely waited until I was seated, and Elspeth kneeling off to one side, before she spoke. With the first word, I remembered Bartu's words about her tongue being a weapon.

"It's said, Lord Wulfgar, that men think with their manhood instead of their brains. I'm not sure you used even that. You not only risked your life needlessly, you risked the future of the Altaii. You nearly allowed your spirit and will to be made into a pendant for the queens to play with."

"I know, Mayra," I said soothingly. Elspeth and Mayra's acolytes were smirking, but I needed her goodwill at the moment more than I needed to stop some girls from giggling. "And I know that I owe my survival of that attempt to you. I just don't know how you did it."

"A simple spell," she said disparagingly. "Once I knew you meant to go ahead with that foolishness, I took a hair from your shaving and a tunic still wet with your sweat and made a simple bond between us. Then I could tell what happened, but vaguely, as if through a silk screen. I couldn't do anything about physical dangers, but when they tried spells, then I could give aid. They were powerful, Wulfgar. I have not seen that much power in a long time. Who were they?"

At least the formality was gone. I wasn't Lord Wulfgar to her anymore. "Sayene was there, and a woman called Ya'shen, and one who looked like somebody's grandmother. Her name was Betine. I've something to ask, Mayra."

She didn't hear me. "Ya'shen and Betine as well as Sayene. I wonder how the Twin Thrones managed to get those three together? And Betine is no one's grandmother, unless it's a demon of some sort. She's as evil as Loewin's breath. Ya'shen is as bad, and I fear Sayene has become the worst of them all. There's darkness there, darkness and power together, and I don't know if I can gather enough strength among the Altaii Sisters of Wisdom to defeat them. There aren't many of us with that much power." She seemed to become aware of me again. "Your question, Wulfgar?"

Quickly I laid out what Elspeth had told me, and what I had made of her words. "Is it true, Mayra? Is it a true way?"

Mayra looked at Elspeth and shook her head.

"The odds are very long, Wulfgar. Even Basrath—" But she took out her bag containing the rune-bones.

Three times presented to the sky, and three times to the earth, the bones were rolled. Mayra sucked her breath over her teeth. Quickly she rolled them again. This time she was clearly surprised. For a moment she waited, as if afraid to see what would be said the third time, but the rune-bones were tossed for the third time. Mayra stared at them as if she wasn't sure what she saw. Twice she reached out to touch them, and twice drew back.

"In the first throw the same pattern duplicated three times. That's unusual. On the second the pattern was there again, six times. On the third throw that same pattern repeated nine times. I've never seen a progression like that. Never."

"The pattern, Mayra?" I asked. "What was the pattern?"

"Lanta must fall, and to your hand. That is specific. It must be your hand which opens the way for the city to fall. If it does, then the Altaii star rises high, and the Lantan star fades. If not, it is the Altaii star which fades and disappears."

"First I must preserve my life as if it was a jewel. Now I must open the way to Lanta with my own hand." I rubbed at my face and let my head rest in my hands. "Do the rune-bones give any guide as to how I'm to do that?" I asked wearily. Something brushed lightly at my shoulder. Elspeth had moved to kneel beside me. She didn't look at me, but her hand rested on my shoulder.

"There is something," Mayra said softly. "The rune-bones indicate, Wulfgar. They don't tell things clearly. They have to be interpreted, and this one I don't know how to interpret. It seems opposed to the other symbols, and it occurs in minor case, but three times din, the minor-case salvation, has rested on top of silte, the minor-case hunt. It might mean salvation rests on the hunt. There are no symbols close enough to the configuration to modify it."

"Hunt? What hunt, Mayra? There's no hunting worth the name in three days' ride of here, except for fanghorns, and there's nothing to do with one of those except kill it."

"The silte symbol is the hunting bow, the long-bow. It could mean salvation rests on the bow. That sounds more likely for war, at any rate."

The hunting bow is just that, a bow used for the hunt. It's longer than a man is tall, too long to use on a horse, but for hunting animals that run when a mounted man is a thousand paces away, it works well. The stalk is made on foot, and then a shaft can be put in an antelope at four hundred paces, or a ku at twice that.

"I once made a joke," I said, "about tearing the walls of Lanta down with Altaii lances. The long-bow seems even less suited to the job."

"That's not so," said Elspeth. "In my world's history, they trained men to use the longbow. With its superior range and power against the shorter bow of mounted cavalry, and the spear and sword of infantry, it's a powerful weapon."

"I can't help you with that, Wulfgar," Mayra said, "but perhaps I can stimulate your thinking."

She sounded angry suddenly, angry and vengeful and in some fashion satisfied. She motioned and two of her acolytes struggled forward with a sack between them. Something inside wiggled. They set it down and slit it open. There was a woman inside, a woman cruelly arched and bound. Elspeth gasped at the sight of her, and her fingers dug into my shoulder. The woman's feet had been pulled up almost to her shoulders, and her wrists were tied to her knees. There was a large gag in her mouth. She looked around wildly when the sack was cut open, and when she saw me, she began to cry. It was Mirim.

"Orne found her," Mayra said. "I told him I'd shrivel his tongue if he spoke of it to anyone, and I see he took that to include you. Don't blame him, Wulfgar. I meant what I said, and he knew it."

"I don't blame any man for failing to cross a Sister of Wisdom, Mayra, but what's so important about a runaway slave?"

Mayra fixed the bound girl with her eye, and Mirim began to sweat. "He found her near the walls of Lanta, Wulfgar. She panicked when he caught her, babbled wildly. After he heard some of the babbling he brought her to me without telling anyone else. Probably the smartest thing he's ever done."

"What did she babble?" I asked quietly, but Mirim flinched as if I'd shouted.

"Nothing, once she was here. Under a truth-spell,

though, she said some interesting things. She was sent to Lanta, to ask at the gates for a man named Ara. They had orders to bring Altaii slaves who asked for that man to him."

"I know the name," I bit off.

"She was to tell him where we went next, when we began our march, and how long we expected to stay in the new camp. She also said that other girls had been sent on the same errand, to help the Lantans know where we went and when."

"Sent," I said. "You said that twice. Sent by who?"

"Talva."

It didn't really surprise me. When she'd said that other girls had been sent I'd remembered the string of runaway slaves, with only Talva to link them. "The Lantans knew I was coming, Mayra. They were waiting for me. To me that shouts betrayal, and right now Talva seems a good suspect."

"Perhaps. As much as I hate to say it, Talva's treason could be no more than letting the caravans know how to avoid us. We'll see, though."

She spoke quietly to one of the acolytes. The young woman ran off and returned in a moment with the tripod and box that Mayra had brought out so long ago. She set the tripod while Mayra took the silver bowl, with its symbolic markings, from the box. When all was in place, she went through the ritual with the oil and the powders. An image appeared in the window of the bowl, and she beckoned me.

"Does it mean something to you?"

All the bowl showed was a bird flying, a falcon. "Nothing," I said.

"I began with the belief that a message was carried to Lanta to betray you. It happened, it appears, and this bird carried the message. Possibly—" She spoke in the ear of an acolyte. The girl went to Mayra's chests and returned with a small bell. "Briskly now, child, as the powders fall."

Mayra dropped a pinch of some powder into the image. It flared, and as it flared, the acolyte struck the bell twice, rapidly. Again a pinch of powder fell, and the bell again rang twice. For the third time the bowl flared beneath the powder, the bell rang, and its last tone went on and on. Mayra put a hand to it to stop the sound. "Look."

In the bowl's window Talva took a falcon from the cage behind her tent. She carried it on a padded glove to a perch, and put it there while she fastened a small cylinder to its leg. Then she took it up again and cast it into the sky. It disappeared rapidly, as if certain of its destination.

"That bird carried the message," Mayra said.

The growl started deep in my chest. It built in my throat, and I could feel my lips pulling back, baring my teeth in a snarl. I whirled and headed for the main body of tents.

"Wait, Wulfgar," Mayra called. "What are you going to do?"

"In the day past I let a woman live although she'd done everything short of killing me. I did it because

I had to, I was fate-bound to her or her sister or both. There's nothing to hold me this time. I'll cut that traitor's head off."

As I hurried toward the tents I was vaguely aware of Mayra hurrying after me, calling to her acolytes to bring this piece of paraphernalia or that. Elspeth was crying, yelling for Mayra to stop me. Between shouted orders to the acolytes I heard her tell the girl I wouldn't hurt anyone. I tried to laugh at that, but it merged with the snarl and was more like the sound of a slavering wolf than any sound a man might make.

I didn't intend to dirty my own blade with Talva's blood. I went out of my way to pass by Hai the Smith's tent, and more especially his forge. As I passed I snatched a long, curved saddle sword, new, with no bonding of spirit and iron with any man. Hai saw my face and let me go. When the deed was done I'd pay the sword price and bury the blade where no man would ever have to dirty his hands by touching it again.

A crowd built behind me as I walked, but I paid no mind to it. I had only one thought, and as fate made it, I arrived at her tent just as she came out to see what caused the commotion. I swept the sword back. Talva saw the blade and my face and fell back screaming against her tent.

And Mayra stepped in front of me. "Women's Justice."

"Mayra," I said hoarsely, "not even you can claim Women's Justice by yourself. This woman betrayed me to a prison and six men to their deaths. I claim blood right on her."

"Your blood-right claim is just, Wulfgar, but I have the ten." She waved frantically, and ten Free Women moved to where I could see them. They were unconcerned, sure that I'd uphold a legal claim to Women's Justice, but I wasn't sure, and neither was Mayra. "Wulfgar, their claim supersedes yours. Any woman can be put under Women's Justice on the demand of ten Free Women, and the men's laws can't touch her."

"There's no need to lecture, Mayra. I know the Books of Safah."

"Then put down the sword, my lord."

Only then did I realize that I still held the saddle sword raised. I flipped it into the air and threw it point-down into the ground.

The ten Free Women who'd made the claim looked concerned for the first time as they realized how close I'd been to violating law and custom. Only Talva seemed to be recovered.

"Am I to be told what this is all about, Wulfgar," she demanded arrogantly, "or do you intend simply to kill me?"

Mayra turned on her. "He has no say in this, now. Or doesn't if you accept Women's Justice. You can reject the claim, and we'll leave you to Lord Wulfgar." She stressed my name to emphasize Talva's omission of the title. There was a murmur in the crowd as they realized the lack of respect in the slave mistress's words, but she didn't notice.

"Of course I'll accept Women's Justice." She was supremely confident. "Whatever the charge, I've done nothing, but Lord Wulfgar"—her stressing of the word was the opposite of Mayra's—"looks as if I'd be killed out of hand if he had his way. And what is the charge?"

"In a moment." Mayra was smiling when she faced me again. There were still several legal ways for Talva to escape, or at least escape punishment, but once Mayra said the words, they'd be beyond the laws of men, to harm or protect.

"Ten Free Women claim Women's Justice, by the laws of the Books of Safah, by the customs of the Altaii people, by their rights as women. The Free Woman Talva stands before Women's Justice." She paused to survey the gathering. "From this moment, for this time, in this place, the laws of men hold no sway. Let no man interfere in the customs of women."

There was silence, men shifting uncomfortably as they always did at such times, women nodding and smiling self-satisfied smiles. Women's Justice was seldom claimed, for it wasn't bound by the laws, but when it was claimed, the reactions of the watchers were always the same.

Talva shifted impatiently herself. "Now will you tell me the charge?"

"Treason," said Mayra.

For an instant fear flickered on the slave mistress's face. Then it was gone as if it had never been.

"I deny it. By any oaths you care to name, I deny it."

"Keep hold on your tongue, Talva, before you swear your life away." Mayra's voice was calm and level, but did Talva listen too intently? "The runaway girl Mirim has been recovered. She says that you promised her freedom and money if she would take the word of this camp's movements to the Lantans."

Talva had relaxed when she heard the charge, I was sure of it. Some of the spectators were muttering among themselves, wondering why such accusations were made on no more than the word of a slave.

"A runaway would say anything to escape her stripes. Of course she claims I told her to run. I'm surprised she didn't claim Lord Wulfgar told her to." She drew herself up to her full height. Though it was no more than chest high on any man, she made it seem impressive. "A girl lies, and I find myself charged with treason. I find Lord Wulfgar not only accepting the lie, but ready to kill me for it. Does anyone here think to ask why he'd accept such evidence? Does anyone—"

"She was under a truth-spell."

Quiet words, but they made Talva flinch. She looked back at her tent entrance. Two of the ten Free Women stood there.

"Under the truth-spell she said that other girls trained by you had been sent to carry similar messages." Talva was visibly nervous, now, but Mayra continued, coolly but relentlessly. "When I discovered that, I made a vision to see if I could find who sent the message that betrayed Lord Wulfgar in Lanta. In the vision you, Talva, fastened a cylinder to the leg of a falcon and sent it on its way. A message of betrayal."

"I refuse a truth-spell," Talva said quickly, then realized how that must sound to the women who sat in judgment on her. "I mean—"

"You can't refuse a truth-spell," Mayra said, "if it was ordered by those you stand before. Remember, Talva, the laws of men, the Books of Safah, can't touch you here, but they can't protect you either. You won't have to submit to a truth-spell, though. There are other ways to get the truth."

"Mayra's in league with Lord Wulfgar," Talva said desperately. "It's well known how close she is to him. She's concocted this to further some scheme of his."

It was a measure of her panic that she would accuse a Sister of Wisdom of lying. If she was frightened then, the burden eight men brought from behind her tent and deposited terrified her.

"This is not permitted," she insisted. "I'm a Free Woman. It's not permitted."

The men set their burden down and quickly got out of the way. It was a simple thing to make Talva's face pale, two uprights with a padded crosspiece, all on a heavy wooden base. The ten Free Women rose as soon as it was on the ground.

"No protection from the laws of men," Mayra said.

"No!" Talva screamed, but the women were on her.

She struggled furiously, screaming all the while that I plotted with Mayra to destroy her for some unnamed reason, that it was all part of a plot to reduce Free Women to the status of slaves. The women paid no attention. They stripped her clothes off and fastened her over the frame, feet corded tightly to the base. Two of them took up positions on either side of the frame, each with a long strap in her hands.

The bound woman tossed her head wildly. "You'll get nothing from me. Do you hear me, Wulfgar? You'll get nothing."

Mayra nodded, and the two women began, taking turns, in a steady rhythm. At first Talva took the blows well, fists clenched, teeth gritted, refusing to surrender so much as a moan. At the sixth stroke, given with the full force of the strap wielder's arm, she gasped. At the tenth she sobbed. At the fifteenth she screamed.

From there she abandoned the attempt to fight the strap. She shrieked and howled. Her fingers clawed at the ropes that held her. Her toes scrabbled futilely at the stand. Her pleas and begging began to trip over each other, to become interspersed with screams in an unintelligible mass.

I started to step forward, and Mayra stopped me

with a hand on my chest. "You have no say here, Wulfgar. Besides, you were going to kill her. Why should this worry you?"

"Kill her, yes, Mayra. Beat her to death slowly, no."

"If she could die from being beaten there," Mayra said, "there wouldn't be a slave alive in the tents. It's a part of her punishment, Wulfgar, the part that satisfies all the people she's offended. Because of this she can be accepted afterwards."

Elspeth leaned against me. Her attention was all on the frame and the woman futilely trying to writhe away from the straps. "I should be furious at this. In my world I signed petitions against the kind of violence you accept as an everyday part of life. I should be horrified, but every time they hit her I remember a time she hit me, and every time she screams, I remember a time I screamed. It's as though she's paying me back."

Mayra spoke. "You see, Wulfgar, it's as I said. Her debts are being paid off so she can still live among us."

"After treason, Mayra?" I found the saddle sword and picked it up. "She'll not survive anywhere."

She smiled. "Let's wait until the Free Women pronounce their judgment."

Talva had been trying for some time to say that she was ready to talk, but the words were garbled and the women sitting in judgment were in no hurry. Finally Mayra motioned for a halt. Talva lifted a wide-eyed, tear-wet face.

"C-cut me free, a-and I'll t-talk," she managed.

"No bargains," Mayra said.

"I'll talk! I'll talk! I s-swear it!" The beating stopped, but Talva babbled on beyond it. "I sent the messages. I let the Lantans know where we would be and when. I sent them word that Lord Wulfgar was coming. The falcons were only to be used for an emergency. They couldn't be replaced. But that was an emergency, wasn't it? Wasn't it?" Her head dropped, shaking with her sobs. "I would have been given a position of power in Lanta. Women rule there. Nothing is denied a woman, no kind of power. I could have done anything, been anything."

Almost before she finished speaking she was unbound and brought to Mayra. She winced when they forced her to kneel and sit back on her heels. The two women stared at one another, one trembling, the other calm.

"Has a judgment been reached?" Mayra asked.

The ten Free Women broke from a group.

"Kill her," said one.

"For treason, death."

"Death."

"Let her serve the man she betrayed," said another.

Laughter greeted that, and Mayra faced Talva with a smile. "How does that sound?"

There was more laughter, louder, and Talva flushed.

"I'm a Free Woman," she said stiffly. "I cannot be

made a slave except with my own consent for the payment of my debts."

"Under the Books of Safah. But, so there are no complaints later, you'd better do it anyway. After all, you do have debts to pay. Of course, we could consider death. There's plenty of support for it." Mayra put her head to one side. "Come along, girl. I'm sure you know the words."

"Don't call me that," Talva snapped. She locked gazes with Mayra. After a minute she shifted. In another she slumped as if defeated. "I renounce my rights as a Free Woman. I renounce my property and possessions. I renounce my freedom. I surrender my life and my will to the one who will own me. I"—for the first time she faltered—"I s-swear it b-by the b-bones of my m-mother, and of m-my mother's mother, and of my m-mother's mother's m-mother." Her head fell forward onto her knees, and her shoulders shook with silent sobs.

For a moment Mayra watched her. Then she laughed. Talva jerked, and her shoulders stopped their shaking.

"I expect you think you've fooled me, girl," Mayra chuckled. "You'd have fooled a man, I suppose. You probably fooled him. A poor defenseless, defeated woman, ready to take her punishment, meekly agreeing to slavery rather than death." She laughed again. "Two days to lull him, and you'd be gone, sooner if you thought you could."

"I made the renunciations, Mayra. I swore the oaths."

"And they near scalded your tongue in saying them. You knew when you swore you had no intention of keeping them. Perhaps you hoped that Sayene would find a way to free you of them. Well, there'll be no freeing you from this." Her acolytes came to stand behind her. "Let her serve the one she betrayed. Are there any who disagree with that?"

The ten conferred among themselves, then settled back shaking their heads. None disagreed.

I had to step in myself, though. "Mayra, I have a claim to her. You've admitted it, and she's made it legal. She's renounced herself. Stop all of this and let me have her. The only escape she'll make is when I put this sword through her evil heart."

"You stop, Wulfgar. Stop, or I will stop you." She raised her hands as if for a spell, and I stopped where I stood. "This is not yet of your concern. It is ours. And if you feel there's been a slight to your honor or your manhood, perhaps it'll ease when this one crawls on her belly to you."

"Him?" Talva whispered. "Him?"

"The one you betrayed, girl. The others are dead. Of those your message betrayed, only Lord Wulfgar lives. Here I have the essence of him, sweat, hair, spittle, blood, and fingernail clippings. With the mixture they make, you will honor your oath."

Easily, for Talva seemed too shaken to struggle, they lifted her and painted the mixture in simple patterns on her skin. Arrows ran up her arms, and others up her thighs and down across her belly. Spirals circled her breasts. On her cheeks, and again between her eyebrows, were a three-point and a rod. Then they let her sink back to her knees.

Once again Mayra produced the bone wand that she'd used on Elspeth. She touched it to Talva's forehead, and the kneeling woman made a rising, inquiring sound of indrawing breath. The wand lifted, and Talva came with it, forcing herself up like an acrobat with only the strength of her legs.

When she'd risen to almost her full height Mayra stopped the wand, holding her bent back in an arch, muscles straining. Suddenly the wand darted back, and a spark of fire leaped from it to the point on Talva's forehead it'd touched. Talva began to drop, but the wand moved back to touch the tip of her breast, and she rose again to her backward-bending arch. The wand pulled back, and again the spark leaped. As it struck Talva groaned, and as she fell the wand moved to the other breast to pull her back again.

"No," she whimpered, "not him. Please, not him. Please."

Mayra's wand moved again to Talva's forehead and began its journey over, and finishing it began again, and again, and again. Now Talva's hands moved, followed the wand, fingers stroking her cheeks as it touched her forehead, fanning across her belly, sliding along her thighs. At each journey of the wand her breath came faster. At each journey of the wand her eyes became farther and farther away.

Mayra brought the wand up again to Talva's forehead, and held it there. An ululating cry began deep in her throat, rising and falling as if she was on the edge of pain, but always getting higher, higher, until Mayra pulled the wand back, the spark leaped, and with a scream Talva sank to the ground.

"You know it, now, don't you, girl?"

Talva lifted her head to look at Mayra, a questioning, wondering look.

"In your head, in your heart, in your belly, you know it."

Sweat was running off Talva until she looked covered in oil. "Yes," she whimpered.

"You betrayed him, as you betrayed your people, sold him to torture for a chance of power."

Again the whimper. "Yes."

"Then go to him, girl. Abase yourself. Beg for his mercy."

Talva turned, twisted on the ground to face me. Another whimper was stifled in her throat. And she crawled to me, on her belly, and put her head on my feet.

"Please," she whispered.

I lifted the sword in both hands. A straight downward plunge and it would pierce the spine, end her treachery forever.

"Please."

She pulled herself up to throw her arms around my legs. Her eyes seemed large enough and soft enough to fall into. One stroke would finish it.

"Mayra, what've you done? Why do you thwart me in this?"

"I'm not thwarting you, Wulfgar. She knows what she did, and why she did it. Inside her the same ambitions still burn, the same hatreds. But there's something else added, something that supersedes everything else, outweighs all her hate and ambition put together. You. She worships you now, worships you like a god, only more than most people worship their gods. She hates you, but she'll do anything to please you. Anything. Isn't that punishment enough? To still have all of her hate and all of her ambition, and to know that she can't do anything about it, because she'd rather please the object of her hate than breathe? If you want to kill her, she probably won't try to stop you. If you want to kill her, go ahead." She said it casually, casually enough in the circumstances for it to be important.

Yet, if Mayra thought it important, so did I. Brion and Hulugai and the other four were there to remind me how important it was. The pit was there to remind me.

The sword slashed down, and quivered in the ground a hairsbreadth from Talva. She fell forward on my thigh. She was shaking with relief. I was shaking with frustration.

Once they led Talva away, the crowd began dispersing. Mayra stayed, though, and I waited also, until we were the only two there. There were things I had to say that I didn't want to say in front of the others, but it appeared she also had something to say.

"It won't work, Wulfgar."

"What won't work?"

"Selling her to someone who'll make her life a misery, someone cruel, perhaps, or vicious. It's written clearly enough on your face, even if you don't realize that's what you intend, but it won't work."

I hadn't thought clearly about what I was going to do about Talva, but this idea sounded like a good one. "Why wouldn't it work?"

"Because," Mayra said patiently, "she's been attuned to you, not anyone else. If you sell her, no matter how well she's trained, she'll manage to escape. She's an intelligent woman. Not only could she find the means to escape, if she wanted to, but I'll wager she could avoid being retaken and possibly find some way to have the spell taken off her. She'd escape punishment altogether. As long as she's owned by you, though, she won't even try to escape. She might think about it. She might wish for it. If, however, she could be free by saying one word, she won't open her mouth. If you want to make certain she pays for what she's done, you must keep her." There was an air about her that said she'd not only known this from the start, but intended it to end so.

"Mayra, she owes a blood debt. Even if I forget her betrayal of me, even if I could forget her betrayal of our people, she sold six warriors to their deaths. It's got to be paid, and you've fixed it so it can't be paid. Why, Mayra? Tell me why."

"Because there are things more important than a blood debt, difficult as it might be to convince a man of that. No, don't ask. The whole fate of our people still rests on the razor's edge. In a year, none of us may be alive, and I won't increase the chances of that by bringing in things that may never come to pass."

"Once again you pull me in directions I've not even considered," I said wearily. "You make your spells, and I stand there too weak to do what must be done. Tell me, Mayra, do the king and the lords run the Altaii nation, or do the Sisters of Wisdom?"

"You Lords of the Altaii command and control the Altaii nation, Wulfgar. We Sisters of Wisdom can only advise and help where we can. I advise you in this and with Elspeth, you must keep her with you always. She will offer advice critical to the Altaii survival. And as for that weakness, it's a weakness of all men," she said wryly. "Few men can kill a woman on her knees. I'd never have taken the chance with a woman."

I laughed in spite of myself. "Well, whatever you've got planned for my future, you've given me more than enough to think about for now. I'm going back to my tent to consider how to tear down the walls of Lanta and open the Iron Gates with hunting arrows."

# XIX

## A GLIMMER

On the next morning I was still considering the hunting bow. It's too long to be carried strung on horseback, too stiff to string while mounted and too unwieldy to use from the saddle. In short, they're not weapons as the Altaii consider them, not instruments of combat. In the hands of a fully grown man the wire-wrapped bow can send a broad-head shaft a full fifteen hundred paces, but no one could hit a specific target at that range. It has power enough, power to drive through a fanghorn's hide at two hundred paces, but not enough to make a mark on stone blocks five times a man's height in every dimension.

I took aim at a round, iron-bound shield hanging on a post a hundred paces away. The shield leaped from its peg and fell to swing from the arrow that had driven through it into the post. It did have power. I drew another shaft, fingers against my cheek. The shield leaped again when it struck. A third, between the first two, only made it quiver.

All three shafts had driven through the shield a good two handspans or more and pierced the wooden posts at least half that distance. It wasn't enough to make a mark on stone walls of the Iron Gates, but a glimmer of a thought was beginning to come to me.

"My lord." Orne lumbered up to stare at my mark in surprise. "That was a good shield to be used as a target, my lord. Do you intend to hunt fanghorn?"

"Something more dangerous, Orne." I pulled the shield loose, with the arrows still stuck through it. "I want you to see that every man in the tents begins to practice with the hunting bow. Everyone must work until they can draw it in their sleep."

"The longbow, my lord? What would we hunt with so many men?"

"Perhaps nothing, Orne, but—"

A rider came galloping into camp, sliding to a halt in front of my tent in a cloud of dust. He had an escort of a dozen of my lances, but they made no move to hinder him in dismounting and approaching me. He was an Altaii, and from the gold-and-green scarf tied around his upper arm I knew from whom he came.

He raised an open hand in salute. "Lord Wulfgar, it's good to see you alive." He pulled out a scroll. "This is for you, my lord, from King Bohemund. Another like it has been sent to Lord Harald."

"Harald is still in the hands of our enemies," I said.

"Then it will be given to whoever leads in his stead. It's urgent, my lord. I was told to see that you read it at once, without a moment's delay."

The scroll had been pierced in three places for cords, and each cord sealed with three lead seals. If the scarf had not been Bohemund's, the seals would still have identified the message as from him. I cut the cords, unrolled the scroll and read the message hurriedly. Then I read it again, more slowly, in surprise.

"It's addressed to me," I said finally, "or to whoever commands in my place if I am still missing. If I still haven't been found, the search is to be called off immediately." I looked at the messenger. "If a similar message has been sent to Lord Harald's tents, then they're being ordered to abandon the search for him."

"I'm sorry, my lord, but it is urgent."

"I am to proceed south to join the king at the last fork of the River Varna. I must be there in no more than two tendays."

"Two tendays!" Orne shouted.

"If they will slow the march too much, the herds are to be abandoned. In the last extremity the lances will leave the rest of the march and press on alone. No matter what stands in the way, every Altaii capable of seating a lance must be at the Varna in twenty days."

"It's an ingathering of the lances, my lord," the

messenger said. "Word has been sent to every encampment from the mountains to the fertile lands, and from the snow country in the north to the dunes in the south. Most couldn't make it if they left their herds and tents on getting the message and rode with nothing but changes of horses, but the message is the same."

"But why? What's the reason? Is it the Lantans and Morassa?"

"I don't know, my lord, but there was a verbal message to be delivered after the other was read. 'Ride, or the Altaii nation dies.'"

"Then we ride. Orne, send a messenger to Bohemund—"

"I can return, my lord," the messenger said.

"Are you sure? You can have a meal and a breath here and ride with us." He shook his head. "Well, then, tell Bohemund we'll be there in twenty days, all of us. Orne, get him a fresh horse, and a string of five or six for changes."

Orne quickly turned the messenger over to a warrior who would see to his needs and was back at my shoulder. "Twenty days, my lord. I don't see how we can make it."

"We'll make it, Orne, every one of us, just as I said." For a moment I felt again as I had on the Plain outside Lanta, awaiting Harald, with Loewin in the sky and the Wind coming early. "The earth moves, Orne. The sky is shaking. The Nine Corners of the World are collapsing. Nothing is certain. All drifts on the wind."

"My lord?"

"See that we leave no women and unbranded youths to die alone. We take everyone with us. And since the herds can move as fast as the baggage animals, we'll not abandon them either. We may yet die, Orne, but we'll not die like tabaq fleeing before the Wind."

"It is good, my lord."

"Send word to Harald's camp. Tell them to join us on the march. And spread the word to break camp. In an hour I want nothing here but hoofprints and the holes of our tent poles."

We made that hour limit, though with nothing to spare. I chivvied the camp from horseback to see that it was met, and, with the cries that tents could not be folded so quickly and the complaints of herd guards that the animals couldn't be gathered and put on the move in so short a time, it was.

On the third day the people of Harald's tents joined us. They faded quickly into the march, our column simply becoming larger, the trailing mass of the herds swelling. The lances rode in three main masses, one on either side of the column, one to the head of it. A cloud of single warriors was spread around the whole, and at the head of the march, almost out of sight of the rest, rode a dozen lances.

If our formation on the move resembled a lance, they are the point of the lance. They guard the way, finding the path to water, avoiding the forty types of sand that can kill, the one hundred and eight that can slow the march to a crawl. To them also goes the honor of first contact with an enemy. I spent most of my waking hours on the march with the point.

We didn't stop our march except when the herds had to be rested, and then only for the hours needed and no more. If they lost weight, it could be regained at the Varna. Sleep was taken in hammocks slung on frames hung between the horses, or more frequently, in the saddle. Women and children slept on top of baggage piled on draft animals. Food was dried meat and raiding cakes. There were no stops for cooking.

On the tenth day we did stop, for to have continued would've meant the end of our march. I was riding with the point. The wind was blowing strongly, carrying sheets of dust, and coldly for all that winter was a mild thing that far south. Because of it we didn't hear the warning hoots and whistles until we neared the top of a rise, barely enough to hide our march from what lay on the other side.

Quickly I signaled, and we all fell back from the rise. Many of the older warriors were pale at the narrowness of our escape, if escape it was to be. The younger men were more excited. A warrior rode back to the march to warn them. Behind us movement stopped.

Dismounting I moved forward, some of the men of the point with me. The calls, like some eerie temple chant, grew louder. A rhythmic pounding vibrated in the ground. I looked over the edge of the ridge. Below me a blue mass flowed across the Plain. Runners.

# XX

## THE LAST FORK OF THE VARNA

~

They were tall, taller than any man, and their skin glistened in the sun like finely tempered steel. If the wind or the cold affected them I couldn't tell it, but then I couldn't tell a male from a female. The Sisters of Wisdom say they aren't sure there are two sexes. They don't like to make visions concerning the Runners. It makes them queasy and gives them pains in the head.

They ran at a steady pace, in ranks like soldiers from some city on parade, each in perfect step with the other. It was as if a huge, many-legged insect was rippling by, chanting a ululating combination of hoots, clicks, whistles and moans. If it's a language, no one knows. Whether it is or not, it's still enough to make the hair on a man's neck stand up straight.

None of them wore any kind of clothing, but they

weren't animals. Each wore a belt with its possessions in crude pouches hanging from it. In three-fingered hands each carried a club or war hammer, tipped with stone or jagged metal, the last taken from someone they'd killed.

They have no knowledge of metalworking, taking what they use from their victims, nor any knowledge of fire. Their food, and anything that moves is their food, they eat raw.

They're primitive, but their fierceness makes certain they're left alone. When they encounter any living thing, they attack, human or animal the same. If the Runners win they eat the dead, their own included, and leave no survivors. To be defeated they must be killed, every last one in the pack. They neither surrender nor retreat. Worst of all, Runners can take a dozen wounds that would kill a man without any effect on them.

There's never been the slightest peaceful contact between Runners and humankind. Now and again some ruler has gotten the idea of making allies of the Runners, or at least negotiating a peace. The human emissaries are eaten, often alive. If a Runner is subdued, it will neither eat nor utter a sound, eventually starving to death.

Such are the reasons for avoiding Runners. Many marches have suffered terrible casualties fighting them, and many encampments have disappeared forever beneath a mass of chanting blue death. Only young men see anything useful in them. It's a game with them, and well I remember it, to ride out and entice a pack of Runners to follow. Running the Runners is a way to show bravery for youths not yet old enough to raid. They call it sport. I wanted no sport on this day.

"How many do you think, my lord?" Orne asked.

"Five thousand, perhaps six. Everyone keep low. They can spot the flicker of an eyelash at this distance."

"I'm just glad they don't hunt by ear or smell, my lord, or the same wind that nearly put us in among them would've told them of us by now."

"A cheerful thought, Orne."

"I've never seen so many in one place before," a young warrior said softly. I barely caught his words. "It'd be great sport to run this pack, as great as ever there was."

"Dice with death another time," I said. "We're delayed enough just by their passing."

The last of the Runners trailed from sight into a depression ahead. I held my breath until I saw by the dust that their line was away from our march. They travel a straight line, diverting only for some natural barrier or because they sight prey. So long as they didn't catch sight of us, we'd be safe from an attack. I rose and signaled for us to move forward.

On the ninth day after our encounter with the Runners, the nineteenth after leaving Lanta, tired and dirty, we sighted the last fork of the River Varna. From there the river rapidly disappeared into the dry courses leading into the Plain. From there south it supported a lush belt on its banks all the way to the sea. And there lay the gathering of the lances.

For as far as the eye could see there lay tents, tents by the thousands, arranged in the three-point around the tents of their lords. Around the tents in a huge mass were the herds, the herd guards constantly moving them lest they crop the forage to the roots. On the horizon to the south in two places, and in one each to the west and the east, faint clouds of dust proclaimed more lances coming. Already there had to be at least forty thousand in the camp ahead. The last time so many had gathered had been to march to the Heights of Tybal.

I sent Bartu back to get Elspeth and Mayra. Both would be needed for the information I had to give the king. When they joined me we left the others and rode toward the center of the encampment. The entire spread of tents formed a giant three-point around one central three-point. That one looked no different from the others, except that its largest tent was larger than any other tent ever seen on the Plain, and in front of it stood the nine-horsetail standard of the King of the Altaii.

Riders met us before we reached that tent, warriors yelling and shouting, slipping from their saddles to do tricks. They'd heard I was dead, and it was their way of welcoming me back to the land of the living. It gave me a good feeling that they felt so, and their spirit began to infect me. I kicked my horse into a gallop, and when he reached full speed, stood up on the saddle and let the reins drop.

On a dead run I approached the king's tent. The men in front of it watched at first, laughing. Then they began to get nervous. As they began diving out of the way I dropped back into the saddle, grabbed the reins and pulled to a halt in the middle of the fifty standards taken from Basrath at the Heights of Tybal.

The others were slower in coming to the tent. Mayra was laughing as much as any of the warriors, but Elspeth was glum, almost grim-faced. Orne and Bartu waited with the horses and were deep in talk with the men who'd jumped out of my way by the time I led the two women inside. I took two steps in and stopped.

Fierce black eyes regarded me from a scarred black face, and I wondered what an Eikonan did in the tent of the Altaii king. Before I'd entered he appeared to have been studying a problem in the Game of War. He watched as I pushed on past the hanging that had once been the Raven Banner, the Holy War Standard of Telmark. Their attempt to push their holdings inland at our expense had failed.

On the other side they were waiting: Odoman, the king's seneschal, Moidra, the Sister of Wisdom who traveled with his tents, and Bohemund, King of the Altaii and my foster father.

# XXI

## TO BREAK THE RULES

~

"Wulfgar," he said, throwing an arm around me, "it's good to see you. If only Harald was here, too."

"You've no word of him, then?"

"Nothing, Wulfgar. It's as if the sands have swallowed him."

"Hasn't Dvere been able to find him?" Moidra asked. Her voice was deep and throaty.

"No," Mayra replied scornfully. "She failed to form a bond before he was taken, and by the time she tried his presence was clouded."

Moidra shook her head at Dvere's failure. Bohemund was studying Elspeth.

"This Wanderer, Wulfgar. I assume she's here for some reason?"

Quickly I told what Mayra had seen with the rune-bones, and what Elspeth had told me after I returned from Lanta. Moidra looked to Mayra for confirmation, and Mayra nodded.

"I'd seen some things about a young woman, a Wanderer, who would be important to our people, and so had some of the others, but there's been nothing specific. Certainly nothing as certain as what you've seen. But then," she added ruefully, "we couldn't expect to, could we?"

I started asking what she meant, but Bohemund was leaning forward eagerly. "Have you thought about how this thing is to be done, Wulfgar? With all that's happening, it may have to be tried even if the Sisters of Wisdom decide it's not required."

"I've thought about it, and I have some ideas." I tugged at the beard I still wore. "This, and hunting bows and breaking the most basic rules of war, may give us what we need. But what is happening? Mayra's been able to tell me there's a plot between the Lantans, the Morassa and the Most High, but no details of it."

"The Most High," said Bohemund. He sounded shocked.

"I could see danger for our people," Moidra said, "an attempt to destroy us, but I could not get a clear sight of where the danger lay, or how to counter it."

Bohemund nodded. "That remained to the slow ways of men to find out. At least, about the Lantans and Morassa. About the Most High," he said slowly, "come."

He led the way to a map table. Elspeth started to

follow, but Mayra and Moidra gave her such startled looks that she crept to a corner and waited.

"What of the Eikonan?" I asked.

Bohemund laughed, and for the first time I realized how Harald's disappearance had cut new lines in his face. "The Lantans, it seems, made an offer to the Eikonan."

"Obviously not accepted."

"Not only not accepted, but the Lantans had to ransom their emissaries back. They were clumsy, Wulfgar, clumsy as men with no knowledge of the Plain's tribes could be clumsy. They offered a bribe to the Eikonan to attack us when they did. Not an offer to hire swords, but a bribe."

It was clumsy. An attempt to hire the Eikonan as mercenaries would probably have succeeded. Even a simple statement that at a certain time we'd be occupied elsewhere might have brought them harrying us in the rear. A bribe, though, made it a thing of honor, and that was something a Lantan didn't understand.

"And that one came to tell us they refused?"

"Yes. His name is N'Runa. He says the Circle of Elders debated the offer for ten days. Not whether to accept it, but whether it was insult enough for them to go to war beside us. They decided it wasn't. I could wish they were pickier about their honor." He swept the covering off of the map table.

Along the western edge ran the Sifr Senaka, the Backbone of the World. To the north was the beginning of the snow country, where the land was clear only a few tendays of the year and the tusk-beasts roamed. To the south were the sea and the holdings of the Telmarkers. And along the eastern side lay the cities of the edge of the Plain, Cerdu and Devia, Asyat and Lanta.

"The reason for what happens is commonplace, or I thought it was until you mentioned the Most High. Now," said the king, "I'm no longer so certain. However. It seems that the Twin Thrones dream of power, more power than can be had by a city, however large. They want an empire. To the north of Lanta lies Devia, a trading center of some size itself. In recent years the city has had a long spell of bad luck. Drought among the dirtmen to the east of them has pushed food prices up. Three of the biggest merchant houses have failed, and the others have tried more and more to push caravans to the far mountains, the Sifr Senaka, and that has increased their losses to the tribes of the Plain.

"South of Lanta is Cerdu, much the same sort of city as Devia. Their trade has been going well, but the Malik, their king, has been discovered using money marked as spent for the army on slaves and imported delicacies. Additionally, a scandal has resulted from the discovery that priests at some of the city's temples haven't been making the prayers they've been paid to make.

"The result is that both cities are ripe for plucking, if the right conditions can be arranged."

"And Lanta means to make an empire beginning with those two cities?" I asked.

"They do. According to those of our people who've

traded in those places recently, the Twin Thrones already have agents there, fanning the flames. They've even provided arms to some of the dissidents. All they need is to show up with an army at Cerdu and that city will fall. Little more than that is needed for Devia, especially if they destroy the Plain tribe that's done the most damage to their caravans on the way. Also, destroying us lets them march troops to the cities without fear of our taking them in the flank. And, of course, it would damage their claims to empire if caravans from one city of the Empire to another were being raided by the Altaii."

"And so they move to destroy us," I said. "But how? Mayra speaks as if they've little more to do than open their hands to grasp us. According to her we have only the smallest chance of survival. Well, we won't die so easily, so how will they do this thing?"

"Their movements were clouded, Wulfgar, so once again it was warriors on horseback who found what we needed."

"Let your men scout in a fog where the very shape of the earth changes beneath their feet from moment to moment," said Moidra. "Then let us hear how they've bested us."

Bohemund still had a slight smile, but it faded with his next words. "Have you seen a Morassa anywhere on the Plain? Have any of your lances?"

"None, but they avoid us anyway."

"This time they don't avoid. In the north and the south they gather like locusts. To the north, two hundred thousand. To the south, twice that and more."

I almost choked on the numbers. "So many? The Morassa couldn't gather that many lances if they raked out every dung heap on the Plain."

"No doubt," Bohemund said dryly. "However, half of the northern force is Lantan, and fully one in three of the southern."

"They must have stripped their outlying garrisons and tributary towns." I studied the map closely. "What of Lanta? What of her garrison?"

"They are several thousand. They are sure that Lanta's gates and walls are invincible. That Lanta cannot be taken."

"And how many lances will we have?"

"If all I think can get here do, then sixty thousand. That's why I believe that what you say about taking Lanta is fated. At any rate, if you can get us into the city, we'll take it. Then let them try and retake it. Their armies can wander around until they starve."

"The Outer Wall. It won't work. We could take the city. In fact, that's the least of our worries. But we've no one who knows how to withstand a siege. It wasn't Lanta's walls alone that defeated Basrath. It took men who knew how to fight that kind of war, men we don't have. Let us be bottled up in the city by those two armies combined, without enough food, without the knowledge, and they'll take it back again, and kill us in the process."

"Then what do you suggest?" Bohemund asked calmly, as if I hadn't crushed the plan he'd begun counting on.

"Each force will begin to sweep inward. If we try

to fight either early, we must fight at a heavy disadvantage. If we wait to gather more lances, we must move ahead of them"—my finger traced the line on the map to Lanta—"and they'll finally confront us here, still heavily outnumbered and caught between the two armies and the walls of the city."

"So far," he said wryly, "you've told me what I already know. How do you propose to counter it?"

"Before, when I thought it was just a case of the Lantans behind their walls and the Morassa raiding, I thought to split our forces, part to ride against the Morassa, part to take Lanta."

"Now, of course, you've abandoned that idea."

"No, I still need to violate the most basic precept of war in my plan. I say we divide our forces in the face of a superior enemy. Half of our forces will stay here to harass the southern army. The other half will ride north. Most will harry the northern army while ten thousand take Lanta."

"Ten thousand!"

"Then those who take Lanta will join with those who harass in the north, and if the proper place can be found, they'll be destroyed. After that all the lances join to deal with the southern army."

"Wulfgar, I'm sure there are a few details you're leaving out, but for one, why split the forces so? Why send so many against the northern army? I'll not even mention taking Lanta with ten thousand lances."

"Half must stay here to make certain the enemy in the south can't move north to interfere with what happens there. The number who go north must be large enough to do what has to be done there. Because it's cold, and the fanghorns will be starting to hibernate, they'll be enough to destroy the northern force, if the baraca is with us."

"You talk like you're telling rune-bones. You'll have to give more details before I'll let the King's Council sit on this place."

I leaned forward over the table and began to explain, tracing out the movements of the armies involved. After a time Bohemund began to smile. Then he started nodding. Finally he slapped at the table.

"It'll work. The fanghorns chew my bones if it isn't insane from one end to the other, but I say it'll work. Moidra, will you cast the rune-bones on it?"

"I think we'd better do more than that, if Mayra will go along. We'd better sit the star."

Mayra nodded. "Yes, and I'll want the men who'll command the lances there, the ten thousands."

"They won't like it," Bohemund said, "but if you need them, they'll be there. Dunstan, Otogai, Shen Ta, Karlan, Bran and Wulfgar. Since it's Wulfgar's hand that must open the gates of Lanta, he'll command the lances who go north." It was an honor, and not one I thought I'd get, yet I knew from the first I'd never thought that anyone else might command. Lanta was mine. My destiny lay there.

"We need a third," Moidra said. "Not Dvere."

"Not Dvere," Mayra agreed. "She's definitely not

strong enough for what might be waiting for us. Of course, not many are. Selka, I think. She might do."

"As well as any. Will you prepare the star? It'll be stronger with you."

Mayra smiled. "All right. I'll leave you to bring the men." She motioned to Elspeth. "Come, child."

Together they left, and as they did I remembered what I'd wanted to ask. "Moidra, you said earlier you couldn't expect to see what Mayra saw. And just now you said the star would be stronger if she prepared it. Why?"

She looked a little disconcerted. "Well, there's really no reason to hide it. We usually just don't talk about such things. Mayra is the most powerful Sister of Wisdom among the Altaii. I can't think of many who can match her, certainly not on this side of the Sifr Senaka. Sayene, of course. She's the reason we need Mayra here. Perhaps two others. Ya'shen, of Liau."

"And the third?" I asked, a hollow feeling in my middle. "Is the third's name Betine?"

"Why, yes. From Caselle. How did—Are they the ones we face?"

"They are. Is it bad?"

She shivered. "It could hardly be worse. I'm nearly as strong as they are, but Selka is the next strongest here or likely to get here before everything's over, and she's not even close. I'll tell you, warrior, we Sisters of Wisdom face graver odds in this than you do, for all your enemy's numbers."

# XXII

## THE NEXUS

—

The other men who'd been named were all among those gathered outside the tent when we left. It was a sizable crowd, for the word had spread, as it always does at such times, that I had escaped from Lanta and arrived at the encampment. The rumors also said I'd brought the means of victory with me, though whether that meant more lances or something else none could say. Some even said I'd brought knowledge of a spell that would ensure victory. There was no explanation of what kind of spell it would be to be handled by a man, or why I would be the one to bring it instead of Mayra, but then there never are explanations for rumors.

I knew some of these men and knew of all of them. Dunstan had been with my father at the Heights of Tybal. Otogai and Karlan had raided to the gates of Efheim, in Telmark. All were known men, but they accepted me as one of their number.

"What is it they want with us, Wulfgar?" Otogai asked.

"To find out if my plan for taking Lanta will work."

He started to laugh, but cut it off when I didn't even smile. "By the Nine Hells, man, I believe you're serious."

The acolytes already had the domed spirit-tent up when we got there and were busily sorting through chests under Mayra's eye for the things that would be needed. Moidra stopped us well away.

"You must leave all the iron and steel here. Not so much as an iron brooch-pin may be taken inside, or none of us may leave alive."

There was some grumbling when it became clear that even nails in boots counted, but we added our boots to the pile of weapons and armor. All of it was outside a circle drawn around the spirit-tent to show the safe distance for iron. Then it was time.

The three Sisters of Wisdom led us inside. A plain five-pointed star had been cut into the ground and outlined with some reddish substance that glistened. The Sisters took positions at points of the figure. Mayra motioned Bohemund and the other five to sit in pairs, one pair behind each Sister. Me she directed to the center of the star.

"It's your plan, Wulfgar, so you must be the nexus. There's danger to it, more for you than for any other, because you've already been the focus

of powerful forces not long past. Hold fast and remember that our strength supports you."

I stood in the place she marked. I wanted to say
something, but my mouth was suddenly too dry.
And then they began.

Mayra faced me from the lower point, to form
the base, she said. Moidra was to my left, to protect
my heart; Selka was on the right. Each dropped her
robes and stood sky-clad. They produced candles,
long and white to the point of paining the eyes, and
lighting them they stepped onto the points. They
knelt, each placing her candle carefully a spaced distance in front of her. I noticed that although they
burned with a brighter flame than I'd ever seen before, the candles grew no shorter. For some reason
that was reassuring.

Mayra raised her hands above her head. "Rok
As'han!"

"Rok As'han!" the others repeated.

"Tsouban!"

"Tsouban!"

"Tsha Raas!"

"Tsha Raas!"

Everything outside the star faded and disappeared
in darkness. The other men weren't even shapes or
shadows. Inside the star there was no more light
than before, but everything seemed sharper, clearer.

"Gla'shadan!"

"Gla'shadan!"

"Beelzelye!"

"Beelzelye!"

"Zahl Pa! Comen!"

"Zahl Pa! Comen!"

The voices came faster, no louder but with more intensity. The candle flames were blinding points of light, as if the sun sat in each, but they gave no more illumination than they had before. At the corner of my eyes, images danced, unclear, half seen, skittering away when I tried to look. The chants merged.

"Alduvai! Vukran! Jahen Gol!"

"Alduvai! Vukran! Jahen Gol!"

"Alduvai! Vukran! Jahen Gol!"

The images just beyond my sight shimmered and rushed to merge before me. Two visions danced in the air, first one, then the other, overlapping, brightening then fading. In one the Towers of Kaal, reaching to the sky beyond the Palace of the Twin Thrones, were engulfed in flames, and a rain of smoke rose from the Outer Wall. In the other Altaii warriors trapped in Low Town fought from hovel to hovel, and endless sheets of arrows from the walls cut them down every time they moved into the open.

"I see," I said, and my voice reverberated in the air like a bronze bell.

"Yes."

I wasn't sure who had replied. Mayra, I thought. The question of who faded before a pain that grew behind my eyes. It was as if a rope around my forehead was being tightened, tighter and tighter and tighter. I tried to say something, to tell Mayra, but there were burning coals in my mouth. The world flickered, and I stood in the middle of a star carved into the stone floor of a tower room.

I'd been there before, and I recognized the three sky-clad women who surrounded me. Sayene. Ya'shen. Betine.

"Qarn! Isu! Galaal!"

Their mouths moved, but the words didn't match.

"Qarn! Isu! Galaal!"

They flickered, like a candle in the wind.

"Qarn! Isu! Galaal!"

The tower room disappeared. Once more I was back in the spirit-tent. There was tightness in the air, and a smell of fear. The ground beneath my feet was like a cloud.

"Anivam! Tsukar Mal! Das!"

The ground was ground again, but the fires were back in my throat, and though I couldn't see them, I felt the flames rising around me.

"Anivam! Tsukar Mal! Das!"

The cold was gone, but a giant hand pierced my side and squeezed my heart in its grip. I groaned.

"Vas El! Kutai Machi! Beltar!"

The hand was gone, but something clawed at my sword arm.

"Vas El! Kutai Machi! Beltar!"

The clawing faded to a tingle. Something began to pull at me, at the inside of me, at whatever it was inside me that was me. I could feel it slipping, be-ing drawn away.

Hold fast, Mayra had said. Hold fast. I reached out, though neither hands nor arms moved. In some manner I reached out to hold fast to that which was me. As I grasped and held I shouted the wordless cry that I'd shout in battle, and as I shouted the Sisters of Wisdom chanted.

"Vas El! Kutai Machi! Beltar!"

Suddenly the spirit-tent was just a tent again. Light crept in at the tent flap, and the candles lit everyone. Mayra was covered with sweat. Moidra panted as if she'd run a great way. Selka fell forward on the ground and wept. For the first time I realized how young she was, no older than Elspeth.

The men sitting behind the Sisters of Wisdom looked stunned.

"What was it?" Bohemund asked. "What happened?"

"They were waiting," Mayra replied. "Sayene, Betine and Ya'shen knew we'd try this, or something like it, for proof of our plans, and they were waiting. Once they discovered Wulfgar's presence they concentrated on him."

I rubbed my right arm to relieve the tingling. "At one point I thought I actually was back in Lanta, in the tower room where they had their spell-star."

"For an instant, you were. There aren't many with the power to manage it, but they tried to take you bodily away. What's the matter with your arm? Why do you rub it?"

"It's nothing, Mayra. A little tingle."

"Nothing?" She grabbed my arm and twisted it around as if trying to see how far it could bend.

"Maybe it's nothing. I'll do something about it, just the same."

"It's my fault," Selka said. "I was supposed to guard your right side, but they were so powerful I had to pay too much attention to merely keeping in the circle. Mayra, they nearly tossed me aside as if I was a child."

"It's all right, Selka. You did well. And as for this arm, if this tingling you say you have is left from an attack, I'll definitely have to do something. And since they're still after you, I'd better give you another protection against the Most High."

Protections, or even arms, weren't what was bothering me. "Mayra, did they discover the plan? Do they know how I intend to take Lanta?"

"He was serious," Otogai exclaimed, and the others leaned closer to hear.

"I don't think they did, Wulfgar. They could only have gotten it from you, and they didn't have you long enough."

"Then which was the true vision?" Bohemund asked. "We all saw them, but which one is true? Do we burn the Towers of Kaal or die in Low Town?"

Mayra shook her head. "Both were equally strong. Both have equal chance of happening."

"Perhaps they didn't get the plan," Karlan suggested. "Perhaps they only got that we attack Lanta, and one vision shows Wulfgar's plan succeeding, and the other shows their counterplan succeeding."

"They'd never think of an attack on Lanta,"

Dunstan said. "Certainly not by us, without a siege engine among us."

"They still fear him," Otogai added. "They tried to take him, and failing that, to kill him. That means they know he's dangerous to their scheme without knowing how, because if they knew he was going to attack Lanta, they'd just put their guards on alert instead of going to all this trouble. I certainly don't know of any plan that could get us in with the gates shut and guards standing to."

"Unless they don't know the specifics of the attack," I said, "but do know that my hand must open the Iron Gates. Even if the plan might succeed with them waiting for it, it couldn't succeed with me dead. That might be the way they see it."

They looked at each other without speaking. Finally Dunstan nodded. "I say go ahead."

"Go ahead," Otogai said.

Karlan nodded. "Go ahead."

The other two agreed, and Bohemund smiled grimly. "Then we ride on the morrow. May the baraca ride with us."

"And I ride to Lanta with you," said Mayra. "I claim the first part of your debt."

"You ride with me," I said. "And may the baraca ride with us."

# XXIII

## A CLOUD OF DUST

The bustle of crowds through the Imperial Gate hadn't been lessened by rumors of war or of the gathering tribes of the Plain. This was Lanta the Unconquerable. This was the city that turned back the invincible legions of Basrath. No war could touch her. No bandits of the Plain could affect her commerce. There was only a cloud of dust on the horizon.

A good part of the traffic was that needed for the everyday life of the city. Carts, and even caravans, of food rolled alongside the wide road. A steady stream of oil wagons came, and huge barrels in place of wagon boxes, to keep the lamps burning.

The guards gave little attention to any of it, certainly not to the oil wagon that was slowed to a stop in the gate by the press of the throng. It was certainly no different from any of the others. A tall, bearded fellow with a vacant stare walked beside the horse to guide it in the crowds. On the seat sat the merchant, his wife beside him, bundled from head to foot so not a glimmer of her showed. Occasionally he'd shout to the man by the horse, yelling for him to go this way or that to gain a bit on the rest, or to the man trailing the wagon, for him to be certain no one stole any of the oil.

One of the guards took notice of something and poked his companion amusedly. "Hey, oil seller," he yelled. "You're oiling the road."

The merchant looked at the guard, suspicious of a joke, then stood up on the seat to look behind. The barrel blocked his view of the tap. Muttering to himself, he climbed down and walked back. His shriek of anguish was enough to send the guards into fits of laughter.

"Idiot! Imbecile! Will you drive me to penury?" A thin trickle of oil descended from the tap. The trail it left showed it'd been leaking for some time. "Close it! Close it! Do I have to tell you everything? If I'm forced to lose my profit on this, I'll have every copper from your hide."

Passersby close enough to see joined in the laughter as the servant tried vainly to close the tap. Despite the leak it appeared to be closed as far as it would go. Suddenly the tap twisted in his hands and came out of the barrel. The servant joined in with a wail as a gout of oil as thick as a man's arm poured onto the road.

"Stop it up, witling! Stop up that hole!"

The merchant danced up and down in frustration while the servant tried to force the tap back in against the flow of oil. At last he managed to hammer it in place, but by that time at least half the oil in the wagon lay on the ground.

"Perfumed oil." The merchant gestured helplessly at the puddles in the road as if he could say no more. "Perfumed oil."

An officer of the City Guard who'd come out to see what was causing the commotion confronted him.

"I can tell that," he said, waving a hand in front of his face. "Now get that wagon out of here before I make you haul sand to sop up this mess. Go on. You're blocking the gate."

"But what am I going to do about my oil?" the merchant wailed.

"You're going to go. Now," the officer said grimly.

Snatching off his cap, the merchant struck his servant with it. "Well? Didn't you hear the gracious noble? Go. I don't have all day. There'll be others at market before me, and I must make every copper I can if I'm to avoid bankruptcy."

The merchant continued his tirade as the wagon rolled forward, until he had to run to regain his seat. The crowd began to move ahead, and those behind grumbled on finding they had to pick their way through pools of oil in the road. The cloud of dust on the horizon grew larger.

The oil cart continued on toward the inner gate, but then turned off into a Low Town side street.

Several others in the crowd who might have been expected to continue into the High City also turned off and stopped by the wagon.

I grinned as I let go of the horse lead and moved to the rear of the wagon. Mayra was climbing down from the seat.

"How can city women breathe in these traveling robes?" she complained as she loosened them. "They don't let any air in."

Bartu was stripping off his merchant's garb, and Aelfric, the man who'd found Elspeth, no longer looked the oafish servant.

"We should find a shrine," Bartu said, "and thank the city gods for the crowd. I was afraid we'd have to lose a wheel to get stopped, and I still don't think they'd have let us go so easily if we had."

"Don't worry," I told him. "It's past, and we're in." I wasn't as easy in my mind as I sounded. The dust cloud moved closer.

Finally a guard saw it. He stared in disbelief, then shouted, pointing. Other guards took up the cry, and the alarm bell over the gate began to ring. Deeper in the city more bells joined in, echoing and overlapping. It was a sound not heard in Lanta in the memory of most men.

I stripped off the stained tunic and worn sandals I wore and dug my own clothes and armor from a chest fastened to the wagon's side. Bartu, Aelfric and the others did the same. If any of those pushing deeper into Low Town thought it strange to see men donning chain mail and belting on swords, they didn't stop to question it.

As the bells rang, the great Iron Gates of Lanta slowly swung shut. Panic spread among the people still trying to get in as the way narrowed. Screaming and shouting, they forced their way through the gap, abandoning goods, horses, carts, anything that couldn't advance in the press. The gates clanged shut, and the screams from outside died as the people there began to run along the walls, trying to escape whatever was coming. Did they but know it, they were the safest people in Lanta.

Bartu handed me a crossbow. "It's time, my lord?"

"It's time."

I put a long quarrel on the crossbow, one that stuck over the bow's end and had a bundle of oily rags tied around the head. He struck flint and steel, and the rags flamed.

"With my own hand," I said, and fired.

Even as the bolt was in the air I dropped the bow and was out and running, swords in hand, the others on my heels. The quarrel struck, the oil seemed to explode, and the whole width of the gate was engulfed in flames.

A guard ran out of one of the gate towers and skidded to a halt, staring at the fire. Then he caught sight of us, and his mouth dropped open. Perhaps he thought he'd somehow gotten on the wrong side of the gate, to find Altaii warriors. He tried to shout a warning, but the sound coming out was pushed back by my sword going in.

Shouldering open the door I burst into the lowest chamber of the tower. A startled guard appeared in front of me, then fell back, hands clasping a ruined throat. Another leaped to his feet to receive a boot in the crotch. As he doubled over, descending steel removed his pain and his head. Leaving those behind me to deal with the other guards I bounded up the stairs.

The sound of the alarm bells covered my coming. The first guard died without knowing what killed him. In the space of heartbeats Bartu, Aelfric and the rest were there, and I moved on. Higher we moved, and higher, faster and faster, and we dared leave no one behind but the dead. We raced against the sound of the bells that hid us like a cloak from the men on the wall outside the tower, men in numbers to brush us aside like kopwings. To buy that cloaking, to buy our lives, every man in that tower had to die before the bells stopped. The last man died, and as he died silence came. His fall sounded like thunder.

I froze, staring at the heavy door to the top level of the wall and waiting for the onslaught. A man moved, and I motioned for silence as if he'd shouted. Slowly my breathing returned to normal. The door remained shut.

Aelfric and Bartu hurried to place a balk of timber across the door. As it settled in the slots Bartu heaved a relieved sigh.

"We made it," he said.

I shook my head. "Not yet. There's a door like

this on every level. Every one has to be barred, else we might as well invite the guards in. Quickly, now, and quietly."

I raced ahead of them all the way to the bottom, leaving the doors to them. I'd said I knew the way my hand could open the Iron Gates of Lanta, but I still didn't know for certain if I was right. It could still be that I'd led more men to useless deaths.

# XXIV

## BLOOD AND STEEL

In the road outside there was still some confusion, but the remaining people were fast disappearing, most of them into the High City. Inhabitants of Low Town had long since gone to ground. At the inner gate guards stood among the litter of abandoned peddlers' barrows and pushcarts, looking toward the outer gate, staring at the raging fire. It seemed the baraca was indeed with us. They hadn't seen us, and their gate stood open.

At the Iron Gate itself the great ball of flame was gone, but every crack and crevice in the road held flame, every depression supported a billow. And on the gate tendrils of smoke seeped from cracks between the iron plates.

The Iron Gates of Lanta. For how many centuries had that name gone unchallenged? Even Basrath hadn't questioned it. To his death he'd boasted that only the solid metal of the Iron Gates had stopped him. I had questioned it. Sitting, looking at those gates, I'd begun to wonder how the plates were fastened together, and then how such a great mass of metal could be moved so easily. I'd gambled on a hunch, and so far I'd won. The gates weren't solid iron, only iron plates on a wooden frame. And that wooden frame was burning.

Even as I watched a plate buckled, and a finger of flame appeared. Half the gamble was won. Now I'd only to wait for the fall of the pieces to see if I'd won it all. I was smiling as I ran back up to the third level. That was the lowest pierced with arrow slits. Through one of them the dust cloud was looming large, and the source of the cloud.

Riding on the wheels of twenty carts a huge tree, as thick as a man is tall, hurtled down the road toward the Iron Gate. On either side rode a hundred warriors, drawing on ropes, but in truth the behemoth had life and carried itself forward for its meeting with the flaming gate. Behind followed ten thousand Altaii lances, coming to tear the walls of Lanta down.

From below a sound impinged on my mind, a rhythmic pounding. "They've discovered the doors are barred," I said.

We were moving down the stairs before the words were out of my mouth. I touched the bottom step on the second level just as the door crashed open, and a dozen guards spilled into the room trying to drop the timber they'd used for a ram and draw their swords all at the same time. The room was suddenly filled with flashing steel and shouting men, and more were coming.

I fought to get to the door. A Lantan sprang up before me, and I killed him without ever seeing his face. The door filled my eyes, the door and a hundred more guards pounding toward it. Another Lantan leaped for me. I took the wound he gave and knocked him aside. I had no more than a dozen heartbeats left anyway if that door wasn't shut.

And then I was there, pushing it back, throwing my weight against it, but there was weight on the other side, now. A hand reached through the gap and poked blindly with a sword, blindly, but at me.

"The door," I shouted.

The numbers were too much against me. It began to swing back in. Aelfric threw his weight beside mine, and another warrior added his. Behind us the fight still raged, but our fight was there. Bartu joined us, blood running down the side of his head. The door stopped. For an instant the scales teetered; then the last grain fell on our side. The gap narrowed.

Outside a man screamed, whether from frustration or because he was being crushed against the door by his fellows in their desperation I didn't know. It was the sound of our victory in that small battle, though. His cry was cut off as the door slid shut. The only noises were panting and the futile pounding of fists against the door. Bartu brought another timber to bar the door, and we could turn to find out what had transpired behind us.

Every Lantan who'd entered the room lay dead. A victory, there, too, but not without its price. A young, red-haired warrior named Hotar lay on the floor trying to hold his life in his chest with his hands. I looked to Mayra, coming down the stairs, but she took one glance and shook her head. He was less than a year past his warrior brand, and he'd asked to come for the glory of being one of the first to enter Lanta. Instead I held him while he died. There's little in the life of a warrior. Only blood and steel, that and no more.

"My lord." Bartu tugged at my arm. "My lord. He's dead, and there's no time left. He'll get his funeral fire, but we've got to go now."

"We'll go," I said wearily.

We retreated to ground level, but there was no attempt to follow us, or to break down another door. They were too concerned about what was coming from the outside to worry about a handful of Altaii in one tower.

"It's too bad you couldn't have used a spell against them," I said.

"Stick to your swords and your men's law," Mayra replied, "and leave the laws of magic to me."

There was no more time for talking. Shouts came from the walls above, screams and the sound of panic. Then the tree, loosed by the warriors, struck the gates, a huge battering ram.

Those gates, inviolate for untold centuries, were sheared away as if by the hammer of a god. Like flung cards they spun into Low Town, leaving everything in their path broken and scattered. The ram, many wheels torn away by the impact, careened into Low Town. Its end struck a tavern, and it twisted in the road, rolling and spinning, tearing the fronts from inns and hostels. Halfway to the High City it came to rest, a wall across the road.

At the inner gate guards scurried like a kicked kes hive. The gates began to close, swinging slowly, hesitantly, for they were seldom moved. They moved a little way, then stopped, a mass of broken peddlers' barrows and pushcarts jammed beneath them. Locally alarm bells rang again, but few in the city took up the call. The guards tried frantically, more like kes than ever, to clear the wreckage. They were too late.

Twenty Altaii lances leaped the burning oil and raced toward the inner gate, leaning low in their saddles as the horses cleared the giant log. Another twenty followed, and another, and another. Arrows from the walls emptied some saddles, but there was still confusion there, and disbelief about what was happening. And more lances came.

Then Orne was outside with horses. "It looks to be a restful enough spot, my lord, if resting is what's on your mind, but I don't think the wine's very good here."

"The wine isn't bad," I replied, "but the food's bad, and I've never seen such ugly dancing girls."

An arrow stuck in the door next to me, and I quickly swung into the saddle. I put spur to horse and headed for the High City, the others close behind and more Altaii lances close behind them. I hoped Mayra's powers and charms could protect her. She'd refused steel armor, and I had no way to shelter her.

My horse took the jump over the tree in the road as if for sport. The inner gate was ours already, and some warriors had fought their way up the ramps that led to the road on top and the great weapons there. For the first time Altaii arrows flew from the Inner Wall, and the Lantans fell from the Outer. Altaii lances began to ride unhindered into the city.

I rode through without slowing, and the others with me. Behind followed a handpicked thousand, chosen for a special task. Other lances fanned out as they entered, spreading through the city. Still others rode up the ramps to the top of the Inner Wall.

There weren't many guards on the Inner Wall, for the most part only the crews for the ballistae and catapults. None of those would hold long in the face of horsemen from the Plain. Soon the defenders of the Outer Wall would find their own firepots raining down on them, smashing into the open back of the wall and finding fuel in the wooden walls they'd added. Even then there were plumes of smoke rising behind us.

The streets we rode through were crowded with Lantans, civilians fleeing and not knowing where to flee. We had no danger from them. They only wanted to get away. But they waited to run until they saw us. They didn't believe. They couldn't believe. And so they waited until their own eyes convinced them, when panic-stricken runners pushed through them.

That disbelief was a greater weapon than our swords. On the Outer Wall among the mass of Lantan guards, they'd disbelieve that the alarm bells could mean there was an enemy actually in the city. They'd disbelieve that an enemy could actually manage to fire the Outer Wall. Even when the summons came to move troops into the city, they'd disbelieve. After all, the enemy was outside, and Lanta was the Unconquerable.

The pall of smoke behind covered a quarter of the way around the city. Within, confusion reigned. A body of guards moved to face us, and were taken in the rear and dispersed by lances with gold goblets tied to their saddles, jewels festooned around their necks. More guards passed, without weapons, running. They fought in the crowd to escape and never even saw us. Panic warred on our side.

In the distance faint feathers of smoke began to lift from the Towers of Kaal, and I felt a small easing. No one who'd not seen it had been told of the vision. No one had fired the Towers just to make it true. Then we were at the great square in the center of the city, and across it lay the Palace of the Twin Thrones.

The gates of the palace were shut, but there were still guards outside, peering toward the rising smoke and talking excitedly among themselves. For all the screams and noise of armed clashes, there was no alert at the palace. Disbelief.

I motioned, and a dozen men moved up beside me. "Now," I said.

From a standing start we reached a dead run in no more than half a dozen paces. We were already at the gallop and halfway across the square when the guards realized what it was they saw and managed to believe. They began to scramble inside. A third of the way to go.

Bowmen on the walls began firing, but there weren't many of them, and they weren't prepared for an attack, so it was well short of a hail of arrows. A warrior took a shaft in the throat and rode three more strides before he fell. Another rolled silently from his saddle.

The palace wall loomed over us. I uncoiled the rope that I, like each of us, carried and hurled it upward. The grappling hook on the end caught with a clang, and I leaped from the saddle and began climbing. Above there was still disbelief. We were there. They were shooting at us. But it was insane to think we were really going to scale the walls. We had a good start before anyone ran to stop us.

A knife flashed, and a warrior fell to the paving stones below. The guard who cut at my rope waited too long. I pulled him over the edge, then caught hold of the wall as the rope parted. With a heave I was onto the guardwalk. I cut down a man slashing at the rope below a grappling hook and dashed on.

A guard met me at the head of the stairs. He tumbled to the bottom before I reached it myself. Another ran to meet me, but he was clumsy and lost his weapon at the first pass. Openmouthed he clutched his arm and waited for me to kill him, but I'd more important things that had to be done. A wave of Altaii joined me, and the Lantans at the palace gates threw down their weapons.

Two men attended to binding the prisoners while the rest of us labored to lift the bar across the gates. The gates were thrown open, the signal given, and the rest of the thousand charged into the palace. More guards rushing to defend the gates arrived in time to go down under the rush. Warriors leaped from their horses and pressed on into the depths of the palace. Mayra came to me as I moved to join them.

"We must go down. The place we seek is two levels down."

I didn't ask her how she knew, or even what it was she sought. I'd promised a service. It was for her to name it.

With her leading we found stairs and started down. She moved as if she'd studied a map, or had been there before. Neither was possible, I was sure, but then almost anything is possible to a Sister of Wisdom. I followed her lead without question, down halls, through rooms and side passages. I began to think we could merely stroll to where she wanted to go, and it almost cost my life.

Fire bloomed in my side, and I fell away from the two Lantans who swarmed out of a gallery we'd passed. The blade came free as I fell, but the second man laid open the side of my head, and the first managed to kick my right-hand sword away.

The other sword hamstrung that one from where I lay. He screamed as he fell.

The other guard circled me as I got to my feet. He was more careful than he'd been before, but I'd no time for his caution. The side of my head was wet with my blood, and the wound in my side was soaking my tunic. The hurt I'd taken at the gate tower opened. If he managed to stay away from me long enough, I'd fall on my face in front of him.

He feinted and moved to the side, feinted and moved. He was beginning to move in. Maybe he gained confidence because I still held my one remaining sword in my left hand. He feinted, moved closer, closer. The exchange was sharp and brief. His eyes widened in surprise as my blade slid between his ribs, and the man on the floor stuck a dagger in my leg.

I've no excuse for forgetting about him. The second guard hadn't. He'd maneuvered me right to where his companion could strike at me. It wasn't his fault he hadn't survived the attack.

I finished the one on the ground with his own dagger. As I was reaching for my swords Nesir walked out of a cross corridor. At the sight of him I forgot my swords, my wounds, Mayra, everything. In two strides I hit him, slamming him back against the wall. My fingers dug through the fat of his neck to reach muscle, and dug deeper.

He wasn't a weak man, for all of his fat. He was strong, and full of the confidence of his strength. He took my wrists in a crushing grip and pulled. Most men's hands would've pulled loose. My fingers dug deeper. For the first time he met my eyes. There was still no worry in his. And then he recognized me.

Sweat popped out on his forehead, and it wasn't from the exertion. His eyes bulged, and it wasn't from my grip on his throat. Staring at me he pulled harder, more frantically. He began to claw and hit. And all the while his eyes were locked to mine. At the end he put up his hands to block my gaze, to block the eyes that had looked into the pit.

Mayra looked at his body curiously. "So he was the one."

I picked up my swords without asking what she knew, or how she knew. What was, was. With her there was often no other explanation.

Suddenly my right arm began to tremble. My hand felt numb on the sword grip. It subsided, but the tingling was back, as bad as it'd been since the day it came. I looked a question at her.

She nodded as if I'd confirmed something she already knew. "Yes. We're close, now. She thought these might do it, but she's waiting."

She walked swiftly, obviously going where she knew the way. Two cross passages down the hall she stopped. The door in front of us opened without being touched. She smiled and entered.

I followed close behind her, but I stopped at my first step. Daiman sat on a table across the room. It was Daiman, but in some fashion he was bigger than I remembered, bigger and younger and stronger and more confident. The casual smile on his face said he was waiting for a little casual practice with someone he knew he could beat.

Three sharp claps drew my attention away from him. Mayra stood with her robes around her feet, hands shoulder high in front of her, palms forward. Facing her, Betine stood in the same manner. The confident smile that was on Daiman's lips was on hers also.

"The first part of the service," Mayra said. She sounded strained. "Kill the man."

Daiman swung his feet off the table and got up slowly. He showed no concern, and considering my condition, perhaps he shouldn't have. But I had promised the service, and she had named it. I raised my swords and took a step forward.

With that step the pain of my wounds disappeared. Without looking I knew they bled no longer. The aches were gone, the tiredness. Each breath I took seemed to flush new life and strength through me. I felt in the first flush of my youth again.

We met in the center of the floor. There were no wild rushes, no furious attacks. Carefully each of us felt the other out, probed for weakness, searched for openings. And that smile never left his face.

He had one sword longer than mine, and a dagger. The dagger was held low for the thrust into the belly or under the ribs, but he was in no hurry. His boots whispered on the stone as he circled.

His first attack was a lightning strike to my head, followed an instant later by the belly thrust. He moved faster than I thought he could, faster than

I thought any man could, but I met the attack easily. As fast as he moved, I moved faster, one blade flicking his sword aside, the other opening a cut on his dagger hand.

Whatever Betine had done to him, whatever Mayra had done to me, I knew in that instant I could best him. I moved to the attack.

My blades no longer seemed a blur. They *were* a blur, blindingly quick flickers of light, gleaming fans of blue steel hissing in the air like hot metal dropped in oil. He struck quickly, too. His sword was a flame in the lamplight. But he retreated, and I advanced. That was the difference.

I struck through his guard. Again. Two red patches widened on his tunic. I struck again, and there was a third. I could end it now. I knew it. I closed, and blazing pain swept along my right arm. It trembled uncontrollably, twitching and burning. I tried to hold on to my sword, but it fell from fingers that wouldn't obey, couldn't obey for the molten metal the bones in my arms had become.

In that first instant he knew what happened. With the first tingle in my arm, the first small tremor, he made his attack from my right. He moved, and his sword swept back for a backhand beheading stroke. He forgot that my left-hand blade was longer than the dagger he carried. Four inches slid into his heart. Not much, but enough.

His sword dropped over his shoulder, and he fell to his knees. For the first time the confident smile disappeared. He looked at me in surprise. "You?

How—" He fell forward and was dead when he hit the stones.

I looked for Mayra. She was standing over Betine. The Sister of Wisdom from Caselle lay on her back, staring at the ceiling with a look of indescribable horror on her face.

"She didn't believe it was happening," Mayra said, "even while it was happening."

"He didn't know me," I told her. "Until the end he didn't know me."

"It was as I thought, Wulfgar, once I saw him. I didn't know how I could do what had to be done, but when I saw him—She didn't trust him, not enough to give him free will to fight his battle. She linked with him completely. He was no more than a puppet. She must have been insanely confident to do such a thing."

"Why? I don't understand."

"The link with Daiman. When he died under that link, she died. You might say that you killed her when you killed Daiman."

"I'd rather it wasn't said. I want no name for killing Sisters of Wisdom, no matter the circumstances." The tingling in my arm had faded to where I could pick up the sword again. "Besides, I've still got a city to conquer."

"No longer, my lord." Orne walked in with scarcely a glance for Daiman, though his eyebrows lifted at the sight of Betine. "I've been looking for you to give you the news. The last resistance has collapsed. Lanta is yours."

# XXV

## OATHS

—

From the tower room in the palace that I'd taken for mine I could see the ring of smoke that still surrounded the city. Hundreds of the guards had leaped from the Outer Wall to escape the flames, but they were back out there now, all of them we'd captured and thousands of men from the city, too. The fire had spread to Low Town, sweeping through it like a flood. Most of the inhabitants appeared to have escaped, but those Lantans out there, wearing our chains now, fought to keep the flames from spreading into the High City.

There were fires inside the Inner Wall, small fires for the most part, easily controlled, but one was beyond anything that could be done. From windows on every one of the hundred levels of the Towers of Kaal flames roared as if they were huge furnaces.

No man could get near them. Thousands worked hauling water to the vicinity of the Towers, not for the Towers, but to wet down the buildings around them, to keep the fire from spreading.

Orne walked in muttering to himself. I looked at him sharply, and he shook his head.

"We've turned out every place big enough to hide a man, my lord. We've questioned all of the guards, and as many others as we've been able to get. Nothing, my lord. They know nothing of Lord Harald."

Mayra put down her wine. "I told you that," she sighed. "If you're going to start disbelieving me—"

"It's not that," I said. "It's just that they might have used a spell to hide him. Or they could have clouded his presence. I couldn't take the chance, Mayra."

She smiled and touched my arm. For some reason it made me feel better.

"The rest, Orne?"

"The slave dealers'll start their caravans again, but they're complaining. They say we have so many it'll ruin the market and push the price down for the next five years."

"The price they pay us, they mean," I laughed. "And the food."

"First the dirtmen said they wouldn't sell to us." He made it sound like a personal affront. "Then they said they'd sell, but at about one imperial to one of their stinking roots. I said we'd come and take the roots, if that was how they wanted it, and they said they'd plow the crop under and burn their barns. Then I said—"

"What was the last thing said, Orne?"

"They'll sell," he said sourly, "at only twice what they charged the Lantans."

"It'll suffice, Orne. For now, it'll suffice."

"As far as your personal orders, my lord, do you realize how difficult it is to find one particular girl out of thousands in the palace?" When I didn't answer, he went to the door. "But I found her. In here, girl. Quickly."

A girl ran into the room, head down. Immediately she fell to her knees, face on the floor.

"Get up, Nilla," I said.

Slowly she straightened, her face a study in puzzlement. Elspeth had shaved my beard that morning, but as Nilla studied me recognition showed on her face. "Why, you're the slave—" With a gasp she threw her hands to her mouth and fell on her face again. "I'm so sorry, master. I didn't mean—"

"Get up, girl. I'm not going to hurt you."

She rose to her feet timorously, but she still hadn't lost her tongue. "If you're not going to hurt me, then why was I brought here?"

"Do you want to go back to that farm still?"

"Master, it's cruel to taunt me."

"Do you want to go? Answer me, girl."

"Wulfgar," Mayra broke in, "don't frighten the child to death. Tell me, girl, do you want to go home? I'm not teasing you. I want to know."

"Oh, yes, please, yes." Tears ran down her cheeks. "I do want to, but—" She faded away into sobs.

"I thought you weren't going to upset her," I said dryly. "Nilla, there are a thousand gold imperials in the bag on the table. They're yours. You're not a skinny child any longer. With that money, you'll be able to take your pick of the men in your village. I've made arrangements for you to be taken to Caselle. In the bag there's also a letter to one Henrus Quitillan, a merchant, charging him to see that you return safely to Knorros and your village. Do you understand that?"

"You mean I'm free now?" She sounded almost wistful.

"That's right. Orne will see you on your way."

"Thank you," she said flatly. She didn't look particularly happy as Orne led her away.

"Mayra, did you hear her? She sounded disappointed, actually disappointed that I was sending her home."

"Of course she did." Mayra laughed. "She was hoping to stay with you."

The hour-bell struck, and I started for the door. "Are you coming, Mayra? It's time to deal with the Council of Nobles."

"I wouldn't miss it," she replied.

Bartu met us in the hall. "I was coming for you, my lord," he said, and fell in behind.

There were still Lantan guardsmen at the doors to the great hall, chained to them. Those doors were heavy, taking all the Lantans' strength to open, and no Altaii would want the job.

A gabble of talk came out to meet me as the doors swung open, but it faded to silence when I entered. The room was lined with the full Council of Nobles, all one hundred of them. The noblewomen sat alone, but behind the men sat their wives, three or four hundred in number, and behind them the walls were lined with Altaii.

I could feel their eyes on me as I walked to the dais where the thrones stood. There was hatred there, and contempt, but no fear. They could hardly believe what had happened to their city. They could not believe it could touch them.

Putting a foot against one of the thrones, I toppled it. The crash when it struck the floor rang through the room like a gong. There was a concerted gasp, then silence again.

"Have that removed. I can't sit in more than one at a time."

I sat on the other, Mayra and Bartu standing at my shoulders, and surveyed the room. They were digesting what I'd said, trying to see if it meant more than the words said. We'd taken towns before, but only in raids. Did we mean to stay this time? Was that what I meant? Would an Altaii rule from one of the Twin Thrones? Avarice and arrogance spread over their faces as they began to plot how to manipulate and control stupid barbarians.

Ara, the palace seneschal, stepped forward, smiling nervously. Perhaps he knew more than the rest. If so, he had a right to his nervousness. "Noble sir," he said. "My lord. It's come to the attention of the members of the Council of Nobles that their daughters have been taken prisoner."

"So?"

"My lord, it's our custom to allow ransom of—"

"Your custom, not mine. Lantan custom, not Altaii. And with what will they pay this ransom? What is there in this city of value that doesn't belong to the Altaii?"

"But, my lord—"

"And then there's the matter of oaths." I said it quietly enough, but I might as well have shouted for the effect on the nobles. Dreams of power were replaced with pale, pasty faces. At last they knew fear. Sweat was running down Ara's face. "Oaths were sworn, while I rested in a cell beneath this palace, that I wasn't in the city. The daughters of the Council of Nobles were pledged to that. Those daughters are now forfeit."

"But we didn't mean that," cried one of the nobles.

I nodded, and Mayra produced a bag. From it she took a sky-stone, and set it in front of the throne. Carved with a Terg by a Sister of Wisdom. Blessed by three times three Sisters of Wisdom. Ara moved back from it as if it was a live stingwing.

"Come up here. Put your hands on this," I said, my voice becoming more like a growl with every word, "and repeat that you didn't mean your oaths. Put your hands on it and say anything you like. Come up here, Lantan."

Instead the noble tried to push himself through the back of his chair. He was shaking, and tears rolled down over his chins. The stink of fear was on him.

Suddenly Orne hurried into the hall. He walked quickly as he could without running, and leaned over to whisper in my ear.

"My lord, we've taken some prisoners who demand to see you. One, at least, I think you ought to see." He shut his mouth with a snap, as if he'd started to say something and changed his mind.

"If you think I should," I said, and he waved to a man at the doors.

Once more they swung slowly open, and Eilinn walked in. I knew at once that it was her. How, I couldn't say, but I knew. Her silver-blond hair was piled high on her head, fastened with pins covered in firestones. A heavy necklet and wide bracelets seemed to be solid emerald, and her robe was heavily brocaded and covered in firestones and pale snowstones.

She moved toward me as regally as if she still ruled there, and the rest of us were merely visitors. Six paces in front of me she stopped. Those green eyes were cool and decisive.

"When was she taken, Orne?" I asked.

She answered before he could. "I wasn't taken. I came on my own."

I looked at Orne, and he nodded. "Why? You might have escaped."

She calmly began taking the pins from her hair, throwing them on the floor. "There wasn't much chance of that, was there? And even if I'd managed to get out of the city, I'd have been alone, without money or supporters, and with no way to join my sister." Her hair tumbled down to her waist. "If I was caught, on the other hand, I ran the risk of being killed by the first warrior who recognized me." The emerald necklet and bracelets joined the pins. "I decided there was only one way to ensure my life." She knelt. "I pledge myself to you."

If anything I'd done had startled them, this sent the nobles into shock. Eilinn was the queen. They gave lip service, at least, to her being a living goddess. She and her sister were the embodiment of Lantan supremacy. They couldn't believe she'd meekly surrender, and I didn't believe it either.

"This is just a trick to preserve your life," I said. "You think this will keep your head on your shoulders?"

"I do think it. It'll keep me alive until my army can rescue me, of that much I'm certain."

It was my turn to be surprised. She said it as calmly as if announcing that the wind was from the south. "And now that I know your reason, why shouldn't I have you killed?" Mayra put a hand on my shoulder as if to stop me, but I shrugged it off.

"Because you don't think you'll lose." The corners of her mouth curled in amusement. "And anyway, if you do, you'll deprive yourself of having the Queen of Lanta, for however short a time, and you won't do that."

I was beginning to feel she meant it, but there was something else there, something she wasn't telling, and I meant to have it. "It's not enough. There's more to it, or you'd not come trusting that I won't kill you or put you in the cell over the pit, the one your sister kept me in."

That struck home. The icy mask slipped a touch. "It is. And I wasn't the one who put you there. Remember that."

"It was your sister," I hammered. "And you were the one who sent an assassin after me. A fine lad died that night, just because I jested about making you a slave. You ask me to believe after that you'll come in here and swear yourself to my service? I'll send for your own executioner."

"I wasn't about to die then." She caught her lip between her teeth and fought to regain her composure. "I had to balance being your slave for a short time, a short time only," she said as if trying to convince herself. "I don't want to die. I want to live. Whatever the circumstances, I want to live."

Mayra bent down in front of her. "There's a way." Eilinn stared at her like a child looking at candy she couldn't believe was being given. "If you can convince him, he'll let you live."

She scooped up the sky-stone and thrust it at Eilinn. The other woman clutched it before she realized what it was. Her face paled, and she swayed as if she was going to fall.

"Catch hold of yourself, child," Mayra said insistently. "You had the intelligence to see your one real chance where most women would've been blinded by panic. You had the courage to take that chance when most women would've seen it as suicide. Gather your intelligence and your courage now, and do what you must do!"

Eilinn held the sky-stone cradled as a woman might hold a bunch of flowers. She stared at it as if her eyes were frozen on it. "I—I—"

"The truth, girl. The words must be the truth, and you must know them for the truth."

Sweat beaded on the kneeling woman's brow. "I, I renounce my rights before the law and my rights above the law. I renounce my property and possessions. I renounce my f-freedom. I s-surrender my life and my will to the o-one who will own m-me." Her skin glistened, now, in the sunlight from the windows, and the sky-stone was wet.

"Now swear," said Mayra, "swear by the most terrible oath you know."

"I, I s-swear by m-my flesh and blood and b-bone and spirit."

With the last word she collapsed, the sky-stone falling to the floor. Mayra caught her and smoothed damp hair back from her face.

"What about the other prisoners you mentioned, Orne? Are they as interesting?"

"I don't know, my lord." He motioned to the door. "I've never seen them before."

The man who entered wore a noble's robes instead of armor, but a bandage on his head and another on his arm showed he'd been in some fighting. There was gray in his hair. That surprised me, for I knew him by name, although I'd never seen him before. I'd seen the woman with him. Her name was Leah.

"Did these also come in to surrender?" I asked.

Toran, for him it must be, bristled. "We did not. If a pair of your warriors hadn't managed to get behind me, I'd have had us out of the city by now."

Leah put her fingers across his mouth to quiet him. She took a deep breath and came closer. For the first time I realized she was with child.

"May I speak for us, my lord?" she asked softly.

"If you'll tell me what claim you two have to ask to be brought to me instead of being chained in coffle."

"None, my lord. You might say we presume, or rather, I presume, on the claim of another."

I studied her and counted back the months to the night of my capture. Then I counted a second time to be sure. Mayra was looking at me oddly, but I ignored her.

"That man of yours over there. You love him? Will he make a good father to your child?"

"As good a father as any man could be, my lord. As any man. And I do love him."

"How?" I asked simply, but she understood.

"When reason returns, my lord, even a simple woman can add three ones to make a triplet, and Elana wasn't able to keep all of her secrets."

I nodded and continued to ignore Mayra's scrutiny. A tall, imperious noblewoman caught my eye. Her more-than-generous bosom heaved with indignation as she stared at Leah with eyes that could have flayed at ten paces.

"You have something to say, woman?" I asked her. "You know something of this?"

"I know all there is to know," she spat viciously. "He was no sooner out of the city than she managed to get herself in that disgusting condition, and by a slave it's said. Abhorrent as it is to think of her allowing herself to get that way, it's even more detestable to think it was with a slave." She shuddered to show how detestable it was, and her lip curled in contempt. "Then he returned, and though she was already far gone, he claimed the child was his. They're loathsome, both of them."

Leah had flinched at every word, and Toran appeared ready to start fighting again, against anyone.

"Warriors," I shouted, "have you heard? Do we want two such as these among us?"

"No," they shouted back, sensing sport.

"Then this is my judgment. Take the two of them, along with a cart and a horse, to where my share of the loot is kept. Let her watch while he loads the cart with sacks of coin, gold bars, anything that catches the fancy of those who guard him. Don't let him shirk." The imperious-faced woman was smiling cruelly. "When the cart is half filled, have him finish filling it with furs. Then lay the woman on the furs, put him on the cart seat, and turn them out of the city. After all, we don't want such as they among us, do we?"

"No," shouted the warriors, and they roared with laughter. The cruel smile was replaced on the noblewoman's face with rage. Leah was sobbing, but with gratitude.

I pointed to Toran. "You, man, do you truly want this child?"

He gestured toward the imperious noblewoman. "Despite what Alimia says, a child is the child of those who raise it. I want this child."

I smiled. "It'll be interesting, Lantan, to see which blood wins out." I took off my armband, graven with my name and a record of the portents at my birth and the rune-bones cast on my nameday. Leah caught it in surprise. "Give it to the child. The price of your freedom is an oath that the child will be given the band."

She looked at Toran, then nodded. "I swear that the child I bear within my body will be given this band on its nameday. I swear by my life force and the bones of my mother and my mother's mother and my mother's mother's mother, by the spirit of every child I hope to bear, except the one I now bear, by the temple stones of the gods I worship, by—"

"Enough," I said, with a grin. "That's oath enough to hold you if the ground opens as it stands."

She bowed low, as a Lantan noblewoman would to her ruler, and returned to Toran.

"See that they have an escort of ten lances until they're well on their way," I told Orne.

"Why did you turn them loose?" Mayra asked.

I was saved from answering by the arrival of a warrior who handed Orne a scrap of paper. Orne read it and passed it to me. I read it twice and crumpled it in my hand. I moved to the front of the throne dais.

"You of the Council of Nobles also made some oaths. Our talk of them was interrupted, but not forgotten. You swore by the nails of your temple doors. At this instant those who were once citizens of your city are pulling those nails, and tearing down the temples until no stone rests on top of another and the images of your gods are ground into dust. You swore by the bones of your fathers, and if I could find them, I'd grind them into dust, too, and empty them into the cesspools of the city. But I can't find their bones, so you'll have to do. Take them." And I headed for the door.

In an instant the room was like lisir among the topa hens. The nobles were knocked unconscious by blows from lance butts. My mind was already far from the great hall, though. The Most High had come.

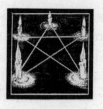

# XXVI

## A THICK TANGLE

Outside I quickly found the man who'd brought the message to the palace. He was a squat, heavyset warrior, with a cropped ear and the cheek tattoo that said he'd fought six years in the arenas of Caselle.

"What happened?" I asked. "This says only that the Most High came and then left without landing."

"It was like this, my lord. I was part of the guard on the Inner Wall, where the catapults are, and all of a sudden one of the Most High's flying carts appeared, coming in toward the palace. Well, we all knew they favored the Lantans. Some say that all the Lantans have been doing, the Most High put them up to. Anyway, we thought they were coming to try to change things back, to give the city back to the Lantans, and, well, the flying cart was right in front of us, so we took a shot at it with the catapult."

Mayra started muttering under her breath.

"And?" I said.

"We hit it, my lord." He grinned suddenly. "Didn't really think we'd do it, but we did. Knocked it three or four hundred paces sideways. Then the rock fell away, and for all it'd been the size of a horse, the cart flew away. But it was fluttering, my lord, fluttering and jerking like a wounded stingwing. Headed east, getting lower all the time."

"Towards the forest?" I asked.

"Yes, my lord, though it's no forest compared to what I saw—Well, it doesn't matter." He paused. "Do you think they'll be back, my lord?"

"I wouldn't doubt it."

He drew his blade and kissed it. "Maybe their spells won't work on cold iron, either. Eh, my lord?"

As soon as he walked away Mayra started cursing. At last she seemed to run down. "You'll have to go after it, Wulfgar. Those idiots on the wall may have caused more trouble than they dream."

"I intend to go. But they're not idiots, Mayra. There aren't many men who'd be brave enough to attack the Most High."

"There aren't many men with enough brains to—" She took a deep breath and got hold of herself. "When you find them, try to smooth things. Don't hurt any of them, can you avoid it. If you must, then kill all of them, cover it as best you can, and return to me as fast as you can ride. I'll try to cover it further."

"Mayra, how do you kill a Most High? *Can* you kill a Most High?"

"I don't know," she sighed. "No Sister of Wisdom has ever been able to penetrate their screens and wards. You'll just have to do the best you can, but only as an absolute last resort." She tapped the bag she'd given me, hanging beneath my tunic. "This will protect you, but I haven't time to prepare anything for whoever else you take. Keep them well away from the Most High. At close range they can do strange things to men's minds."

Remembering being frozen in a corridor of that very palace, I agreed. I'd keep the warriors back. I wanted none of my friends suddenly attacking me.

In minutes Orne had gathered a hundred lances, and we were riding out of the city. Part of that time had been spent in telling other warriors that they couldn't go with us. They felt that as long as the Most High were already against us, and we'd already struck the first blow, it might be well to strike the second as well, before the Most High could strike.

Finding our direction wasn't hard. A pillar of smoke rose to the sky, higher than the smoke from the fires in the Towers of Kaal. It led us east, along the road to Caselle, then to the south, away from the highway. Soon we could see that the smoke rose from a forest, or such as we would call a forest. There was a thick tangle of brush and vines, and trees twice the height of a man, some even three times. I've read of places where there are trees to dwarf those, but I've not seen one, and that was forest enough for me.

We dismounted at the edge of the trees. Immediately all of them wanted to go in with me.

"Only I have Mayra's protection," I explained. "If you follow me in, the Most High may be able to twist your minds so you'd attack me."

"But, my lord," Orne protested, "protections are all very good, but a sword is no weapon at all against the Most High."

"You're right. It isn't." I pulled the unstrung hunting bow I'd begun carrying from beneath my stirrup. Bracing it on my instep and behind my thigh, I strung it. "If a Most High can stop one of these shafts from inside fifty paces, it can have me."

Orne laughed halfheartedly. I didn't think it was such a grand jest, myself. Perhaps a Most High could stop the arrow in flight. There was only one way to find out.

As I entered the wood I nocked an arrow, but I didn't draw it. No man can hold a longbow at full draw for long. I moved from bush to bush, tree to tree, as carefully as if I stalked a fanghorn among the firz. The quarry I hunted could certainly be more dangerous than any fanghorn. Ahead I saw the source of the smoke. If it'd ever been a flying cart of the Most High, it was one no longer. Whatever it was, it burned so intensely I couldn't look directly at it. Even from the corners of my eyes it brought spots and pain. As I moved around it, I saw the Most High.

It sat watching the burning thing, its Staff of Power on the ground beside it. I say it watched, though there were no eyeholes in the hood it wore. Almost in the same instant that I saw it, it became aware of me. A three-fingered hand darted for the Staff, and my arrow took it from its very grasp.

I think that it was as surprised as I was when the pierced Staff began to hiss and crackle. Sparks jumped from it. Fingers of blue flame rose, and an acrid odor.

I was the first to recover, though. When it turned back to me, I had a shaft drawn to my cheek. Its hand moved slowly, as if groping for something else.

"Stop it," I said. "Stop it, or I'll see if those robes can stop this shaft." It stopped. "Now remove the hood."

"Don't you know, human," it trilled, "that it's death to see the face of the Most High?"

"I've heard it said, and I've been told to be diplomatic toward you. With the Most High, however, I don't feel very diplomatic. Remove the hood, and hope that I don't die. I'm holding this shaft by my fingertips. It'll be in your chest before I hit the ground."

Hesitantly it raised its hands and slid the hood off. I stood in shock. The Most High was a most ordinary-looking man, with some sort of box strapped to his throat.

"You won't survive this, you realize," he trilled.

"Remove the box."

With a shrug he unfastened the strap, and swung the box down to smash against a rock. He eyed it regretfully. "I don't think there's anybody left who can repair that," he said in an ordinary voice.

"Why did you do that?"

"Because," he said as if lecturing, "you now have only a man wearing robes like the Most High's. You certainly don't have a Most High to exhibit."

"I've no intention of exhibiting you. Sooner or later your friends would show up if I did. All I want are the answers to some questions."

He laughed. "And how do you intend to make me answer? My friends, as you call them, are already coming to rescue me. If you try to torture answers out of me, they'll be here before you could make me say anything useful to you. If you try to take me away, they'll follow. You won't like having the Most High decide you're a threat to them."

"If you don't answer," I said with a smile of my own, "I'll put this arrow through you, then throw your body in that fire. After that, let the rest of the Most High find out how you died. They'll probably think it happened in the crash."

His face tightened. "I suppose a blasphemous barbarian like you would do—"

"You don't look much like a living god to me right now, just another man. Men have names. What's yours?"

"Che Sen is good enough," he said sourly. "What are these questions of yours?"

I relaxed the draw on the bow, but kept both hands in place. He tensed a little, and I shook my head. "If you want to try your reflexes against mine, go ahead." He settled back immediately. "Now. Why? Tell me that. Why should you plot with the Lantans against us? And don't try denying it, or I'll end this talk now."

He knew my meaning well enough. "I won't deny anything. We did it because it's necessary that the Lantans found an empire."

"Necessary to whom?"

"To everyone. To this entire part of the world. Tribes of raiders, individual city-states, a dozen rulers, all warring. There can be no stability in that. Nations, empires, these bring stability, order."

"And this stability is important enough to destroy my people for?" I asked incredulously.

"Of course it's important enough." His voice rose. "It's essential that the raider culture be stamped out. You can't imagine the harm you'll do if you manage to maintain your hold on Lanta."

"What harm? We might raid a bit further east? We need the city. We need it as a base when the seasons go wild on the Plain. We need it to ensure that we can move our herds to lands with water, lands beyond Lanta, when the great heats come, and the deepest waterholes dry."

Che Sen appeared puzzled. "I'm surprised you thought of that. It should be beyond barbarians of your level. You should loot the city, enslave the inhabitants, and leave with what you can carry. Still, if you think you can remain simple herdsmen and raiders while you hold the city, you're mistaken.

Holding Lanta will destroy what you are as well as anything we can do. For you it might be best to loot the city and leave, after all."

"We'll stay, I think, and we'll stay what we are."

"You'll quit your herds and your raids to become empire builders."

"If that's so, why oppose us? What difference if it's Lantans' empire or ours?"

"The Lantans are traders, for all their scheming," he shouted angrily. "They'll make a stable, orderly empire. You, you're raiders and fighters, for all your herding and trading. Your empire will be turbulent, ever expanding. In ten years you'll be conquering the other cities on the Plain. In twenty years you'll be spreading beyond the Plain, to the north, the south, the east, in every direction. In fifty, who knows. You may challenge Caselle and Liau. Turmoil, constant agitation. This entire part of the world will be in flux for centuries." He stopped, suddenly calm. "You're Wulfgar, aren't you? The one who led the taking of the city?"

"I am."

"I was coming to meet you," he said, taking a small box from under his robe. "I was bringing you this. Just push this and—"

Suddenly the protections Mayra had given me grew warm against my chest. Che Sen gave a yell and threw the box spinning. He snatched off a three-fingered glove and cradled a normal hand to his chest, his face contorted in pain. The box lay on the ground glowing red, and then white. It began to soften and flow, melting a hole into the dirt. In moments there was only the hole, filled with molten metal. The protection grew cool again.

"Shall I take my try now, Che Sen?"

He looked up at me anxiously. "No! It was just a misunder—I mean—You had more questions." He was relieved, as if he knew he'd hit on the right thing. "You must have more questions."

"All right, then. A trade. Your life for answers. If the answers stop, your life does. If this"—I touched the protection under my tunic—"tells me you've lied, your life ends."

"You have something there to tell you if I lie?" he asked curiously.

"A Sister of Wisdom gave it to me," I said, avoiding the lie myself. After all, I didn't say it could tell me if he lied, only that I'd kill him if he did it.

He seemed to believe, though. He muttered something about witch women and settled back. "Ask. I'll answer truthfully as best I can. If that thing says my answer is wrong, it's because what I think is true isn't. Remember that, and don't be hasty."

"I won't be. Now tell me something about the Wanderers. Sometimes they carry strange weapons. Our metalsmiths can duplicate the weapons themselves, but the steel involved keeps the Sisters of Wisdom from telling us how to make the pellets fly. How is it done?"

"You can't. No, I'm not trying to put you off. The force that makes the pellets move comes from a powder. One of the substances needed to make the powder isn't available in this world any longer. At least, it isn't where you can get to it. I'm not even sure that we could."

"If you know that much, you must know what world they come from," I said quickly. "And if they can come here, I can go there and get the substance myself. How can I get there? Where do they come from?"

"They come from the same place you do, or from where your ancestors came, at any rate. And if I could send you there, I would. Only, you'd die on the way. Haven't you thought about the fact that all of the Wanderers are women? Actually, there are Wanderers from other species, too, but all of them are female. Haven't you wondered why you've never heard of one male Wanderer? There's something between their worlds and ours that is inimical to males. They aren't just killed, they cease to exist completely."

He must have thought me stupid not to see a hole in what he'd said. It was time to show him I wasn't a fool. "Your first lie, Che Sen," I said, drawing the bow, "and your last. If the men died when our ancestors came, how was there a second generation?"

"Wait!" He held up his hands like a shield. "Let me explain. Please." For someone masquerading as a living god, he didn't hide his fear very well.

"Then explain."

"Long ago," he began breathlessly, "thousands and thousands of years, we whom you call the Most High were the only inhabitants of this world. Many of the things you take for granted weren't here at all. No Runners, no fanghorns, no tussat. I could list them for hours. Some of us noticed what you call Wanderers, though, people, beings, animals, that weren't native to this world. Those men traced the Wanderers, trying to find out where they came from. They found it.

"Think of this world as a canal, like a dirtman's irrigation canal, dug across a wide flat area that stretches as far as the eye can see. Now imagine that there are other canals, parallel to this one, some wider, some deeper, some moving slower, some moving faster, but none ever touching. Those are the other worlds, the worlds the Wanderers come from, and the rest of you, also.

"The Wanderers were like bits of spray thrown up by a disturbance, caught by the wind and carried to another canal. Those men discovered how to reach out to those other worlds in order to gather specimens for study. Unfortunately, they were like a man standing on a boat in one canal throwing a bucket on the end of a rope at another canal while blindfolded. They could never be certain which canal their bucket would land in, or, if you think of the flow of the canal as the flow of time, when it would land.

"One time they might bring back some strange beasts, the next nothing but primordial slime. One time a group of fairly civilized humans, the next stone-age primitives, or Runners, or fanghorns, or a thousand other things. Several times the people or beings caught had weapons powerful enough to give trouble. There was considerable worry about them, but they were always eventually absorbed into the populations of the sequestrations they were put into."

"Sequestrations?"

"No matter. They don't exist any longer. Something was caught that didn't want to be caught, something powerful enough to fight being drawn here, to strike back. In the space of a single day civilization disappeared from this world. We dug ourselves out of the rubble, but we could barely help ourselves. We had to let the inhabitants of the sequestrations fend for themselves. Your ancestors rode out of one of those sequestrations, just as the ancestors of every civilized or uncivilized being on this world did, excepting only us."

"You've told me quite a lot, Che Sen."

"Have I?" He seemed surprised. "Well, if so, what does it matter? You can't make any use of it. Only one of your Sisters of Wisdom who put a truth-spell on you herself would believe it."

"But I can make use of it," I said. He looked disbelieving. "Perhaps no one would believe me, but what if rumors were spread about what you revealed to me? What if it was whispered that the Most High are only men hiding behind their hoods, that rather than being all-powerful living gods, they're barely hanging on to the scraps of the power they once had? What if the rumors say the Most High dabble in the affairs of men out of fear where men may go without their interference?"

His face was a sickly white. "A flyer would land in front of your tent, and Most High would kill you on the spot for blasphemy. And the word would be spread about what happened to the man who dared lie about the Most High."

"But you wouldn't hear it, would you." I smiled. He looked even sicker. "If they killed me, what would they do to one of their own who revealed all of this? You'd be dead before me."

"But it wouldn't change anything. You'd still die." A crack had appeared in his voice. He was ripe.

"I won't tell," I said, and he nearly collapsed with relief. "I'll just have Mayra make it into a rumor-spell. She won't like acting the rumormonger, but she'll do it for me. If I die by any action of the Most High, those rumors will spread, and every rumor will say it came from a Most High who calls himself Che Sen. So you'd better see that your friends decide it's better that I live, after all."

"But I'm not high enough to have a say in those things," he shouted.

"Try," I told him, backing away. "Try very hard."

The last sight I had of him was sitting there watching me, looking as if he'd like to think of something to make me change my mind. He didn't look happy. I thought he'd do it, though. It seems that Most High or not, men want to live.

Orne and the others were waiting nervously

when I came out of the forest. They were spread in a semicircle, weapons in hand, as if ready to fight should something besides myself emerge. Their relief was palpable.

"It was a Most High, my lord?" Orne asked. He looked me up and down as if to find some injury I might not tell him about.

"It was." I unstrung the bow, returned it and the sheaf of arrows to my saddle and mounted.

"And?"

"And nothing, Orne. I'm sorry, but I can't tell you what happened in there. You can understand that, when dealing with the Most High."

He didn't understand any such thing, but if I wanted no more questions, he'd ask none, and see that no one else asked any either.

"Where to now, my lord?"

"Back to Lanta, but only long enough to gather the lances. By nightfall I want everyone on the move north."

Behind us one of the Most High's flying carts glided like a giant wheel to land in the trees. We didn't even look back.

# XXVII

## A SMALL SPELL

Dawn had yet to come. Mondra had set an hour before, but Wilaf and t'Fie were still up. T'Fie headed north this time, cast aside in the battle with the others. I wished Mayra was there to cast the omens of that.

Below us lay the enemy camp. There was little light from the moons, but enough to see that the Morassa tents and the Lantans' were separate this night, not mingled in groups as they had been. Had a few more been sleeping, I'd have wished I had all three ten thousands with me, and not just one.

I nodded, and Orne put his hands to his mouth and gave the cry of a loto. Those night flyers seldom came this far north, especially once the cold came, but no one who shouldn't hear was both close enough and alive. The outer ring of sentries had already made a last acquaintance with Altaii steel. Answering cries rippled softly, and we moved forward.

The inner ring of sentries, standing within the light of torches ringed around the camp, shifted uneasily, looking at the men on either side of them. No doubt, after the past few days' happenings, they wondered if they actually heard horses walking out there in the darkness. And if they did, should an alarm be given, or would it be another useless stand-to? Finally, in several places along the line, men decided to give warning. They were too late. Before they had a horn to mouth, we were on them.

I lanced a sentry as I passed into the tents and caught another as he ran from a tent buckling on armor. The lance head caught in his chain mail, and I abandoned it. Throughout the camp screams of panic warred with shouts for order. Drawing the curved saddle sword, I pressed deeper into the encampment.

As I dashed down the lanes between tents I struck at those who came close enough, but I went out of my way for no one. I wanted tent ropes and tether lines for horses. Here and there fires flared as a collapsing tent failed to extinguish a burning lamp. Horses running free, panicked by the shouting and the fires, added to the confusion, breaking into the groups of Lantans trying to form, trampling running men.

Then some Lantan and Morassa horsemen began to appear, as warriors managed to gain their horses. One of them spotted me and, yelling wildly, couched his lance and charged. I'd given orders that no one was to accept combat if it could be avoided, but I moved to meet him anyway. I loosed the reins, guiding my horse with the pressure of my knees, and angled my shield across my body, sword arm trailing back. Screaming, the Lantan rushed at me, and, as his lance point touched my shield, I twisted the shield to send his lance over my shoulder. My sword slashed forward, my arm's force added to that of my charge. A shock traveled down my arm, and the Lantan rolled off the back of his horse.

I pulled to a halt, and Orne and my battle drummers joined me. Each of the two had a pair of large kettle drums fastened one on either side of his horse.

"It's time to be out of here," I shouted. The noise in the camp was getting louder, and no little of it was the sound of combat.

The drummers began beating out the message. From another part of the encampment it was answered, then another, and another. Even through the clash of arms and the screams of dying men and frightened horses, they could be heard clearly.

"Now, ride," I ordered.

As swiftly as we'd struck, that swiftly did we melt back into the darkness. Behind us was only death and turmoil. Many of the tents were burning, and no few of the supply carts, and the light they cast showed utter confusion.

Trumpets sounded. Orders came in shouts. Men

ran here and were then sent there. Formations were gathered, then broken up as men left to fight fires or gather horses. Men fighting fires or gathering horses were pushed into formations to await our next attack.

Slowly, though, order began to be restored. Reason seemed to gain the upper hand. Men moved to fight the fires. Others set at gathering the horses. The rest waited in formation, tidy lines and squares for the Lantans, loose groups for the Morassa, against another attack. The fires died, the horses were gathered, and the folding of the camp was begun. They were coming after us, all two hundred thousand or more of them. As I watched it, I laughed to myself. We had them, now. They were ours.

When I'd arrived from Lanta, I'd gone straight to Lord Dunstan, who'd led the two ten thousands who'd harassed the northern army. My first question was abrupt. "What about the fanghorns?"

He smiled. "There's not a one to be found. The last anybody's seen was closing in its den more than a tenday ago."

I heaved a sigh of relief. We needed the fanghorns in their dens and hibernating if we were to win.

The second thing I did was to take a package that Mayra'd given me from my saddle and find a secluded spot. There were two dolls in the bundle, a Lantan guardsman and a Morassa, and a packet of powders. I set a small fire and made an arrangement of cords to burn through slowly and drop the dolls and the packet of powders into the fire. Then

I left. It was bad enough for a man to be dabbling in magic. I didn't want to be around when the spell was actually invoked by the flames.

The enemy had protections and wards, of course, to keep magic from being used against them. If there'd been any hope of divining their next move, of spying on their councils, or better yet, of turning some of them against the others, of even laying a curse on them, Mayra would've come. Their protections and the wards would guard against things of that nature, though.

There was one small chance, a minor one, that their protection didn't cover everything. Often only the major points would be covered, spell-induced treason or plague and the like. The spell Mayra had given me, so minor I could work it myself, was an irritant. It was to make the Lantans and Morassa feel frustrated and on edge, to sharpen whatever natural feelings they had toward each other, but not enough to bring any counterspells into action. A little thing, but it might be enough to make them act without thinking when they desperately needed to think. It might be the edge we needed.

Before my arrival Dunstan and Bran had been harassing the enemy, keeping them off balance wondering where the next strike would be and when. Time and again they'd hit, sometimes with a hundred lances, sometimes with a thousand but never enough to be pinned and brought to battle by the unwieldy mass of the enemy. Foraging parties, wood and water details, scouting parties: None had been safe. When they went out without a heavy guard they disappeared, and when mere wood-gathering details grew to several thousand warriors, the raids shifted to the horse herds.

Forces sent out to hunt these raiders found only what Dunstan and Bran wanted them to find. If they were large, they found nothing but empty ground and campfires of two days ago. Were they smaller, to move faster, they found death.

This northern force hadn't managed to make its move south, yet. In fact, when I arrived they were farther north than they were when Dunstan and Bran first made contact. With my arrival, and the ten thousand lances I brought with me, we moved to full offense.

Some five or six hours after sunset on my first night, I ordered torches stuck in the ground in a huge circle around the enemy encampment. When they were lit, as close in succession as could be, panic reigned in the camp, alarms were sounded and confusion spread. To all appearances they were surrounded by a force as large as their own, or even larger. It was impossible for so many Altaii to be there. They knew that, but their eyes told them differently. All night they stood to arms, in a tight defensive formation, while we retired to our blankets, leaving only a few men on watch. Before dawn the torches were removed. I watched them search the next morning for clues as to who we were and how many, but all they found were the tracks of seemingly countless numbers of horses.

On the second night the torches were put in place again, and the Lantans and Morassa stood to again, waiting. Our watchers said there seemed to be many complaints from the Morassa about having to stay awake. Some of them went back into their tents and were nearly attacked by the Lantans.

The third night again the torches were placed. This time, after what appeared to be considerable arguing, a force of some ten thousand, half Lantan and half Morassa, was sent out. Obviously they were to discover what was there and force a move of some kind.

Between the torches and their camp, we were waiting for them with the short, curved horse bows. They never met the mounted masses they expected, but from behind every rock and bush and fold of ground war shafts emptied their saddles. Our horses were far to the rear, and the orders were to shoot anyone riding. Over a thousand of them fell without harming a single one of us, and when the others returned to camp, from the reaction among the rest of them, they must have told of facing invisible enemies, or of overwhelming numbers. They pulled in to tighter formations and moved their supply carts to form barriers. The whole they ringed with torches, so their camp was as well-lit as any palace room. We might be invisible, but if we used magic to sneak up on them, they'd at least see our presence by what we did. Except for watchers, we slept the rest of the night.

The next night they refused to come out, again awaiting our attack, and the next. On the fourth night there was muttering in the ranks, and on the fifth Lantan units came close to mutiny when Morassa began sleeping by their horses. The sixth day the enemy spent dividing their camp in an effort to keep open fighting from breaking out between the allies. That night most of the warriors were allowed to sleep, and we struck.

Now they followed us through the first light of dawn and into the day, south and east, into the rolling hills of the grasslands. We moved as slowly as we dared, as if keeping our horses rested for a long chase, careful never to break contact completely. The last men in our line, on topping a ridge, could often see the first of them, topping a ridge behind us.

They followed us slowly, but surely. Their slowness was to allow the Lantan infantry to keep up. Our scouts began reporting that the Morassa seemed to be arguing for the mounted warriors to be sent on ahead to close with us. The Lantan cavalry also appeared to be arguing for it. Tempers were flaring, the scouts said. It appeared that small spell was working.

I called for Orne, and he rode up beside me. "How are their infantry keeping contact? I don't want to move fast enough for them to take the Morassa suggestion and leave them behind."

"They're keeping up," he grunted, "but barely. Any warrior on the Plain could keep this pace all day, sleep or no, even a Morassa. What am I saying? Even a boy could keep it. These Lantans are supposed to move and fight on foot, but they're soft."

"As long as they're keeping up. Have the scouts keep a close watch on them. If they begin to lag we'll have to slow our march."

"But why, my lord? Without them it'll just be that much easier for us. And alone, with no horsemen to scout and cover them, they'll be all but useless."

"You know better. You've faced infantry in the open field before. Well led, they're far from useless, and we'd better assume these are well led until we know differently. Anyway, I wouldn't leave them if they were fresh-recruited dirtmen. I won't leave sixty thousand Lantans in an organized body to form a rallying point. I won't leave one thousand."

"Very well, my lord. We'll take the infantry with us if we have to carry them on our horses."

We continued south and east until sunset. Always the enemy stayed at our heels. No doubt they thought they were driving us before them according to their plan. Perhaps they even thought we constituted the entire force that had been harassing them. Whatever they thought, they followed us until sunset, until after sunset, so eager were they. An hour after dark came, our scouts reported that they'd finally made camp. Even then, apparently, there'd been some argument for continuing the pursuit.

They made their camp with no tents and no fires,

a battle camp. We made the same, and fed on dried meat and fruit, with lukewarm water tasting of waterskins to wash it all down. Half of us slept while the other half kept watch. Our scouts were on constant patrol around their camp, but I'd take no chances of being surprised as they had been, with my men trying to wake up and begin fighting all in the same moment.

Before sunrise the chase began again. Our scouts rode in to report that the enemy was breaking their camp without so much as a single torch. They hoped to catch us in our blankets. When they arrived, though, we were gone.

There was something different about their pursuit that morning. They pressed. Despite the tiredness of their warriors, despite the infantry trying to keep up, they pressed. Time and again Lantan mounted units or masses of Morassa broke away to push harder, only to be argued back by the Lantan officers. The Morassa were close to blows with the men who held them in check. The frustrations were boiling, the angers building. If they'd only hold for one more hour. I needed an hour.

I sent Orne for a messenger.

"My lord," the youth said. He'd been chosen for his small size, and given the fastest horse I could find.

"You know the message?"

"Yes, my lord." His mount arched its neck and took two quick steps. He held it back, but he was leaning, waiting for the command.

I handed him my messenger's scarf. "Go."

He dashed away as if the wand had dropped to begin a race, leaning low over his mount's neck. In the flicker of an eye he was over the next hill and gone. I'd no worry about him running the horse out. It had been chosen for endurance as well as speed, and he had brains to go with his light weight to qualify him.

But I still needed an hour. The grasses were taller, now, most as high as a man's shoulder. Some clumps were as tall as a man on horseback. All had their seedpods open, shaking in the wind, dropping the seed that would be covered by the winter snows and sprout in the spring. Shaking in the wind.

"Orne!"

"Yes, my lord?"

"Tell the scouts to get closer. Wherever there's an area of tall grass large enough for them to avoid capture, let them move about in the grass so it sways as if there was more than one man in it. There's nothing else up here this time of year would do it, so they'll have to investigate, and if they investigate, the commanders will slow their march."

"But Lord Wulfgar, won't that make them suspicious?"

"The commanders perhaps, Orne, but I know for certain that their commanders aren't going to give in to their feelings beyond a certain point. I'm counting now on their individual warriors."

"Very well, my lord. It's as good as done."

The sun was hot, although it was early, for this

was the Plain, if the edge of it, but the wind was out of the north. It bit through the bone, then ate into the marrow. The winter coming would be a hard one on the Plain.

The trick with the tall grass no longer delayed them. They were coming harder, now. Their forward scouts had us in sight all the time, now. Soon they'd move.

We rode through an opening in a ridgeline out onto a broad, flat valley surrounded by three ridges in a three-point. We pushed through the grass faster. By the time the enemy's scouts entered the valley, the last of us had disappeared over the far ridge. They galloped wildly across the valley, desperate not to lose sight of us, and wrenched their horses to a halt short of the ridge as we appeared on the crest, ten thousand Altaii lances spread in a crescent and holding the high ground.

The rest of the enemy was pushing hard to catch us, too. The first of them had nearly reached the center of the valley in their haste before they realized that we were waiting. Their officers managed to gain control and stop their headlong charge, but others, following behind, piled into them. Men and horses milled around in confusion. Among orders shouted, and counter-orders, men moved off as if to attack and were forced back by their officers.

I laughed. "Look at them, Orne. The soldiers want to attack, but their commanders fear a trap. Look at them studying the skylines, watching for more of us to appear."

"I'd feel better about it, Lord Wulfgar, if we'd a hundred thousand lances behind those ridges," he muttered. "Are you ready for the signal?"

"Not yet, my friend, not yet. We must wait for their infantry to join."

"If they don't attack first," he grumbled, and moved for a better view through the gap to the Plain beyond. He drew the long-handled ax he favored instead of a sword and rested it across his saddle.

# XXVIII

## A CURTAIN OF STEEL

~

Below, the Lantans and Morassa were beginning to bring order to their forces. The Lantan cavalry had formed into symmetrical ranks, while the Morassa made a great point of not being in anything approaching a formation. They did gather in groups around their battle leaders, though.

Among the Lantan officers and commanders there was much riding back and forth, much conferring. There was no need for a Sister of Wisdom to tell me what they were discussing. What was going to happen next, and even more, why what had already happened had occurred. We obviously couldn't fight so many with so few. But then, why had we turned to face them? On the other hand, if there were more of us hidden somewhere, if there were indeed enough of us to face them, why hadn't we attacked? Why wait and dispel both the element of surprise and the chance presented by their disorder? The discussion went on, but when Morassa entered it, it began to degenerate. The arm gestures grew wider, more strident. Men stood in their stirrups, and fists were shaken. At last they broke apart and cantered back to their respective units. I didn't think they'd resolve their questions, but they were definitely more at swords' points than ever.

"My lord," called Bartu, "the infantry. It comes."

They entered the valley at a walk, their measured tread pounding the ground like a drum. No one had thought to send a messenger to them, but their officers had seen the rest of the army waiting ahead and slowed the step until they could see what it was they faced.

Once they were inside, and could see us clearly, they moved to a trot. Still no one broke the step. They were well trained, these Lantans, for all Orne's contempt for men who walked to fight, as fine as any infantry in the world.

Their death-walkers moved out in front of the formations, taking their huge, stomping steps, whirling the tundun over their heads. The leaping, stamping steps were meant to intimidate. The long, narrow pieces of wood swung on the ends of long cords made noises like blood pounding in a dying man's ears, or like the roar of giant flies settling on corpses. They made a fine show, this Lantan infantry and its death-walkers. I wondered how well they would die.

The horsemen before us split, the Lantans sharply,

the Morassa as if they wondered what was happening. The infantry marched into the gap and halted on a shouted command. The death-walkers faded back into the formation, and as one they swung their shields to overlap, forming a solid shield wall. The front two ranks leveled their spears, and the rest held theirs at the ready.

We were faced then with the whole northern army. In the center was six times our number of infantry. The two wings of cavalry numbered half again that many each. Their banners, whipping colorfully in the wind, seemed to outnumber our lances.

"It's time, my lord?" asked Orne.

"It's time," I replied. With a grunt of satisfaction he returned the ax to its loop on his saddle and dismounted. "Now, drummers," I commanded, joining him on the ground.

As the drums began to pound out their signal I took the hunting bow from under my stirrup and strung it, briefly thinking of Elspeth. With an oversized sheaf of arrows I walked forward onto the front slope of the ridge. Three out of every four warriors joined me there, and each had a longbow in his hand. *Salvation rests on the bow.*

The remaining quarter of the warriors moved behind the crest with the horses. It hadn't been an easy job to convince them to do it. Finally I'd had to say that if any of the horsemen broke through, they were free to take them.

Suddenly shouts rose from the enemy below. Men

pointed, and heads swung round, and with every head that swung there was more shouting. On the ridges behind them were my remaining ten thousands. Like those with me they were split, one in four with the horses, the rest in front of the ridgelines, bows in hand. On the day I arrived in the north they'd split away. Since then they'd waited, impatiently I was sure, for the message the youth had brought, the message to move onto the ridges. Now we stood waiting, and the enemy was below us, surrounded.

Frantically units shifted, formations moved to face this new threat. They were on edge, but there was nothing of panic in their movements. They still outnumbered us heavily. They would roll over us as if we were a pebble on the road.

An argument broke out between the Morassa leaders and the Lantan commanders. Fingers pointed, at the Lantan troops, at the Morassa, at us on the ridges. Evidently there was some dispute over who should be attacked first, and by whom. Morassa fists shook, and Lantans gestured angrily. Might they not finish each other off for us?

Then, as suddenly as it had begun, the argument was over. The Lantans moved back to their units, the Morassa back to theirs. Slowly the Morassa moved away from the Lantans. All of them. They swirled about in apparent confusion, but finally divided themselves into three parts, one facing each ridge. I began to realize that the Lantans intended to dispose of the Morassa as well as us. If they constantly formed the first wave of attack, there wouldn't be enough of them left when it was all over to cause any trouble.

Our drums began to play again, a battle beat, and the war flutes joined in. The masses of horsemen began to move, rolling forward in a tide that gained speed with every step. Their war cries drifted ahead of them, shrill in the cold air.

I nocked an arrow and drew it back to rest on my cheekbone, the bow held high. *Salvation rests on the bow.* Almost gently I released the string, and the long arrow arched high into the air. Fifteen hundred paces away the broad-head shaft, meant for killing fanghorn, fell. By chance it plunged into a Morassa's chest, and he fell to be trampled beneath the hooves of the charge. I don't think any of the others noticed.

They had to notice the flight that followed, though. Twenty-five hundred shafts struck from the sky to tear gaping holes in their ranks. And then another twenty-five hundred. And then another. And then the first rank was ready to fire again. No sooner did one flight rise than another rose to follow. The charging Morassa rode through a curtain woven of steel. Horses and men fell by the hundreds at each flight, never to rise again. On the survivors came.

At four hundred paces we no longer fired volleys. Each man picked individual targets out of the thundering throng. I fell into the rhythm. Nock an arrow, draw, and release. Nock, draw, release.

Saddle after saddle we emptied, and still they came, riderless horses keeping pace with the charge. At one hundred and fifty paces we no longer aimed just for the man, but for the heart, the throat or even the eye slit in his helmet. Of those who fell now, all fell dead, and no fewer fell than before. The hail of arrows continued, but the Morassa came on, wound to the breaking point by frustration, pushed beyond it by friction with the Lantans. They no longer cared about their losses, only the chance of killing us.

At seventy-five paces, at the very foot of the ridge, they hit the stakes. Sharpened on both ends and driven into the ground by those who had waited here, they formed a tangled barrier hidden by the grass. We'd known they were there and picked our way through. The Morassa hit them at full gallop.

Horses screamed and thrashed on the stakes. Many a rider, thrown from an impaled horse, was himself impaled in falling. Those who made it to the ground safely and rose died by Altaii arrows.

The attack had degenerated into a milling mass, swirling at the bottom of the ridge. Volley upon volley we fired into it at point-blank range. Some of them tried to use their horse bows, but so fierce was our fire that not an arrow of theirs reached us.

In a twinkling they broke. One instant they were still trying to fight, to force a way through the stakes, and the next they were streaming back across a field strewn with their dead and dying. From the other ridges also, broken remnants of the attack flowed back to safety in the center of the valley. And all the way, until they were out of bow-shot, our arrows pursued them. *Salvation rests on the bow.*

The Lantan officers rode up and down their lines, exhorting their men, rousing them to fever pitch. They would have to carry the attack now. The Morassa might be induced to charge again, but for the present they would have to carry the battle. Carry it they might. Even with the valley floor covered with Morassa dead, they outnumbered those of us who stood to face them by more than ten to one.

"Orne," I called, "any sign?"

He grunted. I knew as well as he did that the signal we awaited hadn't come. "They're late," he said.

"They'll come. They'll come." I flexed the fingers of my right hand. With so much use the bowstring was cutting them.

"They'd better come soon, my lord. Almost half of our arrows are gone, and I doubt we'll have a chance to recover even those at the foot of the slope."

"They'll come," I repeated.

They'll come. I wasn't as sure of that, myself, as I had been. But then, they had to come. If the signal was never given we couldn't hope to hold. But the wind was quickening. It whipped at our cloaks and rippled the grass that hadn't been trampled in waves toward the entrance of the valley. Toward the entrance. An omen, perhaps. They would come.

In the valley the infantry was moving to the fore. The Lantan horse mingled with the Morassa in an attempt to stiffen them again. If their commanders had thrown off all of the frustration, if battle had cleared their heads, we could be in trouble.

If the infantry was concentrated against my formation in the center, and the horsemen were massed and set at my flanks, the open spaces between my warriors and those on the other ridges, they might succeed in isolating most of my men from the fight. Did it happen, the men with the horses had orders to move to the open areas and use their horse bows. And there were stakes there, also. But the horse bows hadn't the power or range of the longbow. They'd force a way through the stakes eventually. We'd be forced to mount our horses to avoid being overrun. It wouldn't be a defeat, but a great mass of Lantans and Morassa would still be at large, sweeping south. Would the signal never come?

The Lantan infantry split into three parts. I heaved a small sigh of relief. Mayra's charm still worked. The desire to get at those who had eluded them still fogged their minds.

Each formation moved to face a ridge. Their death-walkers were out again, dancing and whirling the tundun. The thrumming noise was loud enough where I stood. Precisely, as if on a drill field, the formations divided, and again, until they were in squares of no more than a hundred men each.

Some thinking had gone on, although in a fog of anger and frustration. Units of that size would be easier to maneuver through the stakes. They expected losses, when the stakes made too many breaks in a shield wall, but they also expected to reach us this time.

Twenty thousand infantry stepped off toward us, the death-walkers prancing between the formations. At a command, each rank in every formation, excepting the front rank, lifted their shields overhead to form what they called the turtle. Every single shield flashed up at the same instant, as one. And they came on, their steps steady and measured.

With the turtle they'd taken away the plunging fire we'd used before. The falling arrows would strike the angled shields and be deflected. They'd march right up to us in safety under a roof of shields, these infantry.

The death-walkers danced more furiously. The tundun seemed solid blurs in the air. They danced the glory of our deaths, the glory of killing us. The shining disks that covered their shins were plain, now, and the fur bands they wore instead of helmets. I could even make out individual saratai feathers hanging from their wrists. They danced the joy of battle.

At two hundred paces I drew shaft to cheek. Along the ridge others did the same.

A rhythmic grunt of cadence could be heard,

and the slap as twenty thousand sandals struck the ground on one beat. The death-walkers leaped high. They danced the drinking of our blood.

At one hundred paces my shaft joined two thousand others and more, and the Lantans learned that a Lantan shield could stop a longbow shaft at that distance no better than the Altaii shield on the post in front of my tent so long ago. *Salvation rests on the bow.*

As grass before the scythe the first rank fell, and those behind, their shields raised, exposed, were swept away as well by the flights that followed. In the space of moments, in the time it took to fire ten arrows as fast as they could be fired, the first row of formations ceased to exist.

The others continued their slow advance. Their steps never faltered or slowed. The death-walkers danced harder, leaped higher. They danced revenge for the blood we shed.

The second row of formations came, and at one hundred paces they died. As the last snow under the first rainfall, they melted away. Their bodies added to the pile stretching across the foot of the ridge.

In the third row, short of the hundred paces, all lowered their shields. They were too close to be affected by the plunging fire. With a cry they rushed to climb over the mound of bodies and close with us.

Their shields weren't any harder, though, than those who'd come before. A shield, pinned to its bearer's arm, dropped slightly, baring his throat, and he died. A man with an arrow growing out of his helmet's eye slit fell back, and falling grabbed the shield of the man behind him, baring his chest to death. As the others had fallen, so these fell, and now the heaped bodies were so high that the last rank broke trying to scramble over them.

Our fire continued unabated, and suddenly the survivors of those under our bows broke. They washed back into the next line, breaking into formations, tearing open shield walls, carrying panic in their hands. The holes they opened made a way for our arrows, and the combination was more than the men could take. Their comrades fleeing, or our fire, either one they could've taken alone, but not together. They broke as the others had broken, and all fled back into the rest of the attack, breaking it in turn.

Our arrows pursued them as they ran. Many a Lantan, his shield thrown away so he could run faster, died with the sight of safety in his eyes and the breath of panic in his throat.

The field before us looked like a slaughterhouse built by a mad god. The tall grass was all trampled, held down by the bodies of men and horses. Had I desired such a thing, I could have walked nearly to the enemy on a carpet of flesh, never once touching the ground.

Lord Dunstan came to me, his cloak wrapped around him against the wind. "The arrows are almost all gone, Wulfgar. It was a grand plan, but we'll not stop them again."

"I know," I sighed. "I'd hoped, Dunstan, that—" I studied the enemy and shook my head. Already the infantry, what was left of it, was beginning to re-form. And the Morassa had recovered enough to be arguing with the Lantan horsemen. "Three to our one still alive and unhurt. Perhaps four. It looks like we'll have to face them, just the same. Dunstan, if you'll—"

"My lord, the signal," shouted Bartu, pointing.

Across the valley, from the crest near the opening out onto the Plain, an arrow rose into the sky, an arrow tipped with flame.

"Drummers," I called, "the second signal. Orne, the prisoners. Quickly, for your lives."

The war flutes fell silent as the drums shifted from battle rhythm to a message. On the other ridges the Altaii there faded over the crest, and on mine all excepting myself, Orne and a hundred men. I stood, watching the entrance to the valley, as Orne and the others raced down through the stakes to begin searching among the bodies there. If they took too long I would have to call them to hide where they were.

The enemy appeared confused. To all appearances we'd been winning. Now we seemed to retreat. Their arguments grew fiercer. They were on the point of drawing weapons.

The men hunting among the dead hurried back

up the ridge. Some now carried burdens, bodies slung over a shoulder or dragged between two men. They disappeared behind the crest, and I followed.

"How many?" I asked.

"Fourteen Lantans," Orne replied. "Eleven Morassa. And all sound enough to survive the march south."

We crept back up to look at the valley. Only the enemy was there. In some way their formation looked like a huddle of men on the edge of breaking completely.

Then, through the entrance to the valley sped riders, Altaii riders. Three, five, nine, a dozen. I breathed deeply and relaxed for the first time in a long time. All of them had made it. I'd not liked what I asked them to do, but they'd all returned, and that made it better.

The riders split, riding in two great arcs around the enemy force. They came on the run, slowing only to make their way through the stakes, and pounding over the ridge. They were young men, all men not so far from youth as to have forgotten how to do what they'd been asked to. When they rode in among us, the warriors raised a cheer, both mine and those from the other ridges, joining us on the backslope.

Some of the Lantan officers, curious as to where those young riders had come from, rode out to the valley entrance. Perhaps they thought that these were the first of our reinforcements. When they saw the reinforcements the riders had brought, their screams could be heard behind the ridge where we were.

Into the valley poured Runners. And more Runners. And still more Runners. Like the sands carried by the wind they came, an endless blue stream. As they sighted the Lantans and the Morassa their chants rose in pitch, the cadence increasing. Without stopping, or even slowing, they waded into the northern army that had come to found an empire. Their great clubs and war hammers swung, and the screams of our enemies were almost loud enough to drown their chants. In minutes the entire floor of the valley was a cauldron, seething with combat, and from this battle there would be no human survivors.

The Runners fear almost nothing that lives, but even so fanghorns fear less, and they're harder to kill. For that reason the Runners don't come north, where the fanghorn's numbers are greatest, until the cold comes and the fanghorns are sleeping the winter away in their dens. Then they come in countless numbers. As the fanghorns seem to need the cold, so too do the Runners, but for what no one can say.

The young men who'd brought them had been sent for that purpose, but their task had been harder than simply running a pack of Runners. They had had to find as many Runner packs as they could, run each of them, maneuver them toward the valley, and yet, by using relays, keep them following in their tireless run until my message that we brought the enemy was relayed to them. If they'd cut it fine, I wouldn't complain. The singers would make songs about them.

The lances were mounted and waiting. All ignored the sounds drifting over the ridge. I lifted my hand, and we rode away without looking back to the valley where our enemies were dying. This battle was past. There was another waiting in the south, and we might yet see defeat and death for our people.

# XXIX

## TO COME SO FAR

When we rode into Bohemund's camp, no little bedraggled from a hard march, we were greeted with cheers and shouts. Women ran out to hold their children up to see us, and men waved banners. Boys ran alongside our horses, strutting as if they, too, were part of our force. Drums and flutes played to welcome us.

We weren't far in before the mass greeting us had pressed in to merge with us. Garlands were hung from saddles, and girls tied flowers in the horses' manes.

I was more interested in what I could learn from the camp. For one thing, it was farther north than I'd hoped it would be. The king must have had trouble in slowing the southern force of the enemy. For another thing, the camp was larger than I'd expected it to be. Much larger.

I managed at last to break away from the celebration and ride to King Bohemund's tent. He was waiting when I swung from the saddle, him and Mayra.

"It's good to see you, Wulfgar."

"And you, also, my king." I started to ask if there was news of Harald, then let the question die unasked. If news there was, he'd tell me. If not, I'd not prod his wounds.

"And me, Wulfgar?" asked Mayra. "Are you glad to see me?"

"You know I am. Why should I not be?"

"There are reasons."

"Let's discuss this inside," said Bohemund. "Shout things to the wind and anyone may hear."

Bohemund waited until his servants had brought us chairs and cups of wine, then sent them away. "What Mayra says is true, I suppose. It's known. Soon it'll be known to everyone."

"What is known?" I asked.

Mayra studied the wine in her cup. Her hands wove a symbol in the air. There was nothing there, but I blinked for some reason, and behind my eyelids I could see the symbol glowing darkly, as an afterimage of fire. "Three times in less than a year, Wulfgar, you've been the nexus and the focus of powers that most males aren't allowed close to once in a lifetime."

"You think it might be dangerous? It doesn't matter. If it's needed, I'm not afraid." I lied when I said it, and I think she knew I lied. A threat I could face

I wouldn't fear, but these unnamed powers were something else.

She sighed and leaned back. "I don't know. I wish I could tell you, yes or no, but I don't know. It's affected you already. Whenever I cast the rune-bones for you now, the patterns are hard to read. There are strange things in them, portents that defy any interpretation I can think of."

And Moidra had said she was the most powerful Sister of Wisdom among the Altaii, one of the most powerful in this part of the world. If she couldn't interpret my rune-bones—I could see she wasn't finished. "What else?" I asked hollowly.

"You've been affected physically, too," she began slowly. "You don't look any younger, but you move like a youth in the first flush of his adult manhood."

It was how I'd felt when she and I faced Daiman and Betine below the Palace of the Twin Thrones.

"You're stronger, too, or else you recover more quickly. The men who rode in with you look like they've fought hard and traveled the length of the Plain, riding hard all the way. A year ago you'd have looked the same. Right now you look as if the hardest thing you've done in the last tenday was tell Sara to bring more wine."

"Those I can live with." I laughed. "In fact, if that's all there is, I recommend every warrior go through it."

"And then there's the matter of your eyes," she went on as if I hadn't spoken. She sounded troubled, more so than before. "They look the same, unless you stare into them. I noticed it first before you left Lanta, but it wasn't until I became aware of the other things that I realized what it might mean. When I stare into those eyes it's as if there's something behind them, a tunnel stretching off into forever, a feeling of limitless space and endless time."

"And what does all of that mean?" The hollow tone was back.

"You've become a link, Wulfgar, a connector between this world and powers beyond. I'm not saying you have any powers of your own," she added quickly. "You're not the first male to become a Sister of Wisdom, or would it be brother, but I've never heard of a male being such a link before. You're going to be the focus of events, and not always events of your choosing or liking. You'll be a catalyst, setting off things by your mere presence, even if you do nothing."

"Considering that, will it be safe for me to ride with the lances in the battle to come? Could my presence turn the tide against us in some way?"

Bohemund spoke before Mayra could. "If you're stuffed with enough magic to draw lightning bolts at every step, I still want you with me. I'm beginning to think that, that Harald is dead, though Mayra says she can find no sign of it. But if they've taken the son of my blood from me, I still have the son of my raising."

"And the son of your raising won't bring defeat to the Altaii rather than stay away from battle," I said gently. "And I swear to you, I'll return the son of your blood to you or bring you the head of him who killed him."

"Before you go any further," Mayra broke in, "it will have no effect that I can find on the outcome of the battle. If you're there or somewhere else, we still have small chance of winning."

We sat in silence on that. There wasn't anything to be said. Mayra looked tired, and Bohemund seemed resigned. If I looked the way I felt, I looked worse than either of them: To come so far and through so much, and still find that it might not be enough.

Bohemund sent for the other commanders, and they arrived with Moidra, who swept to a seat beside Mayra. We sat in an arc in front of the map table, Dunstan and I, Bran and Shen Ta, Otogai and Karlan. Bohemund faced us grimly.

"Since we all met last, there have been changes in what we face. The Lantans have stripped every guardsman from every post and garrison they have." He smiled tightly. "It'd be a time for raiding, with none but boys and old men to stop us. But we're not raiding, and the men they've pulled away have joined the army. That army now numbers more than six hundred thousand."

There were involuntary gasps. At the Heights of Tybal both armies together had not been so many. None of us had ever heard of an army that large, not even in Caselle or Liau.

"To face them we have some ninety thousand.

That's more than I believed could possibly get here, but many of them are weary from the march."

"We've fought at worse odds," Bran said.

"But never with so much riding on the outcome. I'll let Mayra speak to you now, but not a word of what she says must be repeated outside this tent. She's put wards around it to prevent eavesdropping. She can't do it for the entire camp, so don't tell your most trusted men."

Mayra stood, but for a moment she smoothed the front of her robes and looked at the rugs, silently. When she looked up her face was bleak. "Normally, I wouldn't be speaking to you. These aren't normal times. Both armies have been screened against being found by magic. I've clouded things so that ours can't be found by the spell-tracks of the screening, and the enemy's Sisters of Wisdom have done the same for them. So much is normal."

"And what is not normal, Sister?" asked Otogai.

"In this battle, magic will play a part. In the actual battle."

Silence greeted her words. Stunned silence. It was unheard of. Wards and protections were set to stop the use of magic and spells to hinder. The presence of so much iron and steel was enough to stop any direct magic against an army. It couldn't be.

"How?" I asked at last.

"I told you that Sayene had tapped powers greater than are normal. What I didn't say was that she intends to use those powers against you in the battle. She's so confident now she doesn't take enough precautions. Her actions and intentions are detectable."

From Bohemund's face I could see he'd heard this before, and hadn't liked it then any better than now. Dunstan and the others looked like men watching their own funeral fires being built.

"What can she do? Or more importantly, what can we do?"

"You can win, Wulfgar. In fact, you have to. Moidra and I will try to block Sayene, but with this new power of hers, we have to draw on something. We intend to draw on you, on the lances. While you fight with steel, we will fight Sayene and Ya'shen with magic. So long as you're winning we'll be able to hold them. If you begin to lose, our block will fail. Their Sisters of Wisdom will be able to reach you with the new power."

"And if they do?"

"I don't know," she said wearily. "It's hard for me to read anything concerning this power. All I can say is that it will be horrible."

Bohemund spoke again. "Now you know. We face more than we've ever faced before, and if we lose, we may cease to exist. Our entire people may cease to exist."

"Death is death," Karlan said. "Some ways are worse, some are better, but in the end they're all the same. When do we march?"

"You brought the prisoners?" Bohemund asked, and I nodded. "Then tonight they'll manage to escape and steal horses. With fear to speed them they should make it to their army in two days, judging by what our scouts tell me. You all know how the rumors of Wulfgar's victory outran him coming south. In the close confines of an army on the march, there'll be no way for Brecon or Elana to get to these men before they've spread it that the northern army is no more. Whatever magic Sayene has, the individual horsemen and infantry will know themselves alone. And once they're questioned by Brecon and the queen, they'll tell how fast and how hard the forced march was that Wulfgar made. The logical assumption is that we'll remain in camp, or if we move, move slowly away from them in order to rest the lances who've come from the north." He grinned wolfishly. "Therefore, tomorrow we will cross the River Xandra, and in another day we'll bring them to battle before the Great Ravine."

# XXX

## DRUMBEATS

—

The Great Ravine is a gouge, such as might be made by a rock thrown down the side of a sand hill. But it's not on the side of a hill. It stretches across the southern Plain, through dirt and clay and rock. All the way to the sea it stretches, wider and deeper, until it runs into a great bay. It's not a dry riverbed, or any other thing I know. But it made a good place to hide an army.

All of us were there, mounted and waiting. All except Dunstan. With ten thousand lances he'd continued on down the Ravine. Never split your forces, so say the maxims. But we'd done it and won two great victories. Perhaps we could do it again and win another.

Mayra walked up to my horse. She was already sky-clad. Her acolytes were laying out the five-pointed star on the bottom of the Ravine with Moidra guiding them. They, also, were sky-clad.

She pressed a bag into my hand. "Take this. Keep it with you. I just cast the rune-bones for you. The signs are just as strange as before, but one thing is clear. You're going to need this."

It was heavy, and I was certain I'd seen it before. "What is it?"

"The sky-stone from Lanta, the one with the Terg carved into it. Keep it close by you at all times."

I couldn't see how I'd need the oath-stone in the middle of a battle, but if she said it was needed, I'd carry it. I hung the bag around my neck.

The sky was darkening, strange, oily black clouds boiling from out of nowhere. The wind was growing sharper, too, but it seemed unpleasantly warm, and it had a foul smell. My horse shifted nervously. He wanted to leave this place.

Mayra looked at the odd clouds, too. "Sayene's new powers don't like the sunlight." She shivered slightly, despite the warm wind. "Come back from this, Wulfgar."

I touched her shoulder. "I'll try, Mayra."

She moved back toward her spell-star, and I toward the Ravine's edge. We each had our own place in the battle to come.

———

At the bottom of the slope lay nearly half a hundred Lantans and Morassa, tightly bound, most nursing wounds. They were luckier than their fellow scouts. The rest of the enemy's advance screen hadn't survived. These didn't seem grateful for their sparing.

Near the rim Bohemund sat waiting patiently. While the rest of us waited nervously for we knew not what, he merely waited. What came, came. I think he'd decided for certain now that he'd never see Harald again. He waited for the chance to get in among those who'd taken his son.

Slight sounds drifted to us over the edge, slight at first, that is, but growing louder. Jingling of armor. Clatter of hooves. Creak of harness. Tramp of feet. Louder they grew, sharper, closer. They came thinking the way was clear to the Xandra. If it wasn't, wouldn't their scouts have reported it?

"Now," said Bohemund.

Down the ranks ran a sharp cry, and we spurred up and over the rim, forty thousand strong. As we came onto level ground our enemy was spread out before us, no more than a thousand paces away.

They were in marching order, strung out and disorganized. The sight of us sent them into utter confusion. Some units tried to form to face us. Some merely spurred toward us, trusting to their numbers to drive us under.

The numbers didn't save them. Those who came to meet us we rode down. The rest had little time to re-form their ranks, tangled and broken from the march, before we were on them, and then in among them, carving deeper and deeper into the body of the enemy.

The Lantans abandoned the attempt to form. The Morassa never tried. The battle became a thousand individual fights, ten thousand, forty thousand. Soon their numbers would begin to overwhelm us.

My lance took a Morassa in the chest, and a Lantan, trying to close with me on foot, went down under steel-shod hooves. A small knot of infantry attempted to form in front of me. Before their shields could form the wall, I broke through, the sheer weight of my horse sending some flying, scattering the rest. For now we ranged free, but soon the numbers would begin to tell. Soon.

A sound came to me above the clash of steel, above the cries of dying men and the screams of horses. The sound rose, growing louder, coming closer. The sound of Altaii drums. The last thought of the man who faced me at that moment must have been that I was mad, for I laughed. Beating his sword from my throat, I laughed. If the war gods of Lanta smiled, they smiled on the Altaii.

Dunstan, who'd gone south, was coming. Dunstan and his ten thousand lances, who'd circled far to the south and east to come up behind the enemy, was coming. As we fought deeper into our foe's ranks from the front, they struck from the rear.

Every Altaii who heard those drums redoubled his efforts. Before we'd no idea how long we must stay in the cauldron until Dunstan arrived. Now we knew the linking was only moments away, and every heartbeat seemed to take an hour. For that short, endless space of time we fought and bled and killed and died, clinging to our tenuous hold in the midst of our enemies. And then he was there.

Bursting out of the middle of a knot of Morassa he came, lancing one, knocking another flying with his shield. He pulled up with a flourish. "Is this private sport, Wulfgar, or can I take a hand?"

"The sport is now a race," I called back. "Ride, if you've a thought of seeing tomorrow."

We'd hacked our way into the Lantans and Morassa. Now we had to hack our way back out again. The drummers signaled the fallback. Men broke away from fighting in mid-sword-stroke to start on the way. Enemy warriors, pressing to keep contact, jammed in on their own ranks. Confusion ran higher than at any time in the battle. The enemy didn't seem to understand what was happening. They flowed like a mindless mass, thickening and swelling while we pulled away.

Those of us who still lived smashed our way out of the tangle and sped back toward the Ravine. None followed us from the Lantans or Morassa. Their officers and leaders frantically tried to bring some order out of the chaos we'd created. They raced along the column, harrying men into ranks, hurrying before we could attack again.

From the lip of the Ravine I looked to where Mayra was. She stood facing Moidra, within the spell-star. Their lips moved as if they shouted the spell-words and charm-sounds, but I could hear not so much as a whisper. Their acolytes knelt in a circle around the star to keep unprotected men or any iron a safe distance from it. The wind was whipping dust down the Ravine, but inside their circle all was calm.

Bohemund had a trickle of blood running down his face. His eyes looked at something beyond the seeing of others, but he was still outwardly as calm as if he was sitting in his own tent. "They didn't expect steel for their next meal, Wulfgar. They're finding it hard to digest."

I nodded. "And it appears to be time to feed them again."

In the short time they'd had, the Lantan officers had managed to set their ranks to face us. The ease with which they'd been penetrated had left its mark on them. The ranks were deep and narrow, so narrow we could cover their entire front. It was a formation for defense, not for attack. They were too concerned with caution, with what they had riding on the outcome, and not enough with winning. But overhead the evil-looking clouds still roiled and eddied ominously, and the wind smelled of things long dead. If the soldiers thought too much of their own lives, there were others who still thought mainly of ending ours.

Bohemund raised his lance, and the drums and war flutes began to sound the wild song of battle once more. We attacked. The ground pounded under our hooves like a drum beneath the palm of the drummer. A steady, wordless roar poured out to sound our coming.

Their banners lifted high, a hundred colors fluttering in the foul wind. Suddenly the shield wall opened. The banners dropped, and as they dropped their horsemen poured through the gaps to meet us.

We came together with the grinding clash of steel on steel, the slashing sounds of swords cleaving flesh, the rattling death cries of falling warriors. Like two walls of sand carried by the winds we clashed, and swelled, and merged into a maelstrom.

A blade seeking my heart skittered across my shield, striking sparks. My lance caught in the armor of a Lantan, and he pulled it out of my grasp as he fell. I drew the curved saddle sword barely in time to block a slash aimed at taking my head. The fever of battle was on me, but in one corner of my mind I watched the sky grow ever darker and wondered how that other battle went.

Our drums changed their rhythm, once more signaling the fallback. Once more we must disengage before their sheer number could grind us under.

Two Morassa pressed their attack on me hard. There was no way to break free without taking their blades in my back. They closed in, hacking at me together. I caught a slashing cut on my shield and in the same motion thrust the shield out to slam its iron-bound rim into the man's neck. He fell with his head twisted at an impossible angle. The other found to his horror that the death of his companion bared his side to my blade. I turned and was riding away before he finished falling.

Many of us were already streaming back across

the Plain to the Ravine. The Lantans and Morassa, flushed with the heat of conflict, believed us broken, fleeing the battle. As soon as they realized we were breaking off they sped after us, seeking to complete the rout they thought had begun. We ran our horses hard to keep ahead of them. They spurred wildly, striving to catch us. And then death began to fall among them.

The forty thousand warriors who had not ridden with us stood on the rim of the Great Ravine, and each held in his hands a longbow. They erected a corridor of steel behind us for our enemies to ride through, a constant rain of death. Mayra had predicted Elspeth's advice would be key. Elspeth had shown how our salvation would rest on the bow.

It was as though a giant hand swept through the enemy ranks, taking men in huge fistfuls. By the thousands they died. Some, too close to us in their pursuit, were spared the arrows. Instead we fell on them with sword and lance. Those on the far side of the hail of death, the great mass of them, chose not to follow their companions into the shadows. Turning, they fled back to their army, pursued now themselves by the hunting shafts.

The fighting had moved them back from the Ravine, and that added distance gave them safety. Failure when victory appeared firmly gripped had brought change to their thinking. As the horsemen rode back into the mass of their army it began to shift and alter. Units marched to the beat of the cadence call. Morassa began moving to the flanks, and the Lantan cavalry with them.

Though the light of day was still with us, the sky was black with the malevolent clouds, and the noxious wind left a feeling of vileness where it touched skin. Mayra and Moidra still stood, chanting, fighting their fight as we fought ours, but the air inside the star shimmered like the air over a fire, and several of the acolytes, still holding their circle, wavered and cringed as if too near a great heat.

We formed again, but our ranks were severely depleted. More of our foemen died than we did, but our numbers dwindled while theirs seemed unchanged. In the end, it appeared, we'd die there on the rim of the Ravine, and there'd still be an army left to retake Lanta from those we'd left to hold it.

They'd swung their lines into a huge crescent, now, stretched out before us. The center was anchored with the infantry, and the curving wings were horsemen. Wherever along that curving line we struck, the rest of it would curl around us, surrounding us. Even if the bowmen came with us it would only change the time of the end. There'd be no stakes, this time, to slow a charge, no ridgeline to give height.

Orne leaned over to clasp my hand. "Fare you well, my lord. We will drink together in the Land of the Dead. We will eat lamb in the Tents of Death."

He started to say something else, then stopped and leaned forward intently. "My lord," he said sharply, "their lines."

At that distance it was impossible to see clearly,

but a large man was riding out in front of the lines. He was followed by a palanquin borne by eight men, and by a body of riders. I didn't need to see the woman who stepped out to know who she was. Elana.

Out of the lines came another group of men on foot. From the glitter of their armor they had to be from the Palace Guard. Not all, it seemed, had remained in Lanta. They carried something, and when I saw what it was, the marrow in my bones froze. It was a bound and struggling man.

A stir passed through the enemy, and a ripple of sound ran down their ranks. Roughly the guards forced the captive to his knees. The big man motioned, and a rider went to him. The rider received the big man's sword and dismounted to stride to the kneeling prisoner. The sword flashed in the air. A sigh of despair ran through us.

The executioner handed a cloth-wrapped bundle to a Morassa, and the rider galloped toward us. On a staff he had green branches tied, a sign of parley and truce. No sound but the creak of harness leather could be heard among us. He stopped short of us, flinging the bundle and whirling to ride away in one motion. It twisted in the air and fell, rolling and unwrapping before us. A head spilled out almost at our feet. It was Harald's.

The Morassa's horse hadn't taken five paces before horse and rider alike were pierced by a thousand arrows. Neither was recognizable for what it was as they lay like giant spine-crawlers.

Bohemund shut his eyes rather than look at what lay in front of him, but tears ran down his cheeks. I gritted my teeth until they ached, but a low, moaning cry still escaped.

One by one the bowmen slipped away, running to get their horses.

Pain built in my chest, an unbearable pressure. Through a red mist I saw the riders and the palanquin disappear back into the safety of their lines. My sword slid back of its own accord, slicing away the saddle scabbard. An oath. Only in the flesh of my enemies. It would be sheathed again only in the flesh of my enemies.

Already some men had started toward their lines alone, men who'd sworn blood-oath to Harald, men who'd sworn to guard his life with theirs and not leave alive the field where he died.

Images flashed in my head. Two boys wrestling on the rugs of a tent. Two youths in the shallows of the Xora, thinking there was no more water in the world than that. Two young men, riding on their first raid together, taking their brands together. The band of pressure inside me exploded, and I kneed my horse forward.

With the silence of one already dead I rode, not caring if I rode alone, not noticing that the warriors of the Altaii rode with me. No sound was uttered, for the rage was on us. We rode to die, and to kill as we died. As a silent wave of death we rolled forward.

Their flanks began to curve around us, moving

to encircle us. The infantry stood firm, shield wall solid, a hedge of spears presented, ready to hold us until the horsemen could finish our destruction.

The first Altaii warriors reached them, the blood-oath men, and flung themselves from their saddles, impaling themselves on the spears. Their hands clawed at the shield wall, and dying, they opened holes in it.

Into those holes we rode, pressing our attack, shearing deep, ripping the gaps wider. Their cavalry hadn't made contact before the infantry was falling back, trying desperately, uselessly to regroup and re-form.

I brushed aside a lance with my shield as the first horsemen reached us, and decapitated its owner with a backhand blow in passing. Another rode to meet me, a Lantan. He fought well, but death rode at my shoulder, and I little cared if it was mine or another's. There was a look of horror in his eyes as I pulled my steel from his body and let him slide from his horse.

Near me Dunstan wove a circle of flashing steel around himself. All who entered that circle died. Then, with a sweeping blow, a Morassa severed his sword hand, sending sword and hand spinning. Laughing, the Morassa raised his sword for the easy kill, but Dunstan, pushing the stump of his wrist into his face to blind him, broke his neck with a blow from his shield rim. Dropping the shield, he bent low from the saddle to snatch up a sword in his left hand and disappeared into the swirl of battle, heedless of his life pumping out. Die, but die killing your enemies.

Thunder was added to the boiling clouds, a low, growling, unnatural thunder. Light flashed in the clouds, as lightning, but not lightning. The foul wind grew stronger, swelling into a storm.

My horse screamed as a Lantan infantryman put a spear through his side. As he rolled to the ground I stepped from the saddle and put steel through the Lantan's ribs. Many now fought on foot, Lantan cavalry and Altaii alike. I saw a group of Morassa, trying to maneuver like the infantry, ridden down by a mass of Altaii and Lantans intent on their fight. Here and there Lantan infantry tried to form squares and defend against the death that rode around them. None lasted beyond the first attack.

Through the carnage Bohemund cut his way with his intentions written on his forehead. He gave no heed to the death struggles taking place on every side. He didn't slow to strike down an enemy unless that man tried to get in his way. In the midst of the battle he searched only for the men who'd killed his son.

A Morassa came riding down on me, screaming a war cry, lance leveled. Dropping my sword I grabbed hold of the lance just behind the head at the last possible instant, and falling, I pushed the blade to the ground. His cry of triumph turned to a grunt as the impact shivered him out of his saddle. Dazed, he tried to rise, only to find his own lance pinning him to the ground. I left him pawing weakly at the shaft, his life leaking away. My death or another's, it was all the same.

A blade struck me on the shoulder, but I killed the one who wielded it almost without noticing him. Before me, almost within reach, stood Ivo. Ivo, of the Street of Five Bells. Ivo, the Morassa, and a Morassa had murdered Harald.

Wordlessly I advanced on him. He tried to speak, but I wasn't there for talking. I attacked with all the energy I could muster. There was no skill in it, only sheer strength and hacking butchery, for it was butchery I intended. From the first instant all of his efforts had to be directed at stopping my attack, or slowing it, at least, for stop it he could not. Again and again I forced home a blow, cutting at him, tearing at him, forcing him back. He tripped, falling, and I closed for the kill. And he caught himself.

It was impossible, but he caught himself. He twisted aside from my blow, nearly kicked my legs out from under me, and took a cut at my chest that laid me open to the bone, severing the bag Mayra had given me. Almost before I could turn to face him he was ready. More than ready, I saw.

Like Daiman below the Palace of the Twin Thrones, he suddenly had a look of utter confidence. Before my very eyes he seemed to grow, to become taller. His wounds no longer bled, and he had an aura of strength about him. He was now the tool of a Sister of Wisdom, while I faced him on my own. And if he killed me, with Harald already dead, it might well extinguish the last hope of my people. That thought cooled me. Sanity returned. I wanted him still, but I was now all that might stand between the Altaii and oblivion. He smiled and moved toward me.

I circled him carefully, watching. He moved as if he was at practice, casually, almost negligently. Neither of us was aware of the battle any longer. For each only the other existed.

He feinted. Again. I took neither. I could afford to take no chances. Suddenly he leaped in, swinging at my head, trying for decapitation. I met each swing, one after the other, and it came to me that I shouldn't be able to. He was moving with blazing speed. His sword, his hand, his arm was a blur, but I still met each of his blows. And slowly I began to attack, to counter his strikes with strikes of my own. There was only one possible explanation. In some fashion Mayra had found that I needed her. In some way she was taking a part of her attention away from her own battle to aid me in mine.

We sprang apart. The confidence was still on his face, but it seemed less complete than it had. There was wariness, now, in his circling, caution. This time I made the attack.

We stood toe-to-toe, and each swing was a try for the kill. If his blade was a blur, mine was too. Sparks struck whenever they met. His lips began to twitch, from anger or frustration, and he tried to press harder. I moved to meet him, on ground churned into mud by a thousand hooves and countless feet, and my foot slipped.

I fell, and he came for the kill, raising his sword. Mine was gone in the fall, but my hand had fallen on something. The sky-stone. The sky-stone with the Terg carved in it, fallen from the cut-away pouch. Snatching it up, I threw it at him.

It struck his chest, and he screamed, a scream that pierced the ear like a hot wire, a scream that echoed over the entire battlefield, going on and on eerily. In an instant he was a living flame, a statue of blue-white fire. Another scream, coming from no-where and everywhere, joined his, twinning with it, reverberating.

I thrust my hands over my ears, but it went on, digging into my skull. I closed my eyes, but the burning image scorched even behind my eyelids. There was no escape.

Abruptly, both the scream and the light were gone. I opened my eyes. All that remained of Ivo was a pile of ashes with a plume of greasy smoke rising from it. One mass of melted metal within the pile was his sword, I was sure. Another must be the sky-stone.

I picked up my own sword and looked to rejoin the battle, but it was done. In all directions, as far as I could see, streams of Lantans and Morassa fled, pursued by Altaii. All over the field they were throwing down their weapons, crying quarter, and Altaii were herding them together. And a fresh breeze was breaking up the dark clouds.

# XXXI

## A GREEN BRANCH

The skies over the field before the Great Ravine cleared, but there was still much else to make it a nightmare place. The moans of the injured, the cries of the dying filled the air like babble in a marketplace. There was no escaping it. The dead lay in heaps, like drifts of sand driven by the wind. Prisoners in chains and under guard separated our dead from theirs. Ours would be burned, if wood enough could be found. Theirs would be left to the dril and the insects. That foul wind had gone, but an odor hung over the place. It was an odor of the mind, perhaps, but real nonetheless for that. It was the odor of a superabundance of death.

I sat on a small rock at the edge of the field, trying to bind the gash where I'd been struck just before fighting Ivo. One end of the rag I held in my teeth while trying to fold the other under. The healers were too busy to bother with such trifling things.

"Let me do that." Mayra took the rag and tossed it away with a grimace. "You'll manage to kill yourself yet, if you use that." From under her robe she produced a pouch, and from the pouch bandages and salves. She looked as if she'd just risen from sleep.

"If I can survive this, no dirty rag will kill me."

The salve felt cool at first, then warm as she rubbed it in. "Luck may have kept you alive on the battlefield, but it won't do as much good if you get an infection in your shoulder."

"It wasn't luck, Mayra, as you know well. I thank you. Whatever debt I owed you before, I owe ten times, now."

Her fingers stopped. "What do you mean?" she asked softly, but her eyes were intent.

"Why, when I fought Ivo, of course. You know I—" I stopped. She didn't know. She had no idea what I was talking about. "Then how did it happen?"

"From the beginning, Wulfgar. Tell me everything that happened. Leave nothing out, not the smallest detail."

Haltingly I told her of the fight with Ivo, of the power that aided him and the power that aided me, and finally of Ivo's death by fire. All the while I spoke, I wondered. If my help hadn't come from Mayra, then from where?

When I finished she sighed and shook her head.

"I knew nothing of any of this. Not even a scream such as you described could have gotten into the spell-star, and I suppose everyone assumed like you that Moidra and I had something to do with it, and for that reason it wasn't necessary to mention it. Most men are reticent enough about magic. About magic that won a battle they'd be silent as a tomb. And it did win the battle, you realize."

"A fight with Ivo?" I said, bewildered. "Even with magic—"

"Yes, the fight. Either Sayene or Ya'shen must have been searching for you, even while the battle was fought. Once you were found, she took enough of herself away from the battle to control Ivo. Without his own mind Ivo was a living lie, so the oath-stone burned him—a monstrous lie, so he was consumed, not just burned where it touched him. That must have distracted her. She couldn't have expected anything like it. And that momentary distraction was all Moidra and I needed."

"And you were able to attack?"

"Something like that. We'd both been searching for Harald, so even within the spell-star we sensed his death. Then all of you forgot everything except that insane male attempt to commit suicide. Drawing on your energies we could sense that, too. All we could do was try to bundle that, the insanity, the ferocity, the disregard for life, the almost desire for death, and hurl all of it at Sayene and Ya'shen. It must have struck at the very instant Ivo's death broke their concentration on us."

I breathed deep. The air smelled and tasted good suddenly. Perhaps I'd been reminded of what it could have been like. "The baraca was with us, Mayra," I said softly. "There was more luck in that happening than any man has a right to ask for."

"Luck," she snorted. "There wasn't any luck in it. Things don't just happen, my fine warrior. They're ordered and arranged by higher powers. Sayene directed one such against us. Another aided you, and may have arranged what you seem to think was coincidence."

"But how? Beneath the Palace of the Twin Thrones you were there. Facing Ivo, I was alone." Suddenly the hair stood up on the back of my neck. "Mayra, these powers—You're not talking about gods?"

"Some gods are such powers. Some are just lumps of stone." She smiled and shook her head. "Some are one thing one time and the other another. It doesn't matter, though. Whatever it was, it saved you, and it saved the Altaii people." The smile faded. "This does underscore what I said, Wulfgar. You've become a nexus, a conduit between this world and powers beyond. It can bring you great wealth and power. It can also bring death or worse." She tucked the corners of the bandage under neatly and rose. "We'll talk about it later, and I'll see how I can help you. For now let me try helping some more of the wounded."

She walked away straight-backed, stopping to bend over this one or that one. She limped slightly.

The battle hadn't left her entirely untouched, either.

Orne passed her, riding and leading a spare horse. Stopping in front of me he put both hands on the front of his saddle and looked at me portentously. "My lord," he announced, "we still live."

I nodded. "It seems we'll have to put off the lamb until next year."

"Or even the next, my lord."

"Or even the next." I mounted the horse he'd brought. "But the cost has been very high to avoid eating a meal, Orne."

"Has it ever been small, my lord?"

"I suppose it hasn't," I breathed. "Is Bohemund well?"

"He is. He sent me for you, in fact. Over that way." He turned his horse toward the Ravine, and I followed. "Lord Karlan is dead, though, and Lord Shen Ta and Lord Otogai and Lord Dunstan. There'll be no end to the funeral fires from this day, my lord."

"No end," I agreed, and we rode in silence.

We picked our way around and sometimes over the bodies of men and horses. On every side men sat binding each other's wounds. Captives carried away our dead in numbers to make the bones shake and the stomach grow cold. No matter the alternatives, the smell of death clogged my nostrils again.

Bohemund saw us approaching and rode to meet us. His helmet was off, and his face was full of contempt. "He ran," he said without prelude. "Brecon ran."

I stared in astonishment, and Orne muttered something about carrion eaters. "Why?" I asked. "Even a Morassa wouldn't run from combat with the king in the middle of a battle."

"He was the one who gave his sword for Harald to be killed." His voice was cold and hard. "Three times I managed to get close to him, and each time he avoided me in the press. Finally I was able to meet him face-to-face, and he seemed to have gathered enough courage to fight. He knew why I wanted him, all right. Then that scream came. It was enough to tear at any man's courage, but his blood and bones turned to water in front of my eyes. He actually threw away his shield to run better. It affected many of them that way, it seemed, and there were too many of them, all packing together in their efforts to escape, for me to catch him again."

We were all too disgusted to mention Brecon again. Cowardice, even an enemy's, left a foul taste in the mouth.

"Did any of them manage to retreat in good order?" I asked.

"None that I saw," the king replied, "but that's not to say they won't try to rally somewhere. I want you to make a wide sweep around us. If you see anything that indicates they've still got a taste for fighting, let me know right away."

Bohemund rode away, and I turned to Orne. "Gather as many men as you can in a half turn of the sand glass and meet me there." I indicated a stone outcrop. "We'll have to hurry if we're to cover any distance before dark."

We split, and I rode from place to place, telling this man to fall in behind me, that man to find others and meet me. Three times I met a leader of a thousand lances and told him to find as many of his thousand as he could and join me. At the half turn I rode away from the Ravine at the head of some two thousand lances.

I pushed hard, paying no heed to the ones and twos and threes we saw. It was bigger, more dangerous game I sought. Some of the lances wanted to stop long enough to scoop the stragglers up, as if there weren't already more prisoners chained at the Ravine than we'd likely be able to sell.

"We've no time for them," I said each time. "Let them run."

And run they did, even harder after they saw us. There was no taste for fighting there, no desire for anything but escape. If we found nothing more than those scared remnants, I'd go right back to tell the king our enemy was broken beyond recall. But then, topping a rise, I found the larger game I sought.

Below us several hundred warriors bunched tightly around several tents of the Lantan type and a cluster of that city's wagons, with their big boxy bodies. There was a palanquin nearby, and a cluster of women in white robes. A small knot of slaves huddled under the wagons.

Our appearance above them caught them by

surprise. In spite of what had happened, they had no sentries out. When they saw us the warriors rushed to form a line. The women ran into the largest tent.

"Orne, find a green branch and tie it to a lance. I'll parley with them."

"Parley? My lord—"

"Get the branch, Orne," I said impatiently. "What's here is worth talking for. Bartu, ride to Bohemund, quickly. Tell him to come as fast as he can. Tell him I've a partial repayment for him. I think he'll understand."

Bartu brushed past Orne, who was preparing the truce staff, and sped away, trailing dust. His departure caused some excitement among the Lantan soldiers. Perhaps they thought he went for more lances.

"I still don't see why we don't just ride them down," Orne grumbled.

"Enough Altaii have died today. We'll gain this prize another way, if we can. If it doesn't work—" I shrugged and rode down toward the wagons and tents.

# XXXII

## LEASH AND COLLAR

~

The officer commanding them was young, certainly
no more than a junior officer of the City Guard.
He was covered with dirt and sweat, and there was
blood on a face that showed all too clearly the fa-
tigue of battle.

"You speak for these men?" I asked.

He glanced wearily at the lances spread across
the rise. "I do."

"I will speak here." The one I'd hoped for, the one
I'd known must be here as soon as I saw the palanquin, pushed in front of the young officer. Elana.
She sat a city woman's saddle, one with a back like
a chair and both of her feet on a ledge on one side
of the horse. If she'd suffered any in the fighting,
she didn't show it. Her robes were as resplendent,
the jewels in her hair as flawless, as if she was in

the great hall of the Palace of the Twin Thrones. And she was as arrogant as ever. "You've come to try and take me captive then, barbarian, have you? You'll find I'm not such easy prey as my sister was. I've heard how she comported herself, crawling to you, begging for her life, begging to be a slave. She was always soft. You'll find nothing so easy here. We'll fight you to the last drop of blood." Her voice sank to a hiss. "We'll resist to the death."

"She has a mouth, hasn't she," I said. The officer tried to suppress a smile. Elana flared up, but I cut her off. "I haven't come to talk with this woman. If she remains, I've nothing further to say. I'll drop the truce staff, and my lances will leave nothing alive here."

He looked at Elana, a mute appeal in his eyes. Her eyes flashed. For a moment I thought she'd force the issue. Then, wordlessly, she whirled her horse and rode back to the tents.

"What's your name?" I asked once she was gone.

"Tybert," he replied, "late a shield-square leader in the Lantan City Guard, now commanding the queen's bodyguard, what there is of it."

"That's not a Lantan name."

"Mirzan. I'm from Mirza. It's a small city," he added with a tight smile, "and there's little trade except for the export of swords."

I'd heard of Mirzan mercenaries. That about the swords was like our joke about being simple herdsmen and traders in hides. I smiled politely.

"And your men?"

"Mirzan, Norlanders, Hyksos." He laughed. "We've even a few Lantans."

I smiled in turn. When his laugh faded I asked quietly, "Then what holds you here?"

He drew himself up pridefully. "My codes, Altaii. I've taken gold."

"I, too, have sold my sword, Tybert, and one thing is certain. When I fight for my people I'm ruled only by honor and the warrior codes. When I fight for gold, there are other considerations. Such as will I be paid? Elana has no treasury to draw on, now. She has nothing but what is in her tents. If you fight, you're not doing it for gold, for she's none to give you."

He mulled it over slowly. There was nothing in his codes to make him fight for someone who couldn't fulfill the other part of the contract. There was, I knew, allowance for leaving a leader who bungled the operation for which hire was made.

Finally he sighed and nodded slowly. "I fear you're right about the payment. I'm not certain she'd pay now, even if she could. She seems to think we lost the battle to spite her. Very well, I'll withdraw with such of my men who'll follow. I can't say how many that'll be, though."

"That is all I ask," I said.

"One more thing," he said. "Who do I speak to?"

"I'm called Wulfgar."

His eyes widened slightly. "I am honored, Lord

Wulfgar." And backing away he rode back to his men.

I twisted in the saddle and motioned for Orne to come down. He galloped up in a spray of sand.

"They're leaving, my lord?" he asked incredulously.

"Mercenaries, Orne, and they've just been told there's no hope of payment. Since they probably left their previous pay in Lanta, I doubt many will stay now."

Tybert finished talking to the men. He rode away from the tents, heading east, and by twos they followed. All of them. I suppose the Lantans among them had discovered new loyalties.

Elana stared after the departing soldiers, then spurred in chase. "Where are you going?" she screamed. "Come back, you cowards! Cowards!"

Dashing to intercept her I swept her from her horse and dumped her heavily to the ground. She glared up at me a moment, wild-eyed, then screamed. Maybe she thought I was planning her death. What I was doing was seeing her again, watching Harald die.

She scrambled to her feet and ran toward her tent. Her serving girls and the noblewomen who attended her stood as if in a trance. Too much had happened to them on this day. They couldn't accept it all. Their army destroyed. Themselves abandoned. Now their queen ran as if for her life from a barbarian of the Plain. In truth, though, they seemed more dismayed by the departure of their soldiers than by Elana's fate.

I dismounted and followed her at a leisurely pace. Her robes were made for the grandeur of a palace, not for running, and she made heavy going of it. At the entrance to the tent I caught her, and she whirled on me. A dagger gleamed like a serpent's fang in her upraised hand.

I caught her wrist, tightened my grasp only a little, and her face went white. Slowly her hand opened, and with a whimper she dropped the blade. Terror filled her eyes. She thought I was going to kill her, but she wasn't mine to kill.

Forcing her to her knees I pulled the jeweled pins from her hair, shaking the pale blond mass loose around her shoulders. She closed her eyes and caught her lip between her teeth, fighting to regain composure.

"Wait. Listen. It wasn't my fault. You've got to understand." She seemed to realize she was babbling and began again. "I wasn't responsible for Lord Harald's death. You must believe that," she said insistently. "The Most High ordered it. They commanded it. It was their fault."

Someone said, "That's a lie."

I turned on the women to see who had spoken. All were silent, but one flinched and tried to look away when I met her eye. I pointed at her. "You. Tell me how she lies."

She looked from me to Elana to me again. "I didn't—I mean, I can't—I don't know—"

Unseen, Orne had walked up behind the woman. Now he buried his ax in the ground in front of her. "Perhaps her tongue will loosen if she kisses the ax."

She stared at the ax, less than an arm's length from her, and her words spilled over each other in her effort to get them out. "There was a magic mirror. The Most High appeared on it. They told her not to kill Lord Harald. They said it was too late to do any good by it. They said it was dangerous. But Brecon said they should do it anyway, and she thought so, too. After they left to do it, the mirror melted." She was on the verge of tears. "It set fire to the tent. Burned it down. And then that awful thing happened to the Sisters of Wisdom. It's all her fault. If she'd done as the Most High commanded, none of this would've happened."

"What happened to the Sisters of Wisdom?" I asked.

She suddenly looked haggard. "I don't want to think about—"

"Tell me."

For an instant she tottered on the edge of disobeying. Then she shut her eyes and began speaking. "The Sisters of Wisdom were in the spell-star. I was watching them. Suddenly Ya'shen looked up. She seemed startled by something. It was only for a second, but before she began the chants again, it happened. Something seemed to pick Sayene up and throw her right out of the spell-star. She landed over a hundred paces away. And Ya'shen, Ya'shen burst into flame. And she screamed. There was another scream from somewhere, and the two of them together were horrible. Please, I don't want to talk of it."

"What happened to Sayene? Ya'shen died, but what about Sayene?"

"She was barely hurt," she said in a resigned voice, "but she wouldn't even wait for her bruises to be seen to. As soon as she got up she gathered her acolytes and rode away. After that everyone was running. The army, everyone."

"So you lied to me, Elana," I said softly. "If you're going to lie, I don't want to hear you at all."

I tore a strip from her robe and, before she could move, wadded it into her mouth. Another strip fastened it there. Her robes weren't as pretty now that they were ripped. She watched me wrathfully, but seemed to realize the futility of struggle. One more long piece from her robes served to bind her hands behind her, and her belt made a leash and collar.

Elana, held close to my saddle by her leash, watched mesmerized as the other men ransacked the tents and wagons. There was little to find, though, and we left them burning behind us.

I headed straight back for the Ravine. This prize was worth more than being able to report that I'd seen a few more Lantans running. I meant to take her straight to the king.

We kept an easy pace for the women's sakes, but I fear they didn't think so. Before we'd gone far their breath came in whistles and gasps. They kept up the steady trot, though. No doubt they thought we'd drag them if they didn't.

An hour from the Lantan tents we were met by Bohemund. He'd hurried, indeed, to come so quickly. He had fewer than a hundred warriors with him. He hadn't waited to gather more.

"I have a gift for you, my king," I said. "I found it wandering loose, and I thought you might like to have it."

Another rider moved up beside Bohemund, and I saw that it was Mayra. She seemed very interested in Elana, but Bohemund looked at her in surprise. "Who is this?"

I couldn't blame him for not recognizing her. Her hair was plastered to her head with sweat. Her chest heaved violently as she tried to suck in more air through flaring nostrils. Her knees were trembling, and from head to foot she was covered with a layer of dust.

I handed him the leash. "Her name is Elana, and once she was Queen of Lanta."

He pulled her close and leaned over to peer into her face. Tears pooled in her eyes, but she was too tired to struggle. "Yes," he breathed and his hand went to his sword.

Mayra put out her hand to stop him. Her gaze was still on Elana. "She must live. When we get back to camp I'll attune her to you. Our survival is tied to hers."

"Then she'll survive in chains," Bohemund growled

under his breath as he turned to ride away, Elana forlornly at his side.

Mayra waited for me to join her. We rode together for a time before she spoke.

"You've done it, you realize."

"Done what?"

"Opened the gates of Lanta with your own hand, captured both the queens, ended ten thousand years of Lantan history and as much or more Altaii history. Your hand has changed this corner of the world so it will never be the same again."

"I don't know about changing the world, or even a part of it," I said, "but I've done nothing to the Altaii."

"You think all will go on as before?"

"Of course it will," I replied angrily. But I gathered my cloak around me. The wind had died here, but I felt the chill of a wind blowing somewhere.

"Come to me," she said. "When we get to Lanta, come to me, and we'll talk."

And she spurred on ahead, leaving me with my thoughts and that cold wind that no one else felt.

# XXXIII

## THAT COLD WIND

~

The first day of the first month of the Year of the Fourth Wind dawned cold in Lanta, in the great square surrounding the palace. I wore a redbear robe around my shoulders, but the cold still seeped through, aided by the winds of change. One by one the men of a handpicked thousand went to Bohemund before the gates of the palace to receive a messenger's scarf, a scarf of black.

Mayra stood near me, but her eyes were on me, not the ceremony. She seemed worried, but I don't think she felt the bone-chilling wind that I felt.

We'd returned late to the rim of the Ravine. The cold of night was coming, and fires had been lit against it. A warrior came to Bohemund, the Falcon Banner, symbol of the Morassa people, draped over his saddle.

"A trophy, my king," he said. "The spirit of the Morassa is in our hands."

"Destroy it." There was steel in Bohemund's voice. "Burn it, bury it in a dung heap, but destroy it. We take no trophies from vermin."

With a grim smile the warrior rode to one of the fires. The men huddled around it parted to let him in. He trailed the flag into the flames. Tendrils of fire ran up the length of it. In moments it was ablaze. The warrior dropped the burning mass onto the fire, and it was no more than the other ashes.

Songs would be sung about the battle, and this would be in them, how Bohemund wouldn't deign to accept the Morassa banner, but had it burned instead. He wasn't interested in songs, though. Other fires burned on the Plain than those to warm men, Altaii funeral fires. Bohemund rode to Harald's fire and stayed until it burned out and beyond, far into the night.

It was a time of mourning.

———— ～ ————

The line continued forward to receive their scarves from Bohemund. Each in turn was given the same injunction. "Deliver the message. Deliver it well."

Each in turn gave the ritual reply. "I will deliver the message well. None but death shall stop me." On each man's lips it had the sound of an oath.

A few days earlier I'd stood on the Plain, far from the walls of the city. There I was just another warrior, another of those who'd returned from the Great Ravine. All who had left the field alive were there, forming a great circle.

Within the circle stood the youths who had gone into the battle and survived, three thousand of them. None could have survived that place without having performed the acts of bravery required for the warrior brand. One by one they received it.

It's custom that the youth receive his brand in the presence of those who fought beside him. For that reason we were there, to see them recognized as warriors.

For some reason I could not stop thinking of three thousand more who had crossed the Xandra never to return. Their ferryman's fee had been high, but they'd paid it.

Now the leaders of a hundred lances went forward to receive their own scarves. Each had been chosen from many volunteers. Each had himself chosen the hundred lances who would follow him from the thousands who wanted to go. I saw Aelfric among them.

I'd chosen a palace of my own in Lanta, a palace once owned by a member of the Council of Nobles. It was, I thought, a place to stay when my thousand came to Lanta on its sweep across the Plain. Such was not to be.

The sweeps, the marches—the endless war with the Plain was ending. Every day more and more Altaii arrived at the city, and all had come to stay. The horse herds and the cattle herds had been moved to easy pastures to the east of the city. Altaii lances now held garrisons in towns that once knew Lantan guards. Cerdu and Devia and Asyat sent tribute.

I was sitting in the palace garden scowling at the fountain when Mayra came.

"Look at that," I said. "There've been days when I'd have killed to get that much water for my tents, and here it is being used just for looking at."

"You haven't come to me, Wulfgar. I asked you to, remember? We have to talk."

"There's been much to do. Arranging for the dirt-men to sell us food. Protection for the caravans. Many things."

She sighed heavily. For the first time I looked at her. She looked tired.

"It won't change back, Wulfgar, no matter how much you want it to. It can't." She sighed again and motioned to the shadows. Elspeth came out. "I've come to talk to you about the future."

I peered down into the pool of the fountain. So much water.

"I told Che Sen we wouldn't change. The Altaii will always be the Altaii. Well, we're changing already. We're becoming city people, people with walls and buildings and roofs to hold us."

She was waiting impatiently. "Did you never wonder why I carefully guided you to Elspeth, and talked you into keeping her close at hand?"

"I wondered why, yes, but not the other. And I assumed you'd tell me why when you were ready."

"Well, I'm ready now. All of your children, Wulfgar, will rise to places of power. All of your children." She looked at me then in a way that reminded me of how she'd looked in the great hall when Leah let me know she bore my child. "Your children will rule the cities, found empires. Through them you will start dynasties that will change the face of the world as you've changed this corner of it. Your descendants will rise to rule for a thousand generations and more. And some of them will complete the change you've started for the Altaii, from herdsmen and raiders into empire builders. At certain points, Elspeth's advice and knowledge will be critical to the future they build, and that of all the Altaii people."

"The change I've started," I whispered. I rose and walked over to the women. I cupped Elspeth's chin and forced her to look at me. Her tears ran over the back of my hand. "Do you see what you've done with your salvation of my people, salvation that rests on the bow, what you've made me do with your ideas of the Altaii settling down? Better we should have fought our way out the best we could. Better I'd never found you." I let her go, and she slumped forward, her shoulders shaking with sobs.

"Wulfgar," Mayra said gently, but I didn't want her gentleness.

"Mayra, do you realize what you've done to me? My people are to become something else, something strange and alien, and you tell me that I and my children and my blood for a thousand generations to come will be the instruments of that change. We were free, Mayra, and you say that we must be chained and my descendants must fashion and fasten the chains. We were free."

I turned back to the fountain.

"Your debt to me is cleared, Elspeth. Whether you come or not is your own decision to make."

"I'm sorry, Wulfgar," she said, and there were tears in her voice.

I didn't turn. After a time I heard them leave, but I still didn't turn. So much water.

~

It was time for the one who would lead these messengers to receive his scarf from the king. I threw off the redbear robe.

Bohemund waited, the black scarf in his hands. Swiftly he tied it around my left arm, just below the manhood brand. "Deliver the message," he said. "Deliver it well."

"I will deliver the message well. None but death shall stop me." I clasped his hand tightly. "I swear it. By the bones of my father, and my father's father, and my father's father's father, I swear it."

He gripped my hand back. There were tears in his eyes.

# XXXIV

## AND SO, WE RIDE

—

I mounted and took my place at the head of the thousand. Bartu and Orne took their places at my shoulder, Elspeth and Mayra following close behind. We started down the street, away from the palace, toward the gates. Cheering Altaii lined both sides of our route. They hung out of windows, shouting, and waved from the rooftops as we went by. There were even those in the cheering throng who had been loyal citizens of the city. With the shouts ringing in our ears we rode out of the gates of Lanta.

It's said that six days after the battle at the Great Ravine a body of some five or six hundred horsemen was seen. They showed signs of having been in heavy action. They rode east. At their head was a huge man with a Morassa topknot. At that man's shoulder rode a beautiful woman with an air of strangeness about her. They could be no others but Brecon and Sayene.

And so, we ride eastward, bearing our message. Our scarves are black, the color of death, and the message we carry is darkness and death. They are out there, somewhere. We will find them . . . and we will deliver the message.